THE DEPRAT AFFAIR

by the same author

THE FLOATING EGG:
EPISODES IN THE MAKING OF GEOLOGY

as co-author

THE ATLAS OF EARTH HISTORY
THE ATLAS OF EVOLUTION

THE DEPRAT AFFAIR

Ambition, Revenge and Deceit in French Indo-China

Roger Osborne

JONATHAN CAPE
LONDON

Published by Jonathan Cape 1999

2 4 6 8 10 9 7 5 3 1

First published in Great Britain in 1999 by
Jonathan Cape
Random House, 20 Vauxhall Bridge Road,
London SW1V 2SA

Random House Australia (Pty) Limited
20 Alfred Street, Milsons Point, Sydney,
New South Wales 2061, Australia

Random House New Zealand Limited
18 Poland Road, Glenfield,
Auckland 10, New Zealand

Random House South Africa (Pty) Limited
Endulini, 5A Jubilee Road, Parktown 2193, South Africa

Random House UK Limited Reg. No. 954009

A CIP catalogue record for this book
is available from the British Library

ISBN 0-224-05295-0

Papers used by Random House UK Limited are natural, recyclable products made from wood grown in sustainable forests. The manufacturing processes conform to the environmental regulations of the country of origin

Printed and bound in Great Britain by
Biddles Ltd, Guildford and King's Lynn

For Mary and Alfred

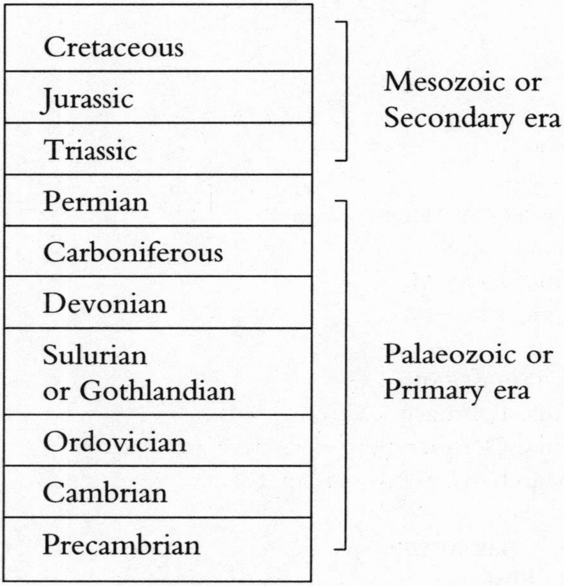

Cretaceous	Mesozoic or Secondary era
Jurassic	
Triassic	
Permian	Palaeozoic or Primary era
Carboniferous	
Devonian	
Sulurian or Gothlandian	
Ordovician	
Cambrian	
Precambrian	

Geological periods of the Mesozoic and Palaeozoic eras, with the oldest at the bottom of the column.

Contents

Illustrations

Maps

Then there is the photograph. Three hundred or so men and women in their best suits and frocks, arranged in rows, in front of a university building on a bright Canadian summer morning. And until you know something of the story lying behind the photograph, it remains just that – row on row of anonymous faces perched above starched collars and beneath wide bonnets in a neatly composed period piece. Jacques Deprat is there, as is Honoré Lantenois, his boss, together with Pierre Termier and Alfred Lacroix. Nearly every leading geologist in the world is in the photograph, brought together to share their knowledge and increase their individual and collective understanding.

You will see thousands of similar photographs framed and hung on walls of scientific institutions, reproduced in conference proceedings and kept in scrapbooks. They all look the same because they all follow the rules of such compositions. They are the passive, visual records of meetings, conferences and congresses. They are souvenirs, but they are also the key to an unspoken code. The official photograph of the 1913 World Congress of Geology is like a map of a strange country. To begin with it is a pleasant confusion of intertwining lines, but when we understand its conventions and begin to pick out its landmarks, it becomes the guide to an unseen landscape.

In the Toronto picture we see Deprat, a 33-year-old researcher from a colonial backwater, sitting on the grass next to

Frank D. Adams, President of the World Congress, at the centre of the front row. The man chosen by his peers as the leader of their science, the king of their profession, has in turn chosen Jacques Deprat as his court favourite. This is no simple matter. Deprat must have been ushered forward, passed up through the ranks. Perhaps it was Termier, his mentor, who introduced him at an appropriate moment to someone close to Adams, or to Adams himself. Science, we need to understand, is a very peculiar combination – an intellectual meritocracy operating in a social oligarchy. Born and nourished by the decline of religious absolutism and the fading divinity of kings, science has retained a touch of the eighteenth-century court in its language and its doings. At every gathering you will see older men with clean-scrubbed youths at their shoulder. These are their favourite students, intended to carry the flame of their masters' work into the next generation. They must be introduced to those who matter, by those who matter. Their entry into the oligarchy must be carefully planned and promoted.

And when it comes to the photograph, the oligarchy is not only asserted, it is itself graded. So the kingpin is at the centre of the front row. On each side, in descending order, are the *éminences grises*. Scattered about the second and third rows are the rising stars, together with those who never quite made it to the top. Behind them and off to the sides are the 'participants' – those who come to the conferences to represent their institutions, but who are not invited to its highest councils.

Deprat must have known, as the lens cap was removed and the glass plate exposed, that everything was now possible for him. Everything that he had worked for in his life – the hours, days and months of tireless, slogging, lonely fieldwork, the manoeuvring, the hateful toadying, the disappointments in France, the sheer expenditure of energy in Indo-China – had led up this moment. And from this moment anything and everything might flow. His colleagues were telling him what he himself had always believed – he was something special, and he was bound for glory.

In contrast Honoré Lantenois is at the far right of the panoramic photograph, as far from the centre as it is possible to be. He has spent a lifetime in the service of his country. Having been an engineer in the Corps des Mines, Lantenois came to geology late in life, but with the passion of the convert. As Chief Mines Engineer in the French colony of Indo-China he fought to gain control of the old, moribund Service Géologique, and then reorganised it into a real scientific institution. He recruited the young Deprat to be its first Chief, and then watched as the young man walked away with *his* prize. Deprat's brilliance, his youth, his energy and his arrogance have made Lantenois feel irrelevant. And now he watches from the sidelines as Deprat, the man he has come to despise, takes his bow on the world stage, ready to take on a leading role in the science that Lantenois has come to love. The world of geology is not very large, Lantenois must know that there will never be any escape from Deprat. The younger man will eclipse him in everything, and will be ever-present in his life.

If we were in a spy film, the Toronto Congress photograph would be projected on to the wall of a darkened room, wreaths of blue smoke wafting across the solitary beam of light. A voice would call out for the technician to zoom in on two faces in the crowd. First Deprat – young, smiling, relaxed, happy, confident – his face refusing to accept the rules of the game, refusing to maintain a dignified restraint; the language of his body telling the story of the days leading up to this moment, of his irrepressible surprise and delight. Then Lantenois, his face similarly beyond the control of convention – angry, resentful, wounded, desperate. He wavers between a rejection of the camera, and a determination to stare it down. Between an instinct to rush away from his enemy's hour of triumph, and his duty and desire to be included in this body of men – it is, after all, an honour to be in the photograph. He is disappointed by something which he finds it hard to understand, because it is something that cannot be allowed for – the unfairness of the world.

And then, as the viewpoint is drawn back again, the two faces in the crowd remain highlighted. All of the others, despite their rank and achievements, are bit players in this drama. The two men are picked out, their faces look at us from eighty-five years away. It is what we know about the things to come that makes them so hypnotic. When we look at this photograph we are not just looking at a snapshot in the flow of events, we are witnessing an event in itself. And we see that in this manufactured event there are motives for the dark deeds that will follow. Here, preserved in one grainy image, are the victim and the executioner. All that remains is to discover which is which.

Part One

Before the Storm

1 *France, 1880–1908*

> You have no idea of the intrigues that go on in this blessed world of science. Science is, I fear, no purer than any other region of human activity, though it should be. Merit alone is very little good; it must be backed by tact and knowledge of the world to do very much.
>
> Thomas Huxley

Jacques François Georges Deprat was born in 1880 in the small town of Fontenay-aux-Roses, on the outskirts of Paris. His father was a teacher of *lettres* at the private college of Sainte-Barbe in the town. The family, of which Jacques was the only child, was not well off, but unusually literate, with extensive and enthusiastic knowledge of the classical world. In later life Jacques Deprat described his father as a Hellenist.

Like so many families in nineteenth-century Western Europe, the Deprats had moved within a few generations from a background of rural peasant life into urban trade and then into the professions. The families of Deprat's parents had made archetypal progress through the layers of French society. Their history reads like the encapsulation of the social history of an entire continent. Jacques Deprat's paternal great-grandfather had been a cobbler, coming from a family of peasants probably originating in the Savoie region. His grandfather was a tailor and, like thousands of other French artisans, he wanted his children to take advantage of the education on offer in mid-nineteenth-century France. Education was the route to becoming a member of a profession – the goal that traders held out for their children so that they would not have to work so hard for so little reward as the generations who went before them. So Jacques Deprat's father Amédée acquired an education, which enabled him to achieve secure, if modest, employment. In three generations the Deprats had lifted themselves from peasants living with the ever-present threat of famine, to schoolteachers in a thriving industrial state. They may have wondered where they might go from there.

The family moved to the town of Moulins when Amédée Deprat found a post at the *lycée*, and then to Besançon, capital of the eastern part of France known as Franche-Comté, in 1893 when Jacques was thirteen. Though Besançon was remote from the great cities and centres of learning of France, its location was a blessing for the young Jacques Deprat. Here, on the lower slopes of the Jura Mountains, he became fascinated by the natural world. And as he grew older he ventured to the high country of the Jura and the Swiss Alps to the south. He had already been given his first geology handbook at the age of eleven, and had become passionately interested in rocks and plants. Now in the Jura natural history in general, and geology in particular, began to be his obsession.

But as well as being an enthusiast for natural sciences, Deprat was also fond of literature, being familiar with Goethe, Schiller and Shakespeare as well as French and classical writers. Throughout his autobiographical novel *Les Chiens aboient**

**Les Chiens aboient* is an autobiographical *roman-à-clef* written by Jacques Deprat under a pseudonym. It was written and published several years after the affair. It is, inevitably, a partial account of the affair, written from one viewpoint and with the benefit of hindsight. Nevertheless, in matters of fact rather than interpretation, it cross-checks accurately with other sources where they exist. Occasionally the account of an event in *Les Chiens aboient* is the only one we have. Where this is the case I have quoted or paraphrased it, with due warning to the reader that its accuracy cannot be absolutely guaranteed. Although Deprat changed the names of all the people involved in the story,

Deprat is keen to show that the two can go together, that a cultured and creative mind could also be a scientific one. He reports that someone said to him when he was twenty years old that you cannot be both an artist and a scientist, you must decide which, or you will end up as neither. But he writes that he always believed these two things co-existed within him.

A 'classical education' was still a strong element of the French school system, but for most students Greek and Latin literature must have been a curiosity. Deprat, doubtless through his father's influence and enthusiasm, seems to have been genuinely fascinated by the classical world, and by literature. His father's enthusiasms fit well with those of a good number of nineteenth-century French schoolteachers. Like Amédée Deprat, most had come from backgrounds which were certainly uncultured and possibly illiterate. Knowledge of, and familiarity with, the classics was the achievement that had lifted their lives above the hum-drum existence of their forebears. Their attachment to the classics, and their fight to keep them on the school syllabus, were less a conservative reaction than a personal expression of indebtedness.

At one point in *Les Chiens aboient*, Deprat paints a charming picture of a scene from his youth:

> Geology strongly attracted the poetic side of his nature, and he had no greater joy than going with his father on an excursion into the mountains, finding fossils and rocks which he would examine on their return. The marl-pits of the Jura, the quarries, rich in well-preserved fossils, enabled him to seek out the remains of vanished ages, while his father, learned, but not attracted to experimental sciences, sat beneath a pine tree and peacefully read some Greek text.

This vision of harmony across the generations belies the

the changes were deliberately trivial enough for anyone with any knowledge of the affair to be able to figure them out. In extracts from *Les Chiens aboient* quoted in this book, real names appear in square brackets.

difficulties and paradoxes that Amédée Deprat faced in his life as a teacher – some of which were echoed in the tempestuous life of his only son. The attitude towards education and towards schoolteachers in France at this time was highly ambiguous. Among the growing middle classes in particular, belief in education, both as a virtue in itself and as passport to success in life, was very strong. It has been said that education was venerated almost to the point of being a substitute for religion as the locus of all virtue.

There is no question that the renowned centralisation of French education promoted a welcome sense of national unity. The Franco-Prussian War, which culminated in the Paris Commune in 1871, had been a national humiliation and was followed by virtual civil war. It has long been held that the 'idea' of France as a unified nation and culture was created and sustained in and by her schools, but the resources given to schools and teachers to carry out this great task were pitiful. Not only was the pay of teachers uncommonly bad (a survey of teachers' salaries in Europe placed France last out of twenty-five countries), their social status was also extremely low. As well as that, the prospects for promotion were restricted, since it was impossible to pass from one grade of school to another without undergoing a rigorous and exhausting set of examinations. Within the system, the only realistic way of advancement was to move. And this is what many teachers, including Amédée Deprat, did.

The consequence of all this was that Jacques Deprat's family gave him the advantages of a fine education and strong emotional support. But they could not give him the two things they did not have – money and status. It was this combination of a highly educated, well-trained and brilliant mind with a legacy of social inferiority that was to prove so crucial to Jacques Deprat's downfall.

Deprat decided to follow a scientific career. He loved the idea of a geologist's life, as an explorer, out in the hills and mountains, using his brain and hands to discover the history of the Earth. He was, no doubt, a romantic, strongly drawn to the natural world, and in particular to its high and remote places:

> The science of the Earth attracted him irresistibly . . . It relied on all the other sciences, and also summarised them all. It was the breathtaking poem of the history of the planet, full of great images. It appealed to the strength of those spirits capable of visualizing phenomena on an extraordinary scale, of embracing at one glance immense successions of events, the life and death of entire groups of animals, the changing of the oceans over thousands of years, the formation and complete erosion of great mountain chains, worn down over countless myriads of centuries, of exercising mental faculties after ingenious analysis, of conceiving in the folds of the earth a prodigious mechanics, out of all comparison with the possibilities offered to men. And the life of the true geologist, was not that of a 'coquillard' [shellfish] living among the drawers of specimens, or the bookish professor of science, but was a wonderful life, spent in large part on long rambles, hammer in hand, on the pathways of the mountains. (*Les Chiens aboient*)

Jacques Deprat had two great strokes of fortune in his scientific education. First, a new university was created at Besançon in 1896 – the year before Deprat left school – and second, a young man named Eugène Fournier was immediately appointed to teach the course in geology. The inspirational example of Fournier confirmed everything that the young Deprat had felt about geology, and from then on he determined that geology would be not just a subject for study, but his life's work.

The state of higher education at this time was highly peculiar to France, and was to have a decisive influence on the explosive events to come in Deprat's life. A book published in 1875 said bluntly that 'there is no higher education in France'. This was only a slight exaggeration of a situation that had come about through the vagaries of French history. In 1789 the national government that came into power after the Revolution closed all the twenty-two universities in France. In their stead a hodgepodge of institutions with a seemingly unregulated set of differing functions came into being. Universities as disinterested places of learning were done away with and replaced by specialised institutions. These new colleges provided vocational training for the liberal and technical professions. But whereas this might have been designed to be a more rigorous and comprehensive system it became, on the whole, hopelessly lax. The old universities were mostly deconstructed into their constituent *facultés*, whose main function was to award baccalaureat certificates to *lycée* students (the head of a *faculté* was often *de facto* Director of Education for a department or region) and to give out degrees, or more descriptively *licences*, i.e. licences to practise. But the *facultés* had almost no students and very few staff. The lectures were open to the public, and were mostly attended by retired people and some students from local *lycées* or secondary schools. The undergraduate population had more or less disappeared. In this sense the 1875 author was entirely correct – higher education did not exist. The exceptions to this sorry state of affairs were the so-called Grandes Ecoles – institutions whose influence in and on nineteenth-century France was pervasive.

While the old universities had been officially downgraded and then left to decay, a new set of institutions was formed, ostensibly to provide technical skills and training. The Ecole Polytechnique with its associated colleges, e.g. the Ecole des Mines and Ecole des Ponts et Chaussées, were literally technical colleges. But soon after their formation, something quite peculiar began to happen. Because the *facultés* were held in such low regard and because there was no other higher education in France, the Ecole Polytechnique with its residential regime, its strict discipline and its intellectual rigour became, along with the Ecole Normale Supérieure, the place where the élite chose to be educated, and where they chose to educate their children. The 'normal' situation was reversed, and a technical education at one of the Grandes Ecoles was proof of membership of, and a passport into, the social élite. Technical education became highly developed, but its exclusivity was rigorously maintained. France did not produce a mass of highly trained technicians, but a small élite of engineers. The number of places in these Ecoles was restricted and the influence of this élite was clear. While graduates of the Ecole Normale tended to go into teaching or perhaps politics, the more avowedly technical Ecoles turned out 'engineers', who in reality became administrators:

> The Polytechniciens and the graduates of the schools of applied science [Ecole des Mines, Ecole des Ponts et Chaussées], of course had their own *esprit de corps*, which, however, was more tied up with control of the state administration . . . Because they were so comfortably ensconced in one sector of the economy they took care not to draw too much attention to their privileges, and they adopted a system of live and let live towards the rest of society. (Zeldin, 1977)

The bureaucracy of the French state and its various colonies was thus largely and quietly controlled by graduates of just a few institutions.

By the 1890s a general reform of higher education in France was desperately needed. The *facultés* had become reduced to the most pathetic circumstances. They survived in tiny cramped offices in the poorest quarters of French cities. Nor did this apply only to provincial institutions. The faculty of sciences at the Sorbonne was reported as occupying 'a few tiny rooms, formerly used as kitchens and bedrooms by students' in the 1870s. The equipment was, by the last decade of the century, at least fifty years old. Libraries had virtually ceased to acquire books and periodicals, and Clermont-Ferrand, one of the largest cities in France, had in 1876 in its Faculty of Letters a grand total of seven regular students.

If he had been born ten years earlier, Jacques Deprat's prospects of higher education would have been dismal. And it is a fair bet that any ambitions he nurtured to become a professional geologist would have ended when he left school. The teaching of science in the *faculté* at Besançon had diminished markedly and the only route to academic or professional status was via the Grandes Ecoles. Although in theory these were open to entrance by examination, in practice getting through the exams involved expensive instruction and private coaching. Then, in 1896, a new Act was passed which created, and gave funding for, fifteen new universities, including the University of Besançon.

The founding of the new University of Besançon and the arrival of Eugène Fournier as tutor of the geology course, were decisive influences in Deprat's life. Fournier was only twenty-seven, and brought with him his friend Arthur Bresson, who was just twenty-five. Under the guidance of these two young teachers, Deprat became further enraptured by geology and was encouraged to follow his enthusiasm. He appears to have been a prodigiously energetic student. By the time he became a Bachelor of Science (Licencié ès Sciences) in 1899, he had already had his first paper published in the *Mémoires de la Société d'Histoire Naturelle* for the department of Doubs, placed three notes on the foothills of the Jura in the *Feuilles des jeunes naturalistes*, and in addition joined the Société Géologique de France. The following year he published a monograph on the Massif de la Serre in the society's journal. By the age of twenty he was on his way to becoming a scientist.

Once he graduated in 1900, Jacques Deprat needed to find work or a place to undertake further study. Despite its natural geological advantages, there was no opportunity for this precocious young man to advance his education or career in Besançon. The new university had no facilities for graduate students, so to get the further qualifications that would enable him to make a living as a geologist, Deprat had to pack his bags and go to Paris. His published work and presumably high recommendations from Eugène Fournier enabled Deprat to get a place in the laboratory of Alfred Lacroix, at the Muséum National d'Histoire Naturelle in Paris. It was not incumbent on Lacroix to take on graduate students and he would not necessarily have done this as a matter of course. We can assume that Deprat's work and personality (he would have attended for at least one interview) were unusually impressive.

Deprat went to Paris in 1900 and remained there until 1904. He would not have received a grant in the form of a living allowance, but may have received some funding from the Académie des Sciences for particular pieces of work, and for the expense of typing and binding his thesis. Otherwise he would have had to fend for himself. Deprat's family did not have the money to support a son living independently in the capital, but fortunately his cousins, the Lefebvres, lived in Paris. The Lefebvres had visited the Deprats in Besançon each summer, and they had travelled through the Jura and Swiss Alps together. Jacques boarded with them from 1900 to 1904. As well as this free accommodation there were canteens, which were really more like soup kitchens, provided for students around the Latin Quarter. The Muséum is on the edge of the quarter, near to the University buildings, so we can assume that Jacques Deprat was able to take advantage of this cheap source of food. Conditions for Parisian students had not changed much from the 1840s when Murger wrote *La Vie de bohème*, later immortalised by Puccini in *La Bohème*. Apart from his work, we do not know much about Deprat's life in Paris. The city was famous for its wild social life at the time, but Deprat would have been conscious of his dependence on his father's meagre salary. He seems to have been a diligent and conscientious student.

In Paris, under the supervision of Lacroix, Jacques Deprat studied for his doctorate. Lacroix was a mineralogist, who was to achieve great success studying the composition of the lava and magma from the Mt St Pierre eruption on Martinique in 1902. Deprat himself became interested in mineralogy – the study, usually through the examination of thin sections under microscope, of the minerals which comprise rocks.

His main interest, though, was in tectonics. The study of the large-scale forces and movements of the Earth's crust that are responsible for the creation of mountain chains, and the raising and lowering of continents, was of great interest at this time, particularly in France. It was French geologists, through their studies of the Alps in the late nineteenth and early twentieth centuries, who unravelled the complexities of tectonic forces, and won international acclaim for their work. For an aspiring geologist in France, tectonics was *the* subject with which to be involved.

In 1902, while studying in Lacroix's laboratory, Deprat applied for and received a grant from the Ministry of Public Instruction to investigate the geology of the Greek island of Evvoia. He spent eight months on the island from April to December 1902 – this was to be the subject of his doctoral thesis. Evvoia (known in French as Eubée) is hardly an island, being separated from the mainland for the whole of its hundred-mile length by a narrow channel. A bridge links the island to Greece at Chalcis. The island covers a total of 4,000 square kilometres (160 kilometres long by 25 wide). Mapping and explaining the geology of such a large island in eight months was a huge undertaking for a relatively inexperienced graduate student. Deprat produced a 300,000:1 geological map which, it is now claimed, 'was considered the best geological map of any part of Greece for many years' (Durand-Delga, 1990).

The island had been studied in 1877 by a geologist named Teller, and Deprat managed to update his work considerably. Deprat found evidence of Palaeozoic rocks on the island, and did important dating work on Permian and Carboniferous rocks using fusulinid micro-fossils – the first time this had been done in Greece. In addition he found important Jurassic reef deposits and dated three stages of the upper Cretaceous period. He presented his thesis to the examiners at the Sorbonne in 1904. While being an impressive piece of work, it also offers a nice example of different types of scientific error.

Deprat dated some rocks on Evvoia as Lower Cretaceous – a period which is now thought not to exist on the island. Guernet's work in the 1960s showed that the fossils Deprat used to date the rocks are Jurassic in age. This was a minor misinterpretation by Deprat.

His analysis of the tectonics of the region was exactly in tune with the ideas of the time – ideas which are now thought to be wrong. It was not until 1980 that, as Michel Durand-Delga wrote in his paper on the Deprat affair in 1990, 'the extra-ordinary piling up of internal nappes in the Hellenides, of which Evvoia offers a beautiful example, was eventually recognised'.

Nappes are slabs of rock formed by folds toppling over, which are then thrust over the top of lower strata (see page 57). We cannot call this an error by Deprat, since it would have taken a huge leap in understanding, for which the evidence may not have existed, for the young student to propose the type of tectonic history that is understood today. Nevertheless the relation between historical time and scientific truth and knowledge is particularly relevant to Deprat's story, and it is interesting to see it emerging early in his career.

Another error in his thesis was potentially more serious. Deprat had something of a feud with a senior geologist named Emile Haug over the age of certain rocks, known as 'schistes lustrés', found in the Alps. The analysis of these rocks was important for untangling the complex history of the Alpine region – a major concern of French geologists at the time. Haug said that Alpine 'schistes lustrés' were Mesozoic in age, while Deprat had argued in 1904 that they were much older – i.e. Palaeozoic. Deprat then used his work on Evvoia to attempt to reinforce his argument. He said that glaucophane and lawsonite schists of Palaeozoic age found in Evvoia were formed in the same way as the Alpine schists. Unfortunately for Deprat, Haug was proved right about the Alpine schists, and this part of Deprat's work was therefore based on an incorrect premise.

In his argument with Haug's views, Deprat marshalled

'evidence' to prove a case. In retrospect his motives seem dubious – and his behaviour would have been as incorrect if he had been proved right as it was when he was shown to be wrong. Although we might presume that Deprat's science became corrupted by his motives, this case is an illustration of the tension that lies at the heart of all scientific work. While we now understand that the simple recording of information is only a small part of a scientist's work, we still underestimate the degree to which the making of acute and perceptive observations depends on a pre-formed idea. This obviously runs both ways – scientists make hypotheses out of facts and then test their hypotheses against more information. But a theory, or a hunch, or an idea, is the essential driving force of scientific investigation. And when a theory begins to conflict with the facts, science gets both interesting and potentially difficult for those involved. Should you fight for your idea in the face of apparently contrary evidence? Should you give it up at the first sign of any inconvenient facts? There is an obvious temptation to over-step the line and make 'wrong' observations to support a theory, as Deprat seemed to do in this case. If we believe he was a little too enthusiastic in his own support, it is worth pointing out that many other researchers shared his views, and that the argument over the age of the 'schistes lustrés' continued among geologists for another forty years.

Inaccuracies are inevitable in every scientific publication. Everyone from the neophyte researcher to the Nobel laureate either bases some part of his or her work on assumptions that are later superseded, or interprets material according to a contemporary authority which gives way to another in time. Nevertheless it is interesting to see that Deprat's thesis contained different types of error, and it is these differences which are fundamental if we are to understand a little of what science is about.

Deprat's thesis was, on balance, an admirable achievement and he was duly awarded his doctorate by the Sorbonne in 1904. It must have been a great and proud moment for his family and for Jacques Deprat himself – the only son of an impecunious *lycée* teacher awarded a doctorate from the University of Paris. He may have been lucky that the new universities came into being at the right time for him, but he had made the most of his opportunity.

By the end of 1904 Jacques Deprat was a 24-year-old geologist with a doctorate from the Sorbonne, a solid reputation, a growing number of influential contacts and a determination to make his living in his science. What were his options? Unfortunately not many. He was about to find out that promising academic achievement was only a small part of what was required to make a career in science. Deprat would have dearly loved to get a teaching post at a university in France, but these were few and far between. The new universities had only been in full operation for six or seven years, so it is fair to assume that not much movement had yet taken place among the staff, while a post at one of the Grandes Ecoles would have been out of the question for a *universitaire*.

The best he could do at first was to take an unpaid job at his old college in Besançon, teaching a course in petrography. This branch of geology is to do with analysing rock content, usually by microscope, and classifying rocks. His old teacher Eugène Fournier gave him the job which, though unsalaried, had some advantages. First and foremost, Deprat had recently married his childhood sweetheart Marguerite Tissier from Moulins. The newlyweds were now able to live with Deprat's parents in Besançon, though the birth of two daughters in 1905 and 1906 must have begun to strain the family finances. Essentially they were all – four adults and two children – dependent for regular income on the small schoolteacher's salary of Jacques's father Amédée. Jacques was able to supplement this income by giving public lectures on geology, at which a small entrance fee was charged. This sideline was boosted by an upsurge of interest in geology among the French public, caused by a catastrophic natural disaster.

In May 1902 a volcano named Mt Pelée on the Caribbean

island and French colony of Martinique erupted. The effect was immediate and devastating. A wall of gas, glass and dust, at a temperature of 800°C, immediately engulfed the nearby town of St Pierre, instantly killing all but two of its 28,000 inhabitants. This type of cloud is now technically known to geologists as a *nuée ardente* (literally 'blazing cloud'). There was little warning, as the side of the mountain was simply blown away and the gas emulsion travelled down the lower slopes at around 100 kilometres per hour. (It is now thought that the people of Pompeii may have died in a similar *nuée ardente* erupting out of Vesuvius in AD79.) Miraculously, there is one eyewitness account of the eruption, by a seaman who was lucky enough to be still on board his ship in the harbour when the eruption happened:

> As we approached St. Pierre we could distinguish the rolling and leaping of red flames that belched from the mountain in huge volumes and gushed into the sky. Enormous clouds of black smoke hung over the volcano . . . There was a constant muffled roar. It was like the biggest oil refinery in the world burning up on the mountain top. There was a tremendous explosion about 7:45, soon after we got in. The mountain was blown to pieces. There was no warning. The side of the volcano was ripped out and there was hurled straight towards us a solid wall of flame. It sounded like a thousand cannon.
>
> The wave of fire was on us and over us like a flash of lightning. It was like a hurricane of fire . . . The hurricane of fire rolled *en masse* straight down upon St. Pierre and the shipping. The town vanished before our eyes. The air grew stifling hot and we were in the thick of it. Wherever the mass of fire struck the sea, the water boiled and sent up vast columns of steam. The sea was torn into huge whirlpools that careened towards the open sea . . . The blast of fire from the volcano lasted only a few minutes. It shrivelled and set fire to everything it touched . . .
>
> Before the volcano burst, the landings of St. Pierre were

> covered with people. After the explosion not one living soul was seen on the land. (quoted in Press and Siever, 1986)

The impact of the disaster back in France was enormous. The photographs of the devastated town, which contained a substantial number of French citizens, brought home the incredible violence of the eruption. This was the age of science, and the public wanted to know how the scientists could explain such an event. How could such a thing happen with so little warning? Scientists, too, were fascinated by the eruption and French geologists made straight for Martinique to study the erupted volcano and its glass and ash and lava. As we have seen, Deprat's supervisor Alfred Lacroix made his name in the study of the mineralogy of the Mt Pelée lavas. The interest in Mt Pelée continued for several years as more discoveries were made.

Though still waiting in vain for the opportunity of a salaried teaching post, Deprat did manage to get some fieldwork while teaching at Besançon. In 1905, through Lacroix's influence, he obtained a grant of 4,000F to travel to Sardinia at intervals over the next two years. Just as importantly, he became a *Collaborateur* in the Service de la Carte Géologique, a government body responsible for the geological surveying and mapping of France. Deprat worked in Sardinia and Corsica at intervals from September 1904 to the end of 1907. His mentor Lacroix had now been elected to membership of the élite Académie des Sciences in Paris, and Jacques Deprat began to send a series of notes on the geology of Corsica to the academy. The protocol was that scientists who were not members could submit short reports (Comptes-Rendus) to the academy, and these would be read to a meeting by an academician – if he thought them worthy of the academy's interest. Some of Deprat's Comptes-Rendus were read by Lacroix, others by Auguste Michel-Lévy, a well-known petrologist, who was an admirer of Deprat's work and Director of the Service de la Carte Géologique.

Corsica was a fascinating place for geologists, and Deprat made a significant contribution to understanding its geological history. The island has two distinct geological regions, east and west. Deprat suggested that the eastern side had been thrust or dragged over the western side. This idea was based on his discovery of a zone of crushed granite, known as protogine, between the two regions. Part of the reason for Deprat's novel discoveries on the island was his great skill at rock-climbing. His upbringing within reach of the Jura mountains had turned him into an enthusiastic mountaineer, and he was simply able to go where other geologists could not. But he also showed a prodigious talent tor the conceptual abstractions that are the most difficult and necessary part of geological fieldwork. The unravelling of the geological history of even a single rock formation, never mind an entire region, can be a fiendishly difficult task with considerable pitfalls for the unwary. The ability to match pieces of evidence which are geographically and temporally separated, and usually intermittent, and to visualise a coherent pattern, comes with experience and confidence. It also requires a proper adherence to the known facts, combined with the boldness to consider novel and adventurous interpretations and explanations of these facts.

Deprat's striking work on the tectonic history of Corsica was well received in Paris, and brought him admirers in the senior echelons of geology. In particular it brought him to the attention of one of the most important geologists of the twentieth century. Pierre Termier was Professor of Mineralogy and Petrology at the Ecole des Mines and assistant to Auguste Michel-Lévy at the Service de la Carte Géologique. His grandiose synthesis of the geological structure of the Alps was to make him, in the words of the standard work of scientific biography, 'the founder of modern tectonics and geodynamics' (Gillispie 1970). Considering the impact that modern tectonics has had, this makes Termier one of the most important geologists of his, or any other, time.

Termier was so impressed with Deprat's work on Corsica, a place where he himself had studied, that he suggested they co-publish a report on a particular part of Deprat's studies – the alkaline granite found in the nappes of the eastern part of the island. From Deprat's point of view, this was a curious and rather annoying request. Deprat felt that the paper he had already published in 1905 contained all he was able to say on the subject. Moreover, he did not feel that Termier would be contributing anything to the paper. In other words the more senior scientist would be conferring some status on his junior colleague by offering co-authorship, and in return would be gaining credit for work with which he had, in reality, little connection. This 'system' of mutual backscratching is common enough in science, but Deprat took a dim view of it. Termier had seen the importance of Deprat's ideas on the famous 'protogine', but the information in their joint paper was, in Deprat's view, little different from what he had published on his own in 1905. Nevertheless Deprat could hardly refuse such an offer from such an eminent colleague. To do so would not only be impolite, it would be positively dangerous to his career. In his autobiography he writes that his father advised him that for once he should swallow his pride and agree. He consoled himself with the thought that, 'After all, it is customary for people to help each other.'

The joint Termier–Deprat report was read to the Académie des Sciences by Michel-Lévy in 1908. To be fair to Termier, even if the paper did not advance the subject much, he was probably genuinely attempting to give Deprat's work a boost by offering to associate himself with it. Termier subsequently did ground-breaking work on the Alpine formations of Corsica with Eugène Maury, using Deprat's ideas, which he was always careful to credit. Nevertheless Deprat clearly harboured some degree of resentment over the incident.

Deprat was becoming established as a researcher, and was building up a body of work on the geology of the Mediterranean, but he found that all scientists did not necessarily behave as he thought they should. He guarded his own priority very carefully, and was easily irritated by any lack of acknowledgement of his work. As well as the Termier incident, he had a number of disputes with other researchers going back to his student days. In 1903 he became annoyed with an experienced geologist, Canon Bourgeat, who failed to cite the work on the Massif de la Serre which he had published as a twenty-year-old. In 1905 and 1906 he crossed swords with Jules Savornin, a young geologist who argued against the prevailing orthodoxy of nappes, and who muddled up the extremely complex structure of Corsica.

Then in 1905 an argument with Maurice Piroutet, a colleague at the Muséum d'Histoire Naturelle, was played out in the pages of scientific journals. Piroutet had brought back samples from a geological expedition to New Caledonia and, as is customary, had shared these with his colleagues. Deprat recognised some micro-fossils known as orthophragmines in some of Piroutet's thin sections. These were the first definite evidence of rocks of Eocene age on the island. Deprat reported this discovery in a note to the Académie des Sciences, and sent a copy to Piroutet. This peremptory publication seems to have upset Piroutet, who then incorporated Deprat's work into a general report on New Caledonia which he was writing at the time. In this report he played down Deprat's role in the discovery of Eocene rocks. Now it was Deprat's turn to feel aggrieved. In June 1905 he published a paper in the *Bulletins de la Société Géologique* about the fossils of New Caledonia (Deprat, 1905). As the basis of the paper, he used material that Piroutet had left behind in Paris while he was on another expedition to the island. Deprat had not, it seems, asked Piroutet's permission or informed him of his plans. On his return, Piroutet criticised Deprat publicly.

What are we to make of this strange and rather petty feud? Michel Durand-Delga writes, 'This is a regrettable instance of a lack of mutual trust, of a certain superiority complex that Deprat possessed, and of rather poor reactions by Piroutet. But to call Deprat a thief in this matter – as the rumour ran later – is excessive, as shown by a close analysis of the texts.'

So, while Deprat was a keen, active and impressive researcher, doing innovative work and making useful contacts, there is no doubt that he was also a little arrogant and was making enemies too.

His own views of other scientists, written up later in *Les Chiens aboient*, were no doubt partially coloured by the events still to come. But Deprat wrote that these views began to form at this time in his life, and the way they are expressed is revealing of his view of himself, as well as of others. He writes about himself in the third person:

> He had kept the same enthusiasm for scientific research. But the respectful admiration that he had held in his younger years for the men of science had been severely undermined. He had met some who worked with the most profound detachment from any scientific vanity, looking into the unknown, endeavouring to see some new light in the darkness. But these types were few in number. The majority have a well-paid job in a distinguished institution as their ultimate ambition . . . He sees men of mediocre intelligence, blinding the public with science, following the received wisdom of the day, never missing a chance to push their own cause. Most of the researchers in the scientific institutions, cross and recross the same places, producing volumes full of banalities. They create a reputation as a specialist in some minor, narrow branch, falling by chance on an interesting piece of data, of which they are incapable of understanding the true scope.

Science has room for different types of minds. And those who beaver away in a narrow and apparently obscure field are as much a part of the necessary structure of science as those who seek the grand syntheses. So did Deprat, in his impatience with the 'mediocre', misunderstand what science was about? Given his own meticulous work in highly specialised areas like micro-palaeontology, this would be an unfair judgement. But there is no doubt that he saw himself as able to grasp the 'true scope' of the information that he uncovered and expected others to be able to do the same.

In the years from 1904 to 1908 Deprat did plenty of research and made a considerable impact. He was in demand for government surveying projects and was highly thought of by the right people, but he still craved a teaching appointment in higher education and his financial and professional situation remained precarious without a full-time job. He later wrote that, at this time, 'he was preparing his future'.

But the future seemed a long way off. The problem for Deprat was that to be a professional academic geologist in France was to be part of a social as much as a scientific élite. If you were not already part of this group, it was extremely difficult to force your way in. However much brilliant scientific work Deprat did, other factors lay between him and professional security. Social mobility in any society is overwhelmingly a one-way process. While the lower orders may move up, the élite fight tooth and nail to ensure that their offspring do not move down. This means that upward mobility can only happen when there is an expansion of opportunity higher up the social scale. Europe has seen large-scale upward social mobility because of the vast expansion of 'professional' jobs, not because the upper and lower classes have swapped around. A social historian of France demonstrates the barriers that the petite-bourgeoisie faced, in this analysis of French society at the end of the nineteenth century:

> Family links and personal relationships continued to be of fundamental importance in the choice of a career and in influencing success. Many social commentators [of the time] stressed the importance of personal ability and success. It was a fundamental element in middle-class ideology, and yet social mobility cannot be said to have been a major characteristic of French society in the nineteenth century. In terms of the proportion of the population affected, upward mobility was achieved by relatively few. Where it did occur it normally took a step-by-step form, a process spread over generations and subject to numerous reversals. Although

> individual ability counted for something, inheritance remained the major influence upon the life chances of an individual. Capital and culture were important. Education and establishment in a profession were expensive. Parental wealth made upward mobility easier and reduced the likelihood of downward movement.

In 1900 only 12 per cent of business and administrative élites

> had middle-class or popular family backgrounds, and these newcomers, of course, succeeded not only because of their intellectual activity and technical competence *but due to their ability to conform, and their skill at integrating themselves, socially and culturally into the élite* [my italics]. The renewal of the élite due to economic and social change was thus extremely limited. (Price, 1987)

To get a university post, and therefore membership of a social élite, you needed more than a few useful contacts in geology. You needed influence and, according to Deprat, you needed the ability to intrigue – neither of which he seemed to have. In the light of later events, we might ask whether Deprat ever did have the skills, or desire, to conform socially and culturally with the élite. His outsider status was brought home to him by two incidents.

In 1904 Lucien Cayeux, a mineralogist whom Deprat knew well, was made Assistant Professor at the Ecole des Mines. This left a vacancy in the same institution as Chef de Travaux. But this post, which Deprat would certainly have been qualified to apply for, was not available in open competition. Instead it was awarded to Robert Douvillé, son of Henri Douvillé, himself Professor of Palaeontology at the Ecole des Mines. In *Les Chiens aboient* Deprat relates this incident to demonstrate another factor besides nepotism. When Cayeux was offered the post of Professor, Deprat wrote to ask whether he might come and work for him. Cayeux's reply is quoted in full in *Les Chiens aboient.* In the letter, Cayeux says that there is hostility to his own appointment because he is not one of the Corps, by which he means he is not himself a graduate of the Ecole Polytechnique and the Ecole des Mines. The Corps, he goes on to say, control everything, and although this is a disgrace, and a hangover from the previous century – that's the way it is. Cayeux's own position was weak and he was therefore unable to help Deprat. If the candidates had been judged by 'our colleagues from the universities' (*'nos confrères universitaires'*) Deprat would have been given the job. This, as Deprat sees it, is the main obstacle to progress in scientific circles in France. If you are one of the Corps you will get the plum jobs. If you are a *universitaire* you will be lucky to work as a technician or *préparateur.* As a *universitaire* himself, Cayeux's appointment at the Ecole des Mines was virtually without precedent in that institution – and did not seem likely to lead to others achieving similar access.

Then in June 1905 the post of Head of Conferences in Mineralogy at the University of Clermont-Ferrand fell vacant. The previous occupant of the post, named Glangeaud, had become Professor on the death of his predecessor – an indication in itself of how hard it was to move up the academic ladder. Deprat later wrote that he had told Alfred Lacroix he would like to apply for the job. Lacroix told him that there was 'no point in hoping you will get the job, but it might help you to get something else in due course'. But that 'due course' went on and on, and he seemed to get no nearer to a full-time job.

By 1908, at the age of twenty-eight, Deprat had an impressive track record, but he was still dependent on sporadic grants and public lectures for his income. Vacancies for teaching posts in universities remained extremely rare and always went to those with the right 'old school' connections. He had a wife and two young daughters to support. In addition his father was shortly to retire from his teaching job at the age of sixty. The Deprat family's only secure source of income was about to be reduced by three-quarters to a minute pension. Jacques Deprat was in danger of being forced out of geology by financial circumstances. At this most difficult time of his career, help arrived from an unlikely and fateful source. Deprat was about to come into contact with the man who would play the leading role in the drama of his downfall.

Honoré Lantenois was in many ways the opposite of Jacques Deprat. Unlike the poorly paid and socially disregarded Amédée Deprat, Lantenois's father was a civilian Captain in the Marines – a reasonable rank in a distinguished service. We may wonder at a society that places a military administrator above a schoolteacher, while proclaiming its devotion to education – but such paradoxes are so commonplace as to be unremarkable, and that is how it was. Lantenois was born in 1863, seventeen years before Jacques Deprat. After secondary school he entered the élite Ecole Polytechnique. It is worth looking at this institution in a little more depth. The Polytechniciens were the *crème de la crème* of French students, but even within this small élite there was a further inner circle. The Polytechniciens ranked slightly above the students and graduates of the so-called *écoles d'application* which, along with the Ecole Polytechnique and Ecole Normale Superieure, were established in the wake of the 1789 Revolution. Of these *écoles d'application*, the Ecole des Mines was the oldest and most prestigious. Graduates of the Ecole des Mines were generally employed by the government and carried the title 'Ingénieur des Mines'.

Apart from teaching its own students, the Ecole des Mines had an arrangement whereby it would take a small number of the Ecole Polytechnique students for special instruction. This opportunity was given only to the very best of the Polytechnique students and was considered a great honour. These double-graduates of the Ecole Polytechnique and the Ecole des Mines carried the title 'Ingénieur au Corps des Mines'. Their relatively small numbers increased their sense of exclusiveness and solidarity. Honoré Lantenois graduated as an Ingenieur au Corps des Mines – and became a member of what was known as the Corps. This was the group whose influence Lucien Cayeux so resented.

The legendary *esprit de corps* of the graduates of these special institutions was founded in part on a sense of exclusivity, and in part on the shared experience of rigid mental and physical discipline. Although the cost of private coaching and tuition for the rigorous entrance exams excluded most of French society from entering the Grandes Ecoles, within the higher social classes which formed their catchment, there was a degree of merit in selection. All entrants had to pass the exams, and therefore only the best students got in. On graduation these students were guaranteed a successful career in the government service or industry. This in turn gave added prestige to the Grandes Ecoles, which increased competition for places. There was, over the decades of the nineteenth and early twentieth centuries, a spiralling effect, the result of which was to give the graduates of the Grandes Ecoles power and influence over the country's affairs.

As for the discipline, descriptions of the Ecole Normale and the Ecole Polytechnique shows the kind of regime that existed:

> Their *esprit de corps* was, and is, legendary. The school indeed consciously sought to create this by its military organisation. Its students lived in groups of about eight, for the two years of their course, with one room in which there were eight desks, a bedroom with eight beds and a bathroom with eight washbasins. On the wall a timetable told them exactly how they would be spending every minute of the day. (Zeldin, 1977)

Students rose at the militarily-influenced time of five in the morning. Mental discipline was important too. Louis Pasteur was a professor at the Ecole Normale in the 1860s, and the register of punishments which he filled out included castigations 'for having read a novel', 'for having read a newspaper', 'for having introduced a periodical into the school'.

The Corps, which was an élite within an élite, not only had influence, but their particular shared experience induced in its members a powerful sense of superiority and solidarity. Deprat was to find that, by confronting one of its members, he incurred the disapproval, if not the wrath, of every *corpsard*.

As a member of the Corps des Mines, Lantenois was given work in the government service as soon as he graduated. He was appointed as an Engineer, working first in Carcassonne and then in Algeria. In 1903, after nearly two decades of government service, he was promoted to Chef de Service des Mines in the French colony of Indo-China.

Honoré Lantenois would have been taught some mineralogy and some geology as part of his training at the Ecole des Mines. And, unlike most of his fellow engineers, he seems to have developed a keen interest in the subject. He joined the Société Géologique de France in his thirties.

When Lantenois first went to Indo-China there was a small geological service in Hanoi, which was part of the Department of Agriculture. Traditionally this service had been the handmaiden of the engineers and agricultural technicians. The geologists, such as existed, were called in whenever a technical problem needed their input. In fact the geological service in Hanoi was fairly typical in having no university-trained geologists on its staff. The staff were technicians who had picked up geological skills in a variety of ways. They were treated as the intellectual servants of the *ingénieurs* – the école-trained corps who were building the infrastructure of the colony and the French Empire.

Lantenois, though he remained an engineer and a *corpsard* through and through, wanted to change the role of geology in the Colonial Service in Indo-China. By 1908 he was well enough established to be able to persuade the authorities to remove the geological service from the Agriculture Department and place it within the Service des Mines, where it would be under his personal control. He then forced the head of the service, Jean-Baptiste Counillon, whom he regarded as not up to the job, to step aside. But Lantenois did not just want to control the service, he had much bigger plans. He wanted to make the Service Géologique de l'Indochine into an independent research centre, mapping the geology of the territory, carrying out its own surveys and investigations and publishing its own journal. He knew that, in order to do this, he would need help. He and his staff, while keen and knowledgeable to a degree, simply did not have the breadth of scientific knowledge and expertise that would be required.

Towards the end of 1907, once he knew that the Service Géologique was to be 'his', Lantenois began the search for a new Chef de Service. It was to Pierre Termier, fellow graduate of the Ecole Polytechnique, and member of the Corps, and Professor of Mineralogy at the Ecole des Mines, that he first turned. Termier, by now established as one of the leading men in world, as well as French, geology, had no hesitation in recommending Jacques Deprat. Deprat gives his own account of the next series of events in *Les Chiens aboient*. Deprat writes that Termier first contacted him in a letter, which came out of the blue, and read:

> Do you want to go to Indo-China? You know that there is a scientific institute over there. The service is a section of the Office of Natural Resources [Mines Service], which is run by my friend the Engineer-in-Chief, Tardenois [Lantenois]. He is an extremely good man. You will get the most kindly help from him in organising a good scientific service. If you accept, the job of Chef de Service is reserved for you. By your work, your determination, your exceptional physical endurance, you are one of the most highly qualified for this enterprise. I would strongly press you to write to my friend Tardenois.

We know that Deprat wrote to Lantenois on 2 January 1908, presumably enquiring about the Service Géologique de l'Indochine and the nature of its work, and offering himself for the vacant post of head of the service. Lantenois replied on 23

March and again in July, probably in response to further enquiries from Deprat.

Deprat procrastinated for a year, with good reason. How would his wife and infant daughters fare in the tropical climate of Hanoi where the summertime temperatures reach 35°C during the day, dropping only to 25°C at night? The humidity is around 85 per cent. If he went, he would take his parents with him. His father had recently retired from his teaching job and was not in good health. Would he be putting his family's welfare at risk? As for geology, Deprat had become something of a specialist on the Mediterranean basin – he had done important work in Greece, Corsica and Sardinia. He would have to give that up. He would also be postponing, and possibly giving up for ever, his ambition of one day becoming a professor in France.

But against all that there was the lure of an interesting life and a new country to explore, where very little geological work had been done. Deprat himself was physically tough, with a passionate love of outdoor life and mountains in particular. There was also the freedom that comes with being in charge – Lantenois's second letter is quoted in Deprat's autobiography as saying that he, Lantenois, would take care of administration and 'as you are more qualified than me from a scientific viewpoint, it is understood that on this side you will have complete freedom. You will be our guide, though we in the Bureau of Natural Resources [Mines Service] will endeavour to make a contribution.'

The mundane deciding factor, though, may well have been money. Amédée Deprat left his teaching job in 1908 and was now on a state pension of 1,000F per annum, compared with his previous salary of 4,000F. The three generations of the family simply did not have enough to live on. Deprat's hand was forced. Lantenois and Termier pressed him to accept, and despite his avowed dislike of all ambition, he felt a little flattered by their insistence. In Indo-China meanwhile, Lantenois wrote a laudatory assessment of Deprat to the Governor-General, Klobukowski. He quoted Termier as saying to him: 'Deprat is, not only as a petrologist, but as a tectonist, one of the brightest of our young people . . . He is an explorer blessed with excellent health, with great physical and intellectual energy; on all points, he is the man we need in this country. I don't think we will find in France a better head for the Service Géologique de l'Indochine.' Lantenois added, 'This is, moreover, what M. Douvillé, one of M. Deprat's colleagues, said to M. Mansuy last year, and repeated to me.'

Deprat finally accepted the terms on offer in late 1908. He was appointed as Principal Geologist at a salary of 12,000F per annum – three times what his father had earned as a teacher – rising to 16,000F in 1915. This was based on university pay scales, excluding *indemnities de terrain* (i.e. field expenses). There was an assurance of complete freedom to publish, and the strong possibility of being made Head of Service the following year. He signed on the dotted line and became a full-time employee of the French government.

On 23 May 1909 Jacques and Marguerite Deprat with their two young daughters boarded the *Armand-Béhic* in Marseilles, bound for Indo-China and for a future of excitement and uncertainty.

2 *Indo-China, 1909–11*

There are no seasons in that part of the world, we have just the one season, hot, monotonous, we're in the long hot girdle of the earth, with no spring, no renewal.
Marguerite Duras, *L'Amant*

What sort of country was Deprat going to in the spring of 1909? Strange, exotic, tropical, hot – but colonised, suppressed and made French. France had controlled Indo-China for only twenty or so years. Having seized the southern part of present-day Vietnam, then known as Cochin-China, in the 1860s, France then fought running battles with China for the next twenty years, each side vying for sovereignty over the territories of Annam and Tonkin, now the northern part of Vietnam. A serious French defeat at the hands of the Chinese in 1885 was enough to bring down the ultra-colonial Prime Minister Jules Ferry. But by 1887 treaties had been signed with China (but not with the local inhabitants) which gave France control over Tonkin and Annam, which they placed in one administrative colonial unit with Cochin-China, Cambodia and Laos. This geographical collection formed the grandly titled Union of Indo-China.

The building of an overseas Empire was not universally popular in France. Resistance to colonial expansion was mostly based on financial factors – the colonies cost more to run than they brought in. This was true of Indo-China in the early years,

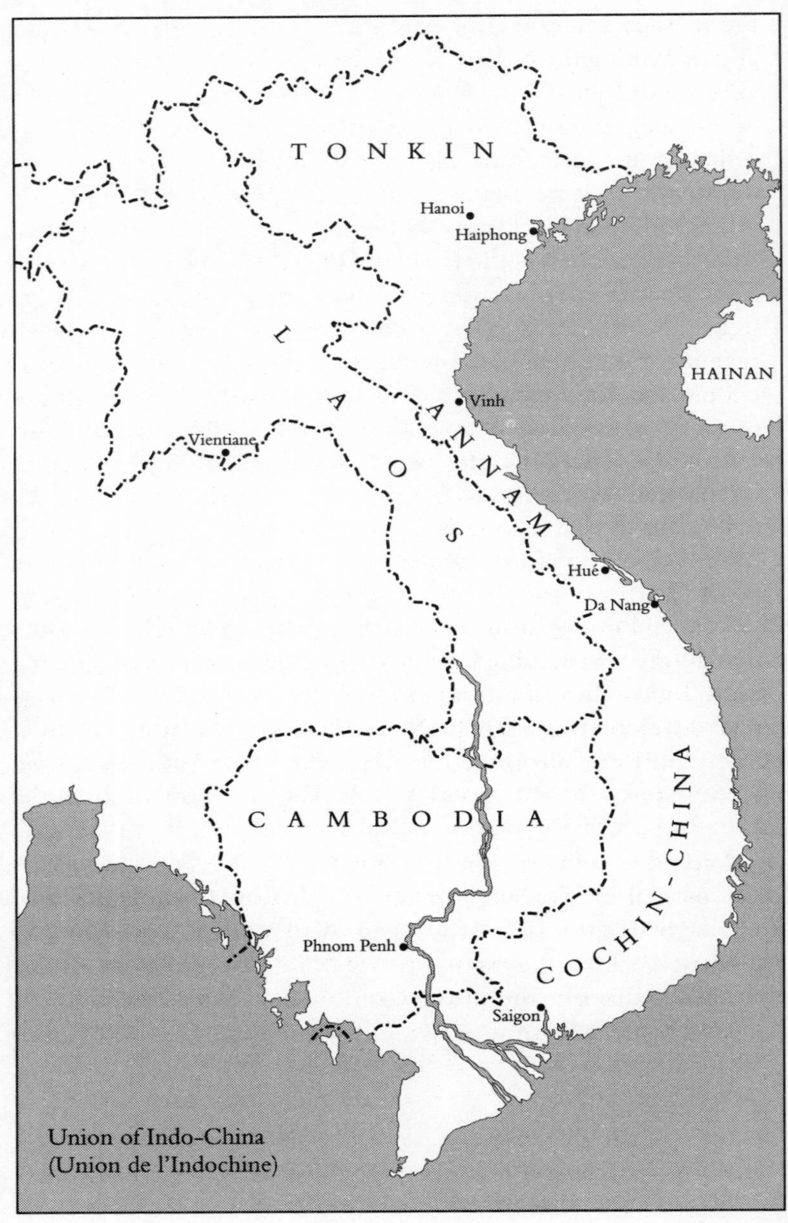
TONKIN
Hanoi
Haiphong
LAOS
HAINAN
Vinh
Vientiane
ANNAM
Hué
Da Nang
CAMBODIA
COCHIN-CHINA
Phnom Penh
Saigon
Union of Indo-China
(Union de l'Indochine)

but in 1897 a new regime was introduced, with the over-riding aim of making the colony pay its way. Paul Doumer, Governor-General of Indo-China from 1897 to 1902 (and future President of France), transformed the infrastructure of the colony, and reshaped its agriculture. Production of rice and rubber was transferred to large estates, controlled by French companies and officials. Traditional and 'inefficient'* village production was largely abandoned as the local people were forced to move away from their homes in order to work on the big estates or in the mines. Rice and rubber in particular became good sources of revenue for the French, while the Tonkinois and Annamite people provided what was effectively slave labour: 'Conditions in some sectors were appalling. Rubber, the second largest Vietnamese export after rice, was produced by virtually indentured workers so blighted by malaria, dysentery and malnutrition that at one Michelin company plantation, twelve thousand out of forty-five thousand died between 1917 and 1944' (Karnow, 1983).

This did not seem to trouble anyone in France because now the colony was making money. After Doumer the French clung on to Indo-China for another fifty years. A sense of the elegance that developed in French life in the colony was given in this interview by an astonished American visitor to the colony in the early 1950s:

> I could see why the French didn't want to give up Indochina. Colonial life was very grand. There was the Cercle Sportif, which was the club. It was restricted to the top colons – the most wealthy, the highest members of the government. Each of them has a beautiful swimming pool, lockers, a dining area, a horse track in some cases, a massage room, tennis courts.

*In fact small-scale rice production was more efficient. In 1898, before the French reorganisation of agriculture, rice yields in Tonkin and Annam averaged 2.5 tonnes per hectare, in 1938 they were 1.2 tonnes per hectare (compared with 1.8 for Siam and 3.4 for Japan).

In the private homes, the French traditions were carried on. If you went to dinner, it was always formal. You dressed in a white jacket and black trousers. The generals and the top military of course observed this very strictly. So if you attended a dinner thrown by de Lattre it was usually in a chandeliered governor's house, with many, many servants, great long tables, the finest of cutlery and glassware. It was like something out of the past . . .

Nobody worked very hard. All the finest imports were available – caviar, French wines and champagnes. A fantastically easy and gracious way of life, because of the tremendous number of servants and the wealth they got out of the rubber plantations and the trading of rice and the other businesses.

Even the military had a beautiful way of life. If you were invited to lunch [at a fort] you'd arrive in the morning, do your work, make the rounds, see the troops, inspect the fortifications, and then at 1 there'd be this fantastic lunch in the officers' mess . . . You'd always start with an aperitif at the bar. Cinzano or sherry or cassis, which was the favourite of the French. Everybody would stand around and have drinks. Then the head of the mess would formally announce the lunch. All the seats were assigned. There were little nameplates for the visitors. All elegantly set up with crystal. This is in the middle of the jungle. Then there would be an officer who would announce *le menu*. He'd stand at the head of the table and say, 'The menu for August 14 at 1:00 p.m. Gentlemen, the menu is . . .' Then he'd recite. 'We will begin with soup. Then we will have fish. Then we will have entrecôte. Then we will have a salad. Then we will have a tart. Then we will have coffee.'. . . That was how it was done. (Sochurek, 1989)

It is not surprising that life was easy for the French. The colony was run by 5,000 civil servants or *fonctionnaires*, while the same number of British ran India, a country with ten times the population. If the earnings from the colony could support them, all well and good – it was not their fault that there was simply not very much for them to do.

But if anyone still harbours the illusion that colonial rule in general was a benign improvement in the government of 'backward' countries and peoples, bringing them the benefits of modern administration in exchange for a little loss of self-determination, there is plenty of evidence to the contrary. For the French, as for other European powers, the colonies were both a potential market and a source of materials – what they were not allowed to be was a source of competition for French home-made goods. So local manufacturing in Indo-China, as elsewhere, collapsed under a deluge of mass-produced cheap goods from the mother country. The only industries to survive which were actually making things were producing pottery, woodwork or basketry for peasants who were so poor they could not afford the French equivalent.

Strict censorship made it difficult for accounts of the life of the Tonkinois and Annamites under French rule to enter the historical record. Paradoxically, it was during the Japanese invasion of Indo-China during the Second World War that local writers seized the opportunity to publish their experiences. The following accounts were collected by Ngo Vinh Long in his 1973 book *Before the Revolution: The Vietnamese Peasants Under the French*:

> Indeed you must go to the poor villages and hamlets to be able to see this tragedy: a husband holds the plough while his wife, his son, his daughter-in-law, and his daughter act as buffaloes, pulling it. They hitch to their shoulders ropes with pieces of matting lest the ropes cut into their flesh. Because of the weight to be pulled, they are unable to keep their balance and must use a bamboo cane to lean on. (Nghiem Xuan Yem)

> *All through the 60 years of French colonisation our people have always been hungry* [original italics]. They were not hungry to the degree that they had to starve in such numbers their

> corpses were thrown up in piles . . . But they have always been hungry, so hungry that their bodies were scrawny and stunted; so hungry that no sooner had they finished one meal than they started worrying about the next; and so hungry that the whole population had not one moment of free time to think of anything besides the problem of survival. (Nghiem Xuan Yem)

Occasional disasters occurred in the villages, which had devastating consequences for those without any resources to fall back on. This account followed a flood and famine in Dan Phuong: 'When I passed the Dan-Phuong market, I saw a number of people – men, women and young girls – who were still breathing lightly, rolled up in mats and lying on the side of the road. They were waiting for death and hoped that by lying there they would be seen by some kind-hearted person who would bury them' (Tran Van Mai).

For European visitors, though, Indo-China and its capital Hanoi were a delicious combination of the exotic and familiar:

> Hanoi has been so often described, together with the imposing scale upon which it has been laid out, as compared with the haphazard way in which British colonial towns in the Far East are left to grow of themselves, that we need not go into more detail. Suffice it to say that, with its broad, well-kept streets, squares, cafés, and abundance of foliage, it makes a most pleasing impression and is a worthy setting to the Government of Indochina . . . Nor must the streets of Annamite shops, picturesque with wonderful paper lanterns like fishes, butterflies or crabs, be forgotten. We drove in ricshas or, as the French call them 'pousses-pousses' to the Hotel Métropole, the best hotel in the Far East, magnificently appointed, furnished and decorated in excellent taste, and with a frontage of 300 feet onto the street. There is also a finely situated club near by – the 'Cercle de l'union' – and a grand opera house being built, at a cost, we were told, of

> £20,000 . . . When one considers that the French have had quiet possession of the country for barely fifteen years, the solid work that has been accomplished is truly surprising. (Little, 1910)

Hanoi was a city of 80,000 inhabitants, including around 3,000 French and 2,500 Chinese. The French had indeed done much solid work – effectively turning Hanoi into an elegant French town: 'Hanoi is virtually a European town, but the broad avenues always have a distinct and artistic character.'

The scores of buildings erected in Hanoi comprised the built paraphernalia of colonial government. Most of them were in the new 'French quarter' to the south of the Petit Lac, and were listed in the *Guide Modrolle*, a tourist guidebook of 1912:

> La Poste, la Trésorie générale, l'Hôtel du Resident Supérieur, le Cercle de l'Union, Banque de l'Indochine, l'Hôtel Métropole, l'Hôtel de Ville, l'Hôtel de la Brigade, l'Usine d'Electricité, Bibliothèque Populaire, Cathédrale St-Joseph, la Mission Scientifique permanente, Chambres du Commerce et de l'Agriculture, La Gendarmerie, le Couvent des Religieuses de Notre Dame de Carmel, l'Hôpital Indigène, la Prison Civile, le Palais de Justice, l'Ecole Française de l'Extrême-Orient, l'Hôtel du Procureur général, la Garde indigène, Bureaux des Chemins de Fer de l'Indochine et du Yunnan, le Musée Commerciel et Industriel, la Loge maçonnique, la Gare Centrale, l'Etablissement zootechnique, le Théâtre, l'Hôtel du General en chef, le Service géographique, le Château d'Eau, l'Hôpital militaire, l'Ecole de Médecine, le Collège des jeunes filles . . .

and so on. Such is the necessary infrastructure of a European society.

To the west was the Citadelle quarter containing the military barracks and the Palais du Governeur-Général. Here too was the Jardin Botanique, twenty-five hectares of beautiful tropical greenery, planted over the rice fields of the nearby village of Chan-cuen. The Jardin was a pleasure garden for the French inhabitants of Hanoi. As well as the plants there were exotic animals in cages, a bandstand where military bands would perform on Sundays, acrobats, *guignols* and cafés. To the south of the Jardin was the Vélodrome de l'Union Sportive d'Hanoi, containing a cycle track and running track, with tennis courts in the centre. And as well as its public buildings, Hanoi offered any number of cafés, restaurants and clubs. For the French it was, in many ways, a highly satisfactory place to live.

This separation of the French and Indo-Chinese populations, cultures and experiences was so complete as to be paradoxically almost invisible. In almost all accounts of French life the Vietnamese are absent, to the degree that any reminder of their presence comes a shock. The rightful inhabitants of the country have been effectively written out of its history – it is no wonder that when we read about the French and the Americans and temporarily forget about the Vietnamese people we feel embarrassed at our connivance in this deceit. This account of the Deprat affair is, unfortunately, no different. Apart from a Laotian assistant of Deprat's named Oun Kham and a Tonkinois artist named Thanh who worked for the Service Géologique, no Indo-Chinese people are mentioned by name in any of the documents relating to the affair. In this sense it was truly an event that happened in 'French' Indo-China.

Jacques Deprat and Honoré Lantenois finally met when the boat train from Haiphong pulled in to Hanoi railway station on 25 June 1909. It is impossible to know for sure what immediate impression these two men made on each other. They had been corresponding for over a year, and must have been eager to meet and perhaps apprehensive about how they would get on. Deprat's later account in *Les Chiens aboient* was understandably coloured by the events to come:

The first impression was good. This was reinforced by

> Tardenois's [Lantenois's] welcome. At Hanoi station Dorpat [Deprat] met a man of fifty years, large, overweight . . . A round head with fair, reddish hair cropped short. Myopic, blinking eyes, speech hesitant and a little embarrassed. His manners were cordial, though appeared a little exaggerated, his smile a little too paternal. Dorpat, warned that Tardenois was 'marvellously good', saw in that eternal smile and his flattering comments, confirmation of that remark.

The expression *merveilleusement bon* had, in Deprat's account, a very different meaning from its literal translation. Termier had described Lantenois this way, and Deprat repeated the expression whenever he was describing Lantenois's less attractive qualities. But despite Deprat's unflattering description of Lantenois, it seems that there was mutual respect between the two men, and a certain warmth in Lantenois's greeting.

The Deprats would have been glad to arrive after four or five weeks at sea, and excited by their totally novel surroundings. Among the layers of officialdom that existed in this highly structured society, the Deprats would have been of upper-middle rank, allowing them to live in some style. The family was installed in a colonial villa in the Citadelle quarter of Hanoi:

> They chose a house on the periphery of Hanoi, spacious, elevated, surrounded by high verandas, in an area of dense greenery. In front of the house, a large garden was filled with old trees. Behind, the botanic garden spread its foliage. Beyond their garden, in view of the house, Lake Tay-Ho extended, a sheet of water sixteen kilometres in circumference, with leafy banks. In the mornings and evenings the calm surface reflected the light from the tropical sky.

The house was on Duong Thuy Kuê, a road on the north-western edge of Hanoi, running along the southern shore of Hò Tây, the Western or Great Lake. Deprat's parents joined Jacques and Marguerite and their two daughters in the villa in

November 1909. With occasional summer breaks in Yunnan, the family were to remain there until 1919. There was never any doubt that Deprat's parents would join him in Indo-China. They were, perhaps in part because he was their only child, an exceptionally close family.

Despite his reservations about coming out to the colony, Jacques Deprat seems to have fallen in love with Indo-China. Though many officials, including Lantenois, went back and forth to France every couple of years, Deprat was, with the exception of one trip to Canada, to remain in Asia for the next ten years.

The same day that he arrived Deprat was shown round the Institute by Honoré Lantenois and introduced to his colleagues. Paradoxically, within the Service Géologique de l'Indochine, Jacques Deprat was something of a novelty in being a fully trained geologist. The new universities had only just begun to produce science graduates in appreciable numbers, so geology graduates with experience were still few and far between.

Like Lantenois, Henri Mansuy, Deprat's most important colleague at the Service Géologique, also came to geology indirectly. Mansuy was from a working-class Parisian background and had acquired all his knowledge of natural history through evening classes and self-instruction. After five years' military service and various short-term jobs he had become friendly with Professor Verneau, an anthropologist at the Muséum National d'Histoire Naturelle in Paris. In 1901 Verneau found him a post as a technician in Indo-China. Mansuy was then forty-four years old, so when Deprat first met him he was fifty-two – twenty-four years Deprat's senior.

Mansuy was, it seems, genuinely pleased to have a man like Deprat come to join the service. In Deprat's account, Mansuy's first words were: 'Very happy to see you arrive M. Deprat, we have waited a long time for you. We have need of you. There are many gaps in our scientific thinking. This slows us down.'

Mansuy, naturally enough, was also caught up in Lantenois's plans for the upgrading of the service. He was to become a scientist with a regular publication outlet for his work. He was, no doubt, proud of his self-taught skills as a palaeontologist; it would be good to show these off to, and have them appreciated by, one of the new breed of young professional geologists.

Deprat was impressed by Mansuy, whom he refers to in *Les Chiens* as 'une force'. And when they talked about palaeontology he wrote that Mansuy 'does not talk idly, he knows . . .' and 'Here is an interesting collaborator. One of the converted! He loves science. We will do good work together.'

Considering that this account was written after the affair, it is a surprisingly complimentary view of the man who was to be, along with Deprat and Lantenois, at the centre of the storm. Deprat's views of Mansuy, as expressed in *Les Chiens*, vary. He gives a generous appraisal of Mansuy's self-taught skills and of his forceful character. But he is first intrigued, and then irritated and bored by the older man's constant complaining about the bourgeoisie, and what he sees as his simplistic anarchist politics. Mansuy had been a boy of thirteen, and presumably living in Paris, at the time of the 1871 Commune. The subsequent events, in which the French army went to war against a section of its own people, must have had a profound effect on any inhabitant of the city. Mansuy was, in Deprat's account, a fervent advocate of Marxist and anarchist views. But he is also portrayed by Deprat as fawning on the upper echelons of the colony, and this, to Deprat, did not sit well with his avowedly left-wing beliefs. This part of Mansuy's character is borne out in the account of the affair written by Michel Durand-Delga in 1990, by the numbers of new species that he named 'without apparent reason, after high-level officials, engineers, administrators, consuls and even Governors such as Klobukowski and Sarraut'. This was unusual practice for palaeontologists or other scientists, and was designed, in Durand-Delga's view, to win Mansuy promotion. In 1912 Mansuy was indeed promoted to the grade of Principal Geologist – the same grade as Deprat, though of less seniority in the service. We have little knowledge of Mansuy's character, except that later in his career he became unpopular with his younger colleagues. His eventual retirement from the service was, according to letters written by those who served with him, greeted with a sigh of relief. His later temporary return to the colony was similarly looked on with dismay. But earlier on he was clearly an important and valued member of the service and, coincidentally, a close friend of Lantenois. Mansuy, for us, remains a shadowy figure who, while lighting the fuse that began the affair, managed to remain in the background.

Among Deprat's other colleagues were two ex-military officers recruited from the Geographic Service, Captains Zeil and Dussault. Zeil had worked with Honoré Lantenois on a previous geological expedition and they had published at least one paper together – but he was eventually pushed out of the service at Deprat's insistence. Dussault, though, was and remained a valued part of the team. There was also a young Italian refugee from the French Foreign Legion, Umberto Margheriti, on the staff. Margheriti effectively became Deprat's assistant.

Writing in retrospect, Deprat records in *Les Chiens* that one of his reasons for hesitating to go to Indo-China was his concern about the rigidity of life as a civil servant – particularly in a colony where the hierarchies of French society would be not so much exaggerated as inescapable. The colony, he knew, was largely run by members of the Corps, and now he was about to experience their influence at first hand. Soon after his arrival, he was taken by Lantenois to meet Louis Constantin, Engineer-in-Chief of Public Works (and Lantenois's and Deprat's boss). Constantin was another member of the Corps. Deprat describes him as a typical bureaucrat, very polite to everyone, but with no enthusiasm for anything, except that everything should be kept running smoothly. Constantin was stiff. He looked coldly at Deprat's assumption of equality with Lantenois, and at his informal manners. For Deprat, writing in his autobiography, Constantin summed up all the correct dreariness of the administrative corps:

> The Director, Maxence [Constantin] a Chief Engineer from the home country, was a small man, slim, dark, cunning, a bureaucrat in every sense of the word. This man, who was administratively in charge of him, left him completely cold. He received him [Deprat] with extreme friendliness, because that was how he received everyone. You never know what political support is possessed by a man you do not know, and in all these types of situation, there is no point in making political enemies, if you want to last. He was not basically a bad man, just a neutral one, without strength, pusillanimous in the extreme, terrified by the rakish style of certain Chief Engineers placed under his command, capable through cowardice of the most debasing and contemptible acts. He contemplated Dorpat [Deprat] with alarm, who not being used to the manners of this milieu, spoke with Tardenois [Lantenois] in a normal fashion, equal to equal, as his position and his work gave him the right to do. Maxence could not conceive that an individual who was not apparently one of the sacred 'Corps', would not keep a modest silence, confining himself to answering when questioned, and prefacing his remarks with a humble 'Monsieur, Chief Engineer'.

The problem was that Deprat did not regard Lantenois as his superior in any way. He saw him as a colleague who ran the administration of the geological service, while he ran its science. It never occurred to Deprat to address him formally, but in this he was out of step with the mores of the colony. A contemporary Englishwoman travelling through Indo-China observed: 'In Hanoi social functions are somewhat spoilt by the importance given to precedence both among government officials and Army officers. The French who pride themselves on the democratic principles are always conscious of their rank even when not on duty' (Vassall, 1922).

In *Les Chiens* Deprat describes an incident at a function held for the colony's upper echelons. We can imagine the scene in one of the colonial mansions, everyone dressed formally, trays of drinks on offer from 'native' servants moving silently beneath glittering chandeliers. Here the apparent informality of limited social mixing only thinly disguised a strict observance of rank and protocol. Deprat, who was clearly uncomfortable with this whole ambience, was introduced to the Résident Supérieur, the official who effectively ran the city of Hanoi, by Honoré Lantenois. Monsieur le Résident was a man named St Chaffray, and was only one rung down from the Governor-General. Deprat quotes the Résident as saying to him, 'I know that you publish work which brings honour to the colony. You cost us a lot of money . . . That's not a reproach. I recognise that it is necessary to have certain services which are luxuries.'

This apparently innocuous comment infuriated Deprat. He knew that the science of geology was disregarded and derided by the *ingénieurs* who ran the colony. He also knew that they had made several major errors in construction work because of this disregard. To make matters worse, the other officials who surrounded the Résident joined in.

'I leafed through M. Deprat's last paper,' he quotes one as saying. 'Very interesting, remarkable speculations on folds. Geology is a poetic science, but without practical results.'

Another, this time the senior engineer in charge of building dikes, says, 'Geology has no practical interest. You do not base the route of a railway on a few antediluvian fossil shells.' Deprat pointed out to each of these senior officials the grave errors they had each made – one in the past and one presently unfolding – which would have been avoided if they had taken the trouble to consult the Service Géologique, or to read the papers that it published. This caused an awkward silence which the Résident Supérieur tried to fill by rounding off the conversation. 'Scientific publications give honour to our country. But frankly, we must not wish them to have practical ends.' Deprat then quoted Henri Poincaré, the great French mathematician and philosopher of science, at St Chaffray: 'The wise scientist never has to research for practical ends. They always come in addition.'

The Résident would not let this junior official have the last word though, and replied that this was a nice saying but that, 'your geology, interesting as it is, does not help to push one more grain of rice in the colony'. Deprat turned away and said to a friend, in the hearing of the collected high officials, 'Yesterday you quoted me some lines of Goethe. Do you remember them?

> "Lass dich nur zu keiner Zeit
> Zum Widerspruch verleiten
> Weise verfallen in Unwissenheit.
> Wenn sie mit Unwissenden streiten."'*

This exchange had the effect of making everyone else feel inferior for not knowing German and for not being able to quote Goethe at the drop of a hat. It was also a tremendous insult to the Résident and the gathered company. Deprat was making enemies.

The whole story may be a fabrication of Deprat's, and there is certain to be a touch of *l'esprit d'escaliers* about his biting comments. But it is an indication of his own analysis of social relations in the colony, the status of his science among the higher officials and the ignorance of the men who were to determine his fate.

Before Deprat left France, Lantenois had written to him about his predecessor as head of the Service Géologique, Jean-Baptiste Counillon. When Lantenois gained control of the service and began its reorganisation, he found that Counillon was uninterested in making changes, and failed to give direction to the service. Lantenois had pushed him to one side. Deprat did not take much notice of all that, though it seems that he did mention it to Pierre Termier, who replied that if Lantenois 'spoke so harshly of one of his colleagues, it must be that he was not too good'.

*'Just do not at any time/ Fall into contention/ Wise people decay into ignorance/ When they argue with the ignorant.'

When Deprat arrived in 1909, Counillon still lived in the colony – he was to remain there until after Deprat left – and still worked ostensibly for the Service Géologique, though he kept himself to himself and was entirely occupied with his fossil collection. Deprat decided to visit him soon after he arrived. Counillon was then living in the indigenous quarter of Hanoi. Deprat wrote that he found Counillon inarticulate and gauche, rather than lazy, with something of the bearing of a peasant. He became very lively when talking about his fossils. Lantenois had told Deprat that Counillon was very angry that a young man had come to take control of the service, but Deprat did not sense any resentment towards himself. Nevertheless, at the time, he took Counillon's apparent guardedness as a slight sign of hostility.

Soon after that Lantenois decided to sack Counillon from the service. The consequences for Counillon were financially disastrous and, according to Deprat, he became extremely angry, accusing Lantenois of persecuting him and of stealing his papers and suppressing his work. Mansuy was also critical of Counillon, which confirmed to Deprat, who knew little of the circumstances at the time, that Counillon must be in the wrong.

However, Deprat wrote that he bumped into Counillon a little later. He had taken a job teaching at a school for Indo-Chinese in order to make ends meet. He insisted on taking Deprat to his house and showing him geological maps which he had compiled, and which Lantenois had used without acknowledgement. Deprat says that this all seemed unlikely, but Counillon's distress made a deep impression on him. He tried to mention these accusations in a casual way to Lantenois. He, in turn, became furious, losing his normal outward appearance of calm. This was the first time Deprat had seen the other side of this '*homme merveilleusement bon*'.

The only account we have of Counillon's treatment and accusations is from *Les Chiens aboient*, and there is no doubt that Deprat is pushing the idea of Lantenois being prepared to get rid of anyone he did not like, by whatever means. Nevertheless, Counillon *was* sacked from the service by Lantenois, and this seems to have simply been on the grounds that he was not dynamic enough.

Jacques Deprat spent the first months of his new life in Indo-China preparing for his first major work on the geology of southern Asia. In November 1909, five months after setting foot in the colony, he left Hanoi for his first major expedition – a geological investigation of Yunnan, the vast and mountainous province of China just over the border from Tonkin.

Yunnan was a place of great interest to the French. It was a prosperous agricultural province of 108,000 square miles (a little larger than Great Britain) and twelve million inhabitants. Its central city Yunnan-fou (now called Kunming) was a major trading centre for goods from all over southern China and from Szechuan to the north. Being remote from the centres of power in Beijing and Shanghai, the province was semi-autonomous and ruled by a powerful local 'governor'. This was not untypical, as throughout the late nineteenth and early twentieth centuries the power of the Chinese centre over its regions waxed and waned. The French made little secret of wanting to take over the eastern part of Yunnan as an addition to their colony of Indo-China. This would give them control over trade to the north and east, easy access to China overland, and a bulwark against British ambitions from India and Burma.

Yunnan held other attractions for the French. Because of its situation on a high plateau, it was and is said to enjoy one of the most perfect climates in the world – a perpetual springtime. For Europeans enduring the heat and humidity of much of Indo-China, its temperate weather was seductive. Median temperatures in Yunnan are 21°C in July and 10°C in January. There are numerous contemporary accounts of the region from European travellers. Archibald Little travelled through Yunnan in 1910, just before Deprat, and came upon Yunnan-fou from the east:

> As is the case with all Chinese mountain cities, the capital of Yunnan enjoys a most picturesque situation. Emerging from

the plain it stands on a limestone ridge along which its north wall runs; the southern wall encloses much flat land, including a considerable amount of paddy fields and lotus ponds, across which run stone causeways leading to temples and tea-houses.

The view over the city and the distant lake is very beautiful . . . Like Peking and Chêngtu, the city is full of fine trees, amidst which glitter the variegated roof tiles of the many temples and guildhalls . . . the population looks well-dressed and well-fed, although the men appear to spend their time mostly in smoking cigars out of inordinately long bamboo pipes, – and a foreigner in the streets attracts no notice whatever . . .

The most remarkable feature of this province of Yunnan is its climate, which is, I should say, the most equable in the world. You can live in Yunnan-fou with open doors and windows all the year round as in the tropics, and enjoy the fresh air minus the tropical heat and damp.

Little openly discusses the 'contemplated occupation of eastern Yunnan by the French'. This possibility was made both easier and more likely by the building of an extraordinary railway from Hanoi to Yunnan-fou. The railway was completed by the French in April 1910. Covering a distance of 520 miles, it was a remarkable feat of engineering, and a major commercial and potentially military artery. The railway climbed the precipitous mountains of Haut-Tonkin, and crossed the Yunnan plateau, linking Indo-China to the interior of the continent. Whereas Chinese goods had travelled by pack animal across the mountains, before being loaded on to river boats for the last part of their southward journey, they could now be loaded on to trains at Yunnan-fou and unloaded on to sea-going steamers at Haiphong. As for the military possibilities, Little wrote of the possible annexation of Yunnan by the French, 'That some such eventuality was the original meaning of the Hanoi–Yunnan railway cannot be doubted' (Little, 1910).

The exploration of the geology of Yunnan was to be a joint

effort, with Deprat taking the leading role, accompanied by Sarromon, a topographer, and with Mansuy acting as the palaeontologist. It was decided that Mansuy should make a study of the stratigraphy and palaeontology along the railway line itself, including the newly excavated railway cuttings between Mong-tseu and Yunnan-fou, while Deprat covered the remainder of the vast territory. Mansuy would return to Hanoi before Deprat, who intended to remain in Yunnan for some time. Deprat would send cases of sample fossils back to Mansuy, who would make preliminary identifications, which he would communicate back to Deprat in the field. This would enable Deprat to have continual interim comments on his fossils, which would help him in his further work in the province. This system was able to work, first, because Deprat continually returned to his base in Yunnan-fou, and second, because the railway (completed during Deprat's expedition) allowed swift communication between Hanoi and Yunnan-fou.

In fact the whole expedition was made possible and desirable by the railway, as Lantenois wrote, a little pompously, in his preface to the subsequent *mémoire* on the geology of Yunnan:

> The mission was however helped to a certain degree by the opening of the new railway line from Lao-kay to Yunnan-fou. As soon as the construction of the line, which establishes an economic link between French Tonkin and Chinese Yunnan, was completed, it seemed opportune that the Geological Service of Indo-China should make a reconnaissance beyond the domain which it was normally allocated. In any case, the study of the geology of China is of truly worldwide interest, and it was right that the French should make a contribution to the edifice so nobly constructed by their illustrious predecessors. (Deprat, 1912a)

Although Yunnan is a plateau in the sense that its altitude rarely falls below 1,000 metres, the region is mostly mountainous and rugged. The territory studied by Deprat was an extensive area of extremely difficult terrain. The expedition was as much an exploration as a geological investigation. As Honoré Lantenois noted, this was a huge area to study: 'This extends over a vast region of 40,000 square kilometres, forming, between Mong-tseu and the Fleuve Bleu, a band 400 kilometres long by roughly 100 kilometres wide. The country is very rugged, particularly to the north of Yunnan-fou, where the altitudes reach 4,000 metres.'

Jacques Deprat himself wrote in the *mémoire*:

> For my part, I explored the whole of the region between Mong-tseu and Yunnan-fou in the first part of my travels. Then I extended my researches to the north, covering the completely unexplored high mountain region, which is an extension of the Alps of Sseu Tchoan [Szechuan] to the south of the Fleuve Bleu. The study of the high regions bordering the Fleuve Bleu was made particularly difficult because of the cold, the considerable altitude and the great difficulties encountered in travelling with wagons.

These 'difficulties' are not enlarged on in what is a scientific paper – to be used only for the passive recording of information and interpretation – but Archibald Little had travelled in the same region and gives a more colourful account:

> Owing to the devious course of the river and the precipitous gorges in which it is in parts enclosed, the path fails strictly to follow its banks, and so has to cross intervening mountain ridges, ascending and again descending, 3,000 to 4,000 feet, by the most miserable path masquerading as a high road that it has ever been my unhappy fate to traverse. Again, when marching along the valley bottom, it often happens that a cliff 500 or 600 feet high has to be surmounted, and in such places a climb, at first sight seemingly impassable to man or beast, has to be made over it. Instead of a short gallery along the face of the cliff itself, which it would have taken hardly more labour

> to cut out, steep steps have been cut, up and down in the hard limestone . . . thus making the path, in places, an ascent – and what is still worse a descent – at an angle of 45 degrees. And over this passes the main traffic between the two rich provinces of Szechuan and Yunnan.

What makes this account simultaneously less sympathetic and more terrifying is the knowledge that Little was being carried in a sedan chair. If this was the main route through Yunnan, we might guess at the territory that Deprat had to tackle in his survey of the region's geology. But from his autobiographical writings it is clear that Deprat revelled in the mountainous conditions and in the difficulties they presented. He went much further than the most energetic geologists in getting to the most inaccessible places, in effect becoming a mountaineer as well as a scientist. We can imagine that Deprat, a man who wrote lyrically about, and seemed always to be happiest in, mountainous country – either the Jura or on Corsica or later in the Pyrenees – would have been thrilled at the prospect of such an expedition. This description of a view over the high country of northern Indo-China in *Les Chiens aboient* is typical of his romantic vision of mountains:

> The country was truly astonishing. Towards the south, the valley continued in narrow sinuous canyons into which the river disappeared. And, above the inaccessible gorges with vertical cliffs cut through the thick limestone, the long steep slopes of schist shining upwards interminably, stairways cut for giants. Here and there, on some narrow ledge, the light reflecting from a terraced rice field taking water from a spring, seemed in the blue mist of the distance to be a small forgotten sheet of glass.

Yunnan was, in any case, worth the hardships. Apart from the beauty of the mountains, Deprat would have been keen to escape the formality and cliquishness of life among the *fonctionnaires*. And then there was the geology. In his *mémoire* Deprat wrote, 'In a general way, the conditions for geological work in Yunnan are favourable, if one puts aside the difficulties inherent in the defectiveness or even absence of roads; the fieldworker, as in the rest of China, is greatly helped in his task by the intense deforestation.'

The exposure of rock in Yunnan was superb, and therefore potentially easier to unravel than the heavily forested and cultivated tracts of Indo-China. Yunnan was assumed to be part of the same geological story as Tonkin and the rest of Indo-China – by studying here Deprat hoped to find the key to the geological history of the entire region. He stayed in Yunnan for a total of eleven months from November 1909 to October 1910. He welcomed Lantenois on the first train into Yunnan-fou from Hanoi on 1 April 1910, and his family came to stay in the city for that summer. They all returned to Hanoi for the winter of 1910–11. Deprat himself then went back to Yunnan to do some more work in 1911. The geology of Yunnan was his major occupation for the first two years of his life in Asia.

The first published record of Deprat's work in Yunnan is a preliminary note read to the Académie des Sciences in Paris (Deprat and Mansuy, 1910). It was and is customary for field-workers who have discovered new species to compile interim lists of their finds for immediate publication. This ensures that they are given the credit for their discoveries, and are thereby given priority in the naming of the new species. A two-page note, listing the fossil species found so far on the expedition, and a suggested stratigraphic scheme based on these fossils, co-authored by Deprat and Mansuy, was presented at a session of the academy on 19 September 1910 by Henri Douvillé, Professor of Palaeontology at the Ecole des Mines, while Deprat was still in Yunnan. We do not know the exact method used to compile this report, but the following seems the most likely route. Deprat sent boxes of fossil specimens from Yunnan back to Mansuy in Hanoi, carefully labelled with their geographic and stratigraphic locations. Mansuy identified the specimens and sent a list of names back to Deprat. Deprat then compiled the paper and sent it to Mansuy, who sent it on to France. This convoluted procedure allowed the pair to make an interim report on their findings, which would give them more time to complete the detailed *mémoire* of the trip.

In this case Henri Mansuy actually went to France on leave in late 1910, so he may well have taken the initial 1910 report with him. He did, in any case, take several of Deprat's Yunnan fossil specimens. Mansuy showed these to Henri Douvillé, who was impressed with the fossils and kept several of the specimens in his own collection at the Ecole des Mines in Paris. When he returned to Hanoi from Yunnan in October 1910, Deprat set about the task of preparing a detailed *mémoire* of his expedition. This was not only the scientific record of his work, it was to be the first full-scale scientific survey published by the Service Géologique de l'Indochine.

During 1911, while Honoré Lantenois was also away in France, an odd dispute arose between him and Deprat. Sometime in the early part of the year, Lantenois visited the Société Géologique in Paris, and discovered that Deprat had submitted some notes for publication in the society's bulletin. Lantenois was furious that this had been done without his knowledge, and without the papers being passed to him first – in this he perhaps displayed the natural instincts of the government *fonctionnaire*, for whom everything must go through the right channels. Lantenois wrote an admonitory letter to Deprat, but received an unexpected reply. Deprat not only pointed out that his contract of employment specifically gave him complete freedom in scientific matters, but also informed Lantenois that he had written to Pierre Termier and Lucien Cayeux enlisting their support. Deprat also referred to the letter Lantenois had written to him in 1908 setting out his responsibilities: 'I consider that our administrative relations are those of a rector and a professor of a faculty.' In other words Deprat was to do the science while Lantenois took care of the administration.

Termier and Cayeux seemed to have intervened swiftly to

calm the situation, and Lantenois backed down. Deprat recounts that this was an important matter of principle for him, and that he felt he ought to threaten to resign. He was advised though, by Termier and Cayeux, to hold back. After all Lantenois was not going to be in the colony for ever.

Two other matters soured relations between the two men at this time. First, Deprat quickly came to the conclusion that Captain Zeil was a liability to the Service Géologique. His scientific training and knowledge were simply not good enough, and he was inclined to make incorrect assumptions rather than consult with anyone who might know better. Zeil, though, was an old friend and colleague of Lantenois. Again, it seems that Deprat forced the issue, and Lantenois gave way by diplomatically finding Zeil another post in the Colonial Service. The other fly in the ointment was the question of Deprat's position. He had understood, and this is confirmed by his correspondence with Termier, that he was to be made Chef de la Service Géologique de l'Indochine a year after he arrived. But come 1910 this did not happen. We do not know the reasons for this, but, although Deprat did protest about it, the fact that such a principled man did not make a huge row suggests that either the promise was not so strong, or that Lantenois managed to persuade him of good reasons for delay. In the end Deprat was promoted in March 1913. These difficulties between the two men seem to have resulted in part from Lantenois's reluctance to accept that, if the Service Géologique was to grow, it must grow away from him. He resented the autonomy that Deprat was exercising, while Deprat resented Lantenois's continued attempts to interfere in his affairs.

Honoré Lantenois returned to Indo-China from France in late 1911, eager to see the *mémoire* on Deprat's Yunnan expedition prepared. It is important to understand how much this work meant for all three men involved. For Lantenois, this was his vision coming into being. He had virtually created a new scientific institution, had procured money for its expansion, had recruited its staff and arranged its expeditions. Now this was to be its first publication, the first tangible fruit of all those labours. As he noted in the preface, a few notes and papers had been published in French geological journals by members of the service, but this was different, it was their own journal. His achievement would be both satisfying for him, and would, he hoped, bring him attention and approbation throughout the French scientific and political world.

For Jacques Deprat too, this was to be a new beginning. He was, in all but name, the head of this newly vibrant and dynamic service, publishing material on a par with, and in many ways more interesting than, any being published in France. Unable to get a decent job in France, he had come out to this isolated colony and, within three years, produced work which the whole of French geology would marvel at. And for Henri Mansuy, a man still conscious of his humble background and self-taught status, this was a further step up into the realm of real scientists. The service had published a one-off paper of his in 1908, but now he had the prospect of years of publication to come.

Lantenois was a little too keenly involved in the *mémoire* for Deprat's taste. He insisted on reading all of the text and suggesting numerous minor changes. Deprat – rightly, in view of his later life – considered himself an excellent writer, and he resented Lantenois's interventions, which simply obscured and worsened the text. Deprat's account of this allowed him to return to one of his favourite themes – the co-existence of artistic and scientific understanding. Deprat took his own writing very seriously, and in *Les Chiens aboient* is scathing about the abilities of scientists to write – 'they write like *boutiquiers*' – and of their knowledge and appreciation of the arts. But he also writes that any artistic ability should be kept hidden from other scientists and engineers, as it is not good to be known to have aptitudes of that kind. On the other hand, he himself believed that it was essential to have a creative imagination in order to be a good scientist. In the event the problem between Deprat and Lantenois over the wording of the *mémoire* was resolved with the assistance of Mansuy, who was, it seems, an ally to both. Deprat wrote the first part of the *mémoire* covering the general geology, Mansuy the second, covering palaeontology (Mansuy, 1912), while Lantenois wrote the preface.

In his preface for issue I, 1, of the *Mémoires du Service Geologique de l'Indochine*, Honoré Lantenois took the opportunity to praise lavishly the work of Messieurs Deprat and Mansuy. He called Deprat's tectonic work 'a magnificent synthesis' and wrote that, 'The works of MM. Deprat and Mansuy have fortunate consequences for the future advancement of geological studies of Indo-China. They have uncovered finally, for our eyes, a corner of the "Face of the Earth" which until now was little explored.'

In return Deprat wrote well in the *mémoire* of Lantenois's previous work – his 1903–4 mission to Yunnan – even where he had to correct it: 'The observations of M. Lantenois are marked by a great precision and are of great interest.' A certain part of the country was, 'Noted as Cambrian by M. Lantenois on his map, a very understandable error since M. Lantenois did not have the opportunity to study the lower Devonian that occurs elsewhere.' And: 'I am happy to record here my indebtedness to the scrupulous fashion in which the observations were carried out, even if I must sometimes differ on points of interpretation.'

What was the main point of Deprat's work in Yunnan? As we have seen, the great questions of geology at this time were tectonic, and this was the discipline in which French geologists led the world. In the 1870s and 1880s work on the structure of the Alps by German, Swiss, French and Austrian geologists had shown that there was folding and thrusting of rock strata from the south to north over the whole region, so that older rocks ended up on top of younger strata, and most strata were displaced by tens of kilometres from their 'original' positions. This idea that mountains were formed by horizontal thrusts, which resulted in piling up of material, replaced the earlier dominant notion that they were the result of vertical uplift caused by molten igneous material pushing up from beneath. Horizontal movements became the key to understanding, not just the formation of mountains, but the geological history of the Earth's crust.

In 1887 the French geologist Marcel Bertrand had shown, mainly through studying the fieldwork of Alpine geologists, that Europe had been subjected to three great episodes of movement, or orogenies, in its history, of which the Alpine orogeny was the latest. The earlier Caledonian and Hercynian orogenies had created the mountains of northern and central Europe. Bertrand also demonstrated that the mountain chains of Europe showed strong relationships to those on other continents. So that, for instance, the Caledonian mountains of Norway and Scotland were linked to the Appalachians. Bertrand even suggested that these ranges were joined by a chain of mountains running beneath the sea.

Pierre Termier was Bertrand's most notable pupil, and it was Termier who was credited with finally solving the overall structural and tectonic history of the Alps. In the 1890s the term 'nappe' (the French word for a tablecloth) was used to describe a solid sheet of strata pushed over the top of existing rock. Geologists visualised the pre-Alpine crust as a flat cloth lying on a smooth surface. If the cloth were then pushed inwards from both sides it would rise upwards in a series of folds which would then collapse sideways. More pushing would make these folds pile on top of each other in a higgledy-piggledy way. In practice, as rocks sometimes behave plastically and sometimes rigidly, the arms of the folds would shear off and be pushed over the tops of others. Thus the tablecloth or nappe became the handy visual model for mountain-chain formation. Pierre Termier showed that nappes had been pushed over much further distances in the Alps than anyone had previously imagined. And in 1903 he published his triumphant explanation for the curious difference between the eastern and western Alps, demonstrating that the nappes of the former had previously overlain the latter and had since been eroded away.

By the first decade of the new century, when Deprat started work as a professional geologist, Bertrand and Termier's work was opening up a new interpretation of the Earth's geological history. Geologists were eager to look again at the mountain chains of the world that had already been explored and to get more information about others. There was an urgent desire to fit all the Earth's mountain ranges into the pattern which Bertrand had described, using the concepts which Termier had so brilliantly exploited. The mountains of northern Indo-China and southern China offered a wonderful opportunity for Deprat to enter the most important debate of his time – the debate that ended up dominating geology in the twentieth century. As Lantenois commented, Deprat succeeded brilliantly.

> In a magnificent synthesis M. Deprat has shown us a great post-secondary* orogenic wave which, coming from Sseu-tchoan [Szechuan] broke against the crystalline primary massif of Haut-Tonkin. Our studies of the geology of Indo-China allow us now to make out that the same pushing force continued, while weakening from the North to the South of Indo-China across the secondary terrain, and that the primary massifs, which appear as geographic islands, covering these secondary terrains, formed the resistant blocks against which the pushing force died out. The tectonic unity of Indo-China and Yunnan is thus revealed.

In other words, Deprat identified a movement or force, which had affected the secondary, i.e. Mesozoic, rocks of the region, and was therefore more recent than Mesozoic itself. The

*The four great eras of geological history were known as the Primary, Secondary, Tertiary and Quaternary eras. The first two names have gone out of use in the Anglo-Saxon world, where the term Primary has been replaced by the Precambrian and Palaeozoic, and the Secondary by the Mesozoic era. Tertiary and Quaternary are still widely used. In France the use of Primary and Secondary has continued for longer. See also geological column on page vi.

folding effects that it had produced in the Mesozoic rocks showed a regular pattern across Yunnan, which probably extended into Indo-China. The older (i.e. primary or Palaeozoic) rocks of the region occurred as blocks within the younger strata. These older blocks were less susceptible to folding, and acted as resistant 'islands' against which, as Lantenois wrote, 'the pushing force died out'. The piled-up folds around the older 'massifs' of Yunnan were named by Deprat as 'the preyunnanaise nappes', and were his most notable discovery.

Quite apart from his synthesis of the tectonic and geological history of the Yunnan and southern Asia, Deprat had discovered fossil species which were previously unknown in the region. These new fossils, some of which were trilobites known from Europe, opened up the possibilities of novel interpretations of the geological history of the entire continent of southern Asia. A species of a marine animal occurring in Europe and southern Asia at the same time in the Earth's history meant that these two places were almost certainly connected by one body of water at that time. This helped to confirm the growing view that a large sea, known as the Tethys Sea, covered a vast area of present-day Europe and Asia, during the early Palaeozoic era (i.e. during the Cambrian, Ordovician and Silurian periods). The extent of the Tethys was known to have altered during its existence and clues to its extent at given times were eagerly seized on. Rocks of this early age had been difficult to date with precision in this part of Asia because they had often been subject to metamorphic change which destroyed their fossil content. The lower Palaeozoic fossils which Deprat found in Yunnan were therefore especially valuable.

Henri Mansuy's section of the *mémoire* showed him to be a skilled and meticulous palaeontologist. For the most part he described minutely the fossils which he and Deprat had brought back from Yunnan, compared them to known types, and allocated them to existing genera and species, or named them as new species. Most lower Palaeozoic fossil species were known from Europe, where the detailed zoning and dating of this part of the geological column had been going on for seventy years. All species were therefore compared to European forms. The discovery of new species was exciting, but the discovery in Yunnan of species known from Europe was more profoundly important.

The *mémoire* was published in 1912, and the introduction included the following notice: 'The Académie des Sciences has awarded the Tchihatcheff Prize for 1911 to MM. Deprat and Mansuy for their work on Yunnan.'

The publication was a triumph for all three men and was to be an important piece of evidence in the events to come.

3 *Indo-China, 1912–17*

Once the all-important first *mémoire* went to press, Jacques Deprat could return to the field. Henri Mansuy decided that from now on he should remain in Hanoi, as a laboratory palaeontologist, identifying and classifying the specimens that Deprat sent back from his excursions. Deprat recorded the findings of his trips over the next four years in a series of papers published in Paris and Hanoi. The Service Géologique de l'Indochine grew steadily in prestige and activity. Its publications were eagerly received in Paris – senior members of the Académie des Sciences and the Société Géologique de France took the trouble to highlight the work of the service in official reports and bulletins. The reputations of both Deprat and Mansuy were enhanced, while Honoré Lantenois reaped the benefit of the confidence and power that he had given to the service.

Deprat's physical toughness helped him in his work, as did his highly developed skill in conceptualising large-scale geological effects in the field. But there is another aspect of the field geologist's, and indeed any practical scientist's, work which often goes unnoticed. As well as being an activity of the brain, field geology is to a degree a manual craft. Students begin to learn the mental aspects of their science by imitating their teachers. Only after a long apprenticeship of approximation, do they acquire the understanding that gives content to the form which they have so carefully learned. The keen beginner will notice the way in which the geologist approaches an outcrop, the search for the bedding and cleavage planes, the measurements of strike and dip, the careful note-taking and, most anticipated of all, the restrained but effective use of the geologist's hammer. All of these are then parodied endlessly with little insight into the meaning of the actions. There is, initially, a lack of understanding of what it means to do these things well or badly; they are just done. But eventually, for some, meaning does arrive. And for those who do acquire the skills of this craft, geology becomes, as Deprat described in his youthful dreams, the discovery of the history of the Earth through the use of your brain *and* hands.

After the first ground-breaking *mémoire*, Deprat's next significant published paper was another short note read to the Académie des Sciences in May 1912 (Deprat 1912b). The title indicates the key element of the report: 'On the discovery of the Ordovician of *Trinucleus* and of Dinantian in North Annam, and on the general geology of that region'. This was followed by a series of *mémoires* on this trip, and another to the Rivière Noire region of Tonkin, published together in 1913 (Deprat 1913c, d, e, f).

The fossil *Trinucleus ornatus*, a trilobite well known from Ordovician rocks in Europe, was an important find as it showed that there were rocks from the Ordovician period in this part of the region, as had also been discovered by Deprat further north in Yunnan. The single specimen was discovered in March or early April 1912 at a place known as Nui Nga Ma (now written Nui Nguu Ma) in Annam, near the main highway that connects the north and south of Vietnam. It was recovered from a bed of grey quartzite, which lay beneath a much younger bed of conglomerate. Quartzite is a form of sandstone made up principally of quartz grains, which can be produced by later mild metamorphism of sandstone or by the conditions at the time of its formation. The specimen which Deprat brought back was recognised as *Trinucleus ornatus*, a species commonly found in the Bohemian section of the Ordovician rocks of Europe by Henri

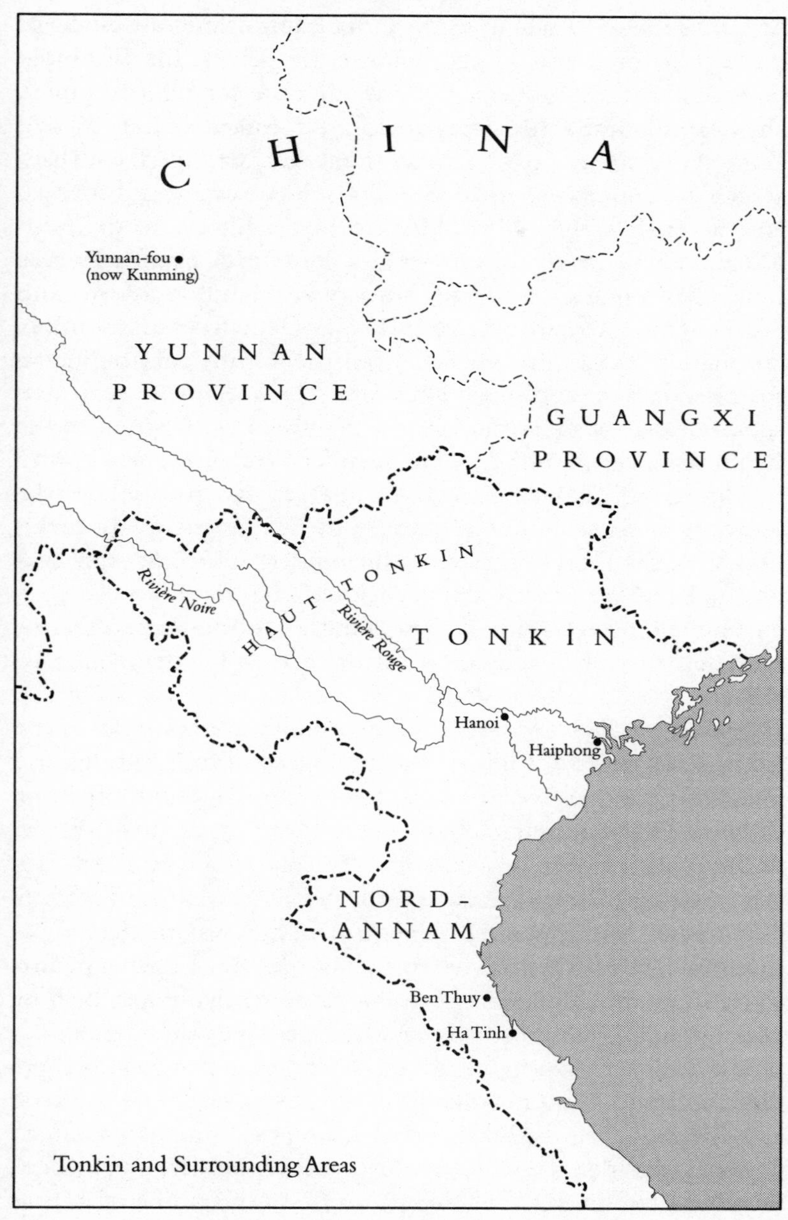

Tonkin and Surrounding Areas

Mansuy. The rocks at Nui Nga Ma could therefore be dated with great precision as Ordovician. Rocks of the Cambrian period are the oldest strata in the Earth's crust which contain shelly fossils and Ordovician rocks are the next oldest. At that time there were no Cambrian beds known in Indo-China which contained recognisable fossils – the quartzites at Nui Nga Ma were thus the oldest definitively datable rocks in Indo-China. The presence of Ordovician rocks in Annam helped to reinforce Deprat's synthesis of the geological history of the south Asian area. Two years earlier Deprat had found a fossil in Yunnan that was also known from the Ordovician period in Europe. This new discovery allowed correlation between two separate parts of southern Asia and reinforced and extended the hypothesis of a marine link between Europe and southern Asia in the lower Palaeozoic era. A stratigraphic pattern for the region was emerging. The finding of this *Trinucleus* specimen was to be the most contentious discovery that Deprat made and of crucial importance in the events to come.

As well as correlating these different fossil finds, Deprat returned to his real specialism. At the end of his 1912 paper he gives a brief account of the tectonics of the Annam region (Deprat, 1912b). He found that there were long (over 80 kilometre), narrow folds in the rocks, with their axes clearly aligned in a north-west to south-east direction – i.e. following the line of the mountain chain which forms the spine of eastern Indo-China, along the border between Laos and Vietnam. There had been two separate periods of folding, with the effects of the later superimposed on the earlier. Folds on this scale occur because of continental movements. In the light of our knowledge of plate tectonics, it is easy to see that two blocks or plates colliding with each other will cause crumpling or folding along the margin where they meet, and that the axes of these folds will tell us a lot about the direction of movements of the plates; but at the time Deprat was writing such movements were not yet considered, so he wrote of 'waves of force' travelling across the continents. The fold patterns of Annam helped to plot the ages and patterns of these tectonic waves. The unravelling of the effects of different tectonic episodes on the same set of rocks is a fiendishly difficult undertaking, requiring a high degree of skill and experience. Deprat's perceptive and pioneering work on the tectonics of the region brought him more admiration from his colleagues back in France.

In June 1912 Deprat made a trip up the valley of the Rivière Noire or Song Da, which runs from the north-west corner of Vietnam down into the delta region on which Hanoi stands. This was another vast area, some 160 by 200 kilometres of mainly dense tropical forest covering mountainous terrain. However, Deprat reported, 'Despite the vegetation, geological observations are made very easy by the exhaustive stripping away at the edge of a mountainous area, which has been subjected to rapid and intense erosion. Travel is sometimes difficult, as it is necessary to make your way up many of the ravines through torrential streams.'

Once again there is no mistaking Deprat's relish for the difficult mountainous country. In his papers he mentions the obstructions that the terrain gives to scientific study, while in his other writings he talks of their beauty. This tension between what Conrad called 'technical language and the language of meaning' is ever-present in Deprat. It is not so much a key to his character, as his expressed view of the world.

The following year he sent a note to the Académie des Sciences, 'On the Palaeozoic terrains of the Black River (the region between the Laotian frontier and the Red River of Tonkin)' (Deprat 1913a). In this short note Deprat gives a typical stratigraphic section with fossil species which he has been able to identify with certainty. He then mentions another site 60 kilometres away, where he has found a section of Gothlandian age (Gothlandian is another name for Silurian). In this section he had come across more trilobite specimens which he believes belong to different European genera – i.e. *Dalmanites*, *Acidaspis* and *Calymene*. In conclusion he writes:

> Among these discoveries, there are some of great importance for the general understanding of the geology of south-east Asia. I would stress above all the discovery of Gothlandian European trilobites; of an extensive détritique Gothlandian series containing fauna with affinities to those of Guelph; of a new important horizon of the lower Devonian containing *Actinopt. texturata* Phill. [a species of bivalve now classified as Pteria (Actinopteria) texturata]; of a middle Devonian Hamilton facies; of Dinantian beds; and of the presence of Ouralian rocks rich in fossils in a region where they have not previously been reported.

Deprat was continuing to find a wealth of new geological material and information in this little-studied part of the world. In his full *mémoire* on the Rivière Noire region, he was able to propose a classification of the primary (i.e. Palaeozoic) rocks of Indo-China, based on his work in the region up to 1913 (Deprat, 1913c). At the time when Deprat was working, rocks from the Cambrian, Ordovician and Silurian periods, which comprise the lower Palaeozoic era, were the oldest rocks in the Earth's crust which could be definitely dated – Precambrian rocks were not thought to contain fossils, and were therefore beyond the reach of geological dating techniques. The lower Palaeozoic, being the most distant in time, was also the most difficult period to untangle. The rocks would have been internally altered, folded, faulted, uplifted, sunk, and generally messed around more than those of later periods. Deprat's discovery of datable fossils from this period, and his unravelling of its stratigraphic and tectonic history, was a notable achievement. Although there was an enormous amount of work to do in Indo-China, Deprat had already, in a remarkably short time, laid the foundations for whoever might follow. The year after his travels in the Rivière Noire region, and after many years of feeling that he was an outsider, he was to experience the warm embrace of the geological establishment.

★

The high point of Jacques Deprat's career as a geologist came in 1913, just four years after his arrival in Indo-China as a respected but junior geologist, unknown outside his native France. In March 1913 Deprat received notice of the XIIth International Congress of Geology, to be held in Toronto and Ottawa in August of that year. He suggested to his superior Honoré Lantenois that he, Deprat, should attend this important gathering in order to present the work of the new Service Géologique de l'Indochine. Deprat later gave his own account of the slightly farcical events that followed.

According to Deprat, writing in *Les Chiens aboient*, Lantenois agreed to his request, and then decided to go as well. Deprat agreed that this would be '*très agréable*'. But then on further consideration Lantenois told him that the Governor-General of the colony would not pay for two of them to go, only one. Lantenois said that this was his last chance to attend, while Deprat was young and could attend future congresses. He had therefore decided that he would go alone. At this point Deprat's wife Marguerite, who seems to have had a healthy impatience with the manoeuvrings of the Colonial Service, stepped in. She insisted that her husband should go, and that he should, if necessary, take unpaid leave while they would spend all of their savings on the fares and expenses. According to Jacques Deprat, his wife went to see Lantenois and told him of their intentions.

Lantenois replied that he could not allow this. He would ensure that they both go – or he would not go himself. That evening Lantenois came to Deprat's house and said that everything had been sorted out. The Governor-General had listened to his arguments (he claimed to have emphasised the importance of Deprat's work) and relented. Later that evening Deprat met the Governor-General at the nautical club (Deprat had an unusually good relationship with the Governor-General at this time), who said that Lantenois had only mentioned the Congress to him that evening, and that he had approved it at once.

Of course we need not take this account at face value, but the fact that Deprat told the story in this way says something about the relationship between the two men. And, as we have seen, whenever there are independent sources for incidents related by Deprat in *Les Chiens aboient*, they tend to confirm his version of events.

Jacques Deprat and Honoré Lantenois embarked from Haiphong in June 1913. Their journey was to take them to Hong Kong, Shanghai, Yokohama, and then on a semi-circuit of the northern Pacific, passing along the southern side of the Bering Sea and Aleutian Islands, before following the west coast of Canada and reaching Vancouver in August. The two men were at sea together for two months, before crossing Canada by train to Toronto.

We do not have to rely entirely on Deprat's 'post-affair' hindsight for knowledge of his views in 1913. During the journey to Toronto and during the conference itself he wrote letters to his parents in Indo-China which have been kept by his family. Deprat's letters from the ships they sailed in are most entertaining when he writes about their fellow passengers. He is deeply impressed by the Japanese, whom he regards as cultured and sophisticated, and similarly unimpressed by certain Americans he meets. Later in his life Deprat returned to this contrast between Asian and European cultures, in which his preference was consistent. As for his relations with Lantenois, they seemed unremarkable. Deprat reports that they got on fairly well, but saw as little of each other as was possible under the circumstances – they clearly had little in common apart from geology. His letters poke gentle fun at Lantenois, but are never overly mocking. Their journey to the edges of the Bering Sea brought them into extremely cold weather and Deprat says that Lantenois bought a huge number of pullovers in Shanghai, and was already shivering by the time they left Japan – but when they get to the Aleutians, Deprat admits that it is so cold that it is hard to sleep. As they were approaching Vancouver he wrote that he was extremely bored and could not wait to land, while M. Lantenois would be happy for the journey to last for ever.

The first International Geological Congress had been held in Paris in 1878. These large-scale conferences are sometimes criticised for their unwieldiness and lack of focus, but, certainly in the early days, there was an urgent need for geologists to come together and sort out some of the basic parameters of their science. As information from the field came flooding in from geologists all over the world, international agreement on questions of naming and categorising was essential. Geology could not exist except as a world science, and to be a world science it must be an international enterprise. An International Congress has been held every few years since. Nowadays this has become an enormous two-week-long jamboree attended by thousands of geologists. But even in 1913 it was a grand affair, with 300 or so geologists from North America, Europe and their colonies, in attendance at Toronto and Ottawa.

The two men arrived in Toronto in August 1913, to be met by some old friends and acquaintances. Honoré Lantenois was, of course, an old friend and in many cases an old student colleague, of members of the French delegation. The cream of French geology was there, and most of them were *corpsards* – graduates of the Ecole Polytechnique and the Ecole des Mines. But it was Jacques Deprat, rather than their old colleague Lantenois, whom the French geologists were eager to meet. Deprat's work on the tectonic history of Yunnan and Tonkin was extremely valuable in the confirmation of nappe theory and in contributing to the organisation of the Earth's mountain chains into a coherent structure. As we have seen, this new tectonic theory was a triumph for French geology and for French science in general. Deprat's part in it had not gone unnoticed. It was, perhaps, only when he arrived in Toronto that Deprat realised the effect that his work was having in France, and all over the geological world.

On the first day of the Congress, having met up once again with Pierre Termier, his old supervisor Alfred Lacroix and other members of the French and other delegations, Deprat returned to his room at the University. There a letter was waiting for him from the secretary of the organising committee of the Congress. The simple one-line message was a dream come true for Deprat and elevated him into the ranks of internationally recognised geologists: 'I have the honour to inform you, you have been elected a Vice-President of the XIIth World Congress of Geology.'

At least one Vice-President was chosen from each country, though the larger countries had several. Deprat was chosen, probably at Termier's suggestion, as the Vice-President representing Indo-China. The choice was between him and Lantenois, so was not in itself a major honour. It was, however, a major snub for Lantenois, though naturally he offered his congratulations to Deprat (Deprat writes in *Les Chiens* that despite this show of politesse, Lantenois was extremely offended). But it did enable Deprat to be a member of the 'Bureau' of the Congress and to sit on the fifty-strong Council of the Congress with Pierre Termier and Alfred Lacroix and the distinguished French geologist Emmanuel de Margerie. This was important since decisions affecting the future development of the subject were taken by this council. The proceedings of the Congress were also bought by every geological library in the world, so Deprat would now be known to everyone in the subject as the principal geologist in Indo-China. Honoré Lantenois's name does not appear on any of the committees of the Congress, or as a contributor. The only record of his existence is in the delegates' list and in the official photograph. This is not unusual, since most delegates come to conferences to listen, learn and meet up with colleagues. But Lantenois's lack of official status is in contrast to Deprat's elevation. Here official rank counted for less than scientific achievement.

In addition, Emmanuel de Margerie proposed to the Council of the Congress that certain geologists should be co-opted as collaborators on the project of a world geological map, which had been set up at a previous Congress. Jacques Deprat's name was included in this list. At the Congress itself Deprat mixed as an equal with the world's leading geologists, including Lacroix, de Margerie and Termier. For Deprat, Termier's patronage was necessary and elevating. In a letter to his parents Deprat wrote, 'So I am one of the Vice-Presidents of the Congress; and this is only given to those who are authoritative in the scientific world . . . I am well launched now and have achieved a place, as Termier himself said, among the leaders of the geological world.'

On his travels to and from the Congress Deprat did not rest from geology. In Japan he visited the volcanoes of Aso-San and Asama-Yama and sent a short review to the Académie des Sciences on 'The mode of formation of two Japanese volcanic centres' (Deprat 1915a). He also collected samples of fusulinid micro-fossils in Japan, which formed the basis of another paper (Deprat, 1914a).

Within a few months of the two men's return from Canada, the period of Honoré Lantenois's Indo-Chinese service came to an end. He was fifty years old and had spent the last eleven years in the colony with occasional spells in France. On 20 April 1914, in what was supposed to be his final farewell to the colony, he boarded the *Atlantique* in Haiphong with an Indo-Chinese domestic servant. He was returning to France with hopes of a further career in the government service. Between Deprat's arrival in 1909 and Lantenois's departure from the colony in 1914 relations between the two men had been outwardly cordial, peppered with the usual disagreements we would expect to find between a manager and his immediate superior. In fact, during those five years, they had spent much of the time away from each other. From November 1909 to October 1910, Deprat was on his major expedition to the Chinese Yunnan, and from May 1910 to August 1911, Lantenois was in France. In March and April 1912 Deprat was in Annam, in June 1912 he was in the Rivière Noire region of Tonkin. They spent more time together travelling to Toronto and back than they did in the rest of the five years.

There is little doubt that Deprat was relieved to see the back of Lantenois. Deprat had been made the official head of the Service Géologique de l'Indochine in 1913, and would have been relishing the chance to run it without interference from above. Lantenois had never really wanted to let go of the service, and had been a fussy, and sometimes unwelcome, presence. Deprat implied later that Lantenois had shown hostility to him ever since his arrival in Indo-China and had tried to block his progress and his work. It is difficult to verify this necessarily subjective view, though it is clear that the two men never saw eye to eye and managed an uneasy collaboration rather than a fruitful working relationship. From Deprat's point of view, it was his own refusal to obey the rules of obeisance to superiors, in fact his refusal to see Lantenois as his superior at all, that was at the root of this difference. He regarded Lantenois as a *fonctionnaire*, a bureaucrat and administrator who knew nothing about science, or about much else for that matter. Mutual respect, that most essential ingredient of good human relations, never did exist between them.

Lantenois had planned to get a job in the Ministry of Industry after his customary six months' 'convalescent' leave in France. But before the six months elapsed, the European powers were engulfed in war. On 11 August 1914 Lantenois was mobilised as a Lieutenant-Colonel Chef d'Etat Major in Algeria. He remained there until December 1916.

Meanwhile, back in Indo-China, Lantenois's replacement as Engineer-in-Chief and Deprat's superior was a mathematician called André Lochard. He was the same age as Deprat, and during the three years they were together, he scrupulously followed the letter of his predecessor's directives – to give absolute scientific autonomy to the Service Géologique and its head. Evidence that relations between Deprat and Lochard were good comes from colleagues, who wrote in letters and diaries that the service was thriving. In a letter to Alfred Lacroix dated 8 April 1915, Jean-Louis Giraud, a young but experienced geologist, newly arrived in the colony, wrote:

> I have found Deprat an enthusiast for the Orient, and he has really done a lot here; the museum which he has set up with Mansuy compares well with those of Universities; there are abundant avenues of study and good work is being done. There is the best understanding between the different members of the Service, Deprat, Mansuy and Commandant Dussault, who all love geology more than the 'world', and with whom I am sure to be on excellent terms.

Deprat expanded his staff by taking on a new laboratory assistant. Mlle Madeleine Colani began to do occasional work for the Service Géologique de l'Indochine in 1914 at the age of forty-eight, after which she became friendly with the Deprat family. She was officially employed full time in 1917 at Deprat's instigation.

For the next two and a half years Deprat continued his relentless fieldwork, going into increasingly inaccessible areas of Indo-China. In June 1915 he took Giraud with him on a long expedition into a mountainous region of Haut-Tonkin, returning to Hanoi in August. On this expedition Deprat discovered another example of *Trinucleus ornatus* between Dong Van and Chang Poung. He had previously found a specimen of the same species at Nui Nga Ma in 1912. This again confirmed the presence of Ordovician rocks in the region, and the possibility of a sea linking southern Europe and south-east Asia during the Ordovician period. Deprat explains this in his 1915 *mémoire* on the northern part of Haut-Tonkin:

> *Trinucleus ornatus* Sternb.
>
> This trilobite from stage d3 of the Bohemian clearly indicates [rocks of] middle Ordovician age. I was particularly interested to discover this species in the North of Tonkin, since it strongly links my observations in Annam on the one part, and Yunnan on the other. I discovered some years ago beds of *Trinucleus ornatus* and *Dalmanites* cf. *caudata* EMMR. in

> yellow quartzites at Nui Nga Ma, the species were described by M. Mansuy. And during my researches in the north of eastern Yunnan, I discovered *Dionide formosa* BARR. in a micaceous black calcschist overlying a series of marls and mottled marls and calcschists very similar to those in the Lou-tçai series [i.e. the series underlying the present find]. Now the formation containing *Dionide formosa* at Si-yang-tang [in Yunnan] is more than 900 km from the *Trinucleus ornatus* formation at Annam; the formation on the climb from Song Nho-qué to Chang-poung forms a link of great interest between these distant points, showing the consistency of this palaeontological horizon from the north of Yunnan to Annam and to the east towards Kwang-si. (Deprat, 1915d)

So now Ordovician species known from Europe had been found in Yunnan, Annam and the north of Tonkin. In January 1917 Deprat was to report another find of a European species in this zone (Deprat, 1917b). The find, a specimen of *Calymene* cf. *aragoi*, was probably made in 1916. The argument for an extensive marine connection between Ordovician Europe and the entire region of southern Asia was becoming overwhelming.

In his autobiography Deprat records this as a settled time. He got on well with his colleagues in the Service Géologique, though he disliked and avoided the higher echelons and cliques who ran the administration of the colony. In *Les Chiens* Deprat writes that by 1916 he wanted to return to France. He was exhausted – having been working without a break for seven years. It seems that his work was suffering too. Michel Durand-Delga writes that at least one of Deprat's *mémoires* is full of small errors and inconsistencies. It is 'difficult to match the text with the figures and there are confusions in the naming of the series'. It is worth remembering that these scientific papers, in common with many others at the time but in contrast to present practice, were not sent for review or to referees before they were published. They were regarded as reports from the field, and were therefore not subjected to rigorous examination.

In a letter to Henri Douvillé at end of 1916, Deprat writes that he weighs only 46 kilograms (7st 3lbs). It was customary for colonial staff to take home leave in France from time to time, but Deprat had not yet done this. Writing retrospectively Deprat does admit that his wish to return to France at the time was formed in ignorance of the true plight of the country. In 1916 the war being fought on French soil was exacting a terrifying price on his countrymen. Futile attempts to break through the German lines were to cost the lives of 1.4 million French soldiers. A vast area of the country was being effectively destroyed. Ten thousand miles away in Indo-China, the scale of this national tragedy was, understandably, difficult to appreciate.

In the summer of 1916 Deprat made his last-ever geological expedition – a six-week exploration of the high plateau of Kwangsi in Haut-Tonkin. In *Les Chiens aboient* he writes that while in the field he received a moving letter from Pierre Termier, whose life had been beset by tragedy. His elder son was killed in an accident in 1906 and in 1916 his wife died after a long illness. The same year his son-in-law, the geologist Jean Boussac, was killed in action. Termier wrote to Deprat about the progress of the war in Europe in emotional terms:

> We must continue to work and to publish all the same. We must not cease living and producing. That would play into the hands of the enemy. But in wishing you a fruitful campaign in China, I ask you to look after yourself. Do not abuse your remarkable stamina. Do not expose yourself unnecessarily to the rigours of the climate, nor to the dangers of robbers. I ask this of you in the name of our friendship, in the name of geology, which has need of you. I have a dream . . . will it come true? I would love to see your great valleys cutting through the piles of folds in the mountains of Indo-China. I won't tempt fate during the hostilities, but afterwards – since we must hope that there will be an end to this sad time – I will make the greatest effort to obtain a mission to the Far East.

It was around this time – in October 1916 – that Deprat heard that Henri Mansuy was to be awarded the prestigious Prix Wilde by the Académie des Sciences in Paris. Deprat was in Yunnan-fou at the time. From there he wrote to Alfred Lacroix in Paris to thank him for his efforts on Mansuy's part, and added, 'He is a great worker and a noble spirit, allied with a generous soul.'

Deprat's relations with Henri Mansuy, his most important colleague, had remained good – though Deprat seems to have seen Mansuy as a slight eccentric whose idiosyncrasies were tolerated because of his age and his good scientific work. In *Les Chiens aboient* Deprat portrays Mansuy as hypocritical: he always spoke up for the working classes and against the bourgeoisie, but at the same time he tried desperately to get himself nominated for the Légion d'Honneur, and he treated the Indo-Chinese staff of the Service very badly. He *did* gain membership of the Légion d'Honneur, but there is no independent evidence of his ill-treatment of his staff. Deprat's benign tolerance of Mansuy was not, however, reciprocated, except on the surface. In all their correspondence Mansuy, who always wrote in flattering terms to his superiors, never addressed Deprat as Chef de Service, though he always used this form of address to Jacob, Deprat's successor. In the rigidly courteous world of the time, this is a considerable omission. Mansuy is a difficult man to pin down because he seemed to inspire contrasting reactions. Some saw him as proud, meticulous and principled, where others disliked him as a bully, a sycophant and a conniver. It is perhaps significant that those in power were in the first group and those who worked for him in the second. His relations with Deprat do not fit easily into this pattern. He may have flattered Deprat until he became suspicious of him, or he may have felt ambivalent about his young superior all along.

While in Kwangsi, Deprat received another letter. André Lochard, Deprat's superior, had been called up to serve in the army and was to return to France. Deprat decided that he must get back to Hanoi. We might wonder why Deprat himself was not called into the French army too. When Jean-Louis Giraud had first arrived in Indo-China in 1915 he remarked pointedly, 'One is struck, on arriving from France, by the number of young and vigorous men circulating in Hanoi.' We do not know for sure, but must assume that Deprat being the breadwinner for a large family and doing a vital job, was excused administrative duties back in France and was too old to be conscripted into the military. Back in Hanoi, Deprat spent the last weeks of 1916 preparing the report of his trip to the Kwangsi plateau. Then in late 1916 a letter arrived from Honoré Lantenois in France with news that was to change the lives of both men. Lantenois was to return to the colony in February 1917 and take up his old job as Chef de Service des Mines. Three years after he had thought he had seen the last of him, Jacques Deprat was to be once again under the control of this meddlesome bureaucrat.

A few weeks after the news of Lantenois's imminent return arrived in Hanoi, Jacques Deprat's name was again being fêted in Paris. On 8 January 1917 General Jourdy gave his inaugural address as new President of the Société Géologique de France. Jourdy was, like Deprat, from the Jura region, and he singled out his fellow Jurassian for praise:

> One of our successors, a young geologist with a great future, left his home town of Besançon to go and discover the surprising history of the great 'preyunnanaise' nappes, created where Tibet comes up against the 'môle' of eastern Tonkin. This grandiose synthesis is the beautiful jewel in the crown, so laboriously carved by this star of the line of Jurassian geologists that began with Thurmann.

Two weeks later, on 22 January, Pierre Termier presented Deprat's *mémoire* on the geology of the southern region of Haut-Tonkin (Deprat, 1915a) to the Société Géologique in Paris. The Comptes-Rendus of the society record Termier's words. It is worth quoting these at length in view of the events to come.

> M. Termier calls the attention of all French geologists to the great importance of the results obtained by M. Deprat: physiographic results, stratigraphic results, tectonic results. The country in which he is working is among the most difficult in the world; one has the very clear impression, after seeing M. Deprat's *mémoire*, that this country, difficult to access and very complex in its structure, is now almost as well known as the countries of Europe. Nothing brings more honour to French science than the geological work accomplished in the last few years in Indo-China; and in this truly gigantic undertaking, in which M. Deprat and M. Mansuy have been the most active workers, the *mémoire* of M. Deprat on the region of northern Haut-Tonkin merits a place in the foreground. (Termier, 1917)

Termier summarises Deprat's tectonic work on the region to date: 'M. Deprat's *mémoire* admirably complements his 1914 paper on the Rivière Noire. The tectonic synthesis of Tonkin is rapidly being worked out; and we now have an overall view of the structure of the whole region.'

Emmanuel de Margerie, future President of the society, also felt the need to comment on the work in Indo-China: 'The works of the Service Géologique de l'Indochine have, as soon as they are published, taken their place among the fundamental documents on the [geological] history of the Asian continent; and one remains struck by admiration in the face of the immensity of the work accomplished over the years, far from any intellectual centres, by two explorers supported solely by their own enthusiasm.'

The President of the Society concluded:

> The Society sends its felicitations to M. Mansuy who, over many years, has worked for the Service Géologique de l'Indochine, and to M. Deprat, a young scientist with a great

future, who is head of the service. The society is unanimous in considering that the science and the fortitude deployed by these two geologists amply merits a national award, such as the Légion d'Honneur, since their remarkable and sometimes dangerous work honours the nation as well as science.

By any measure Jacques Deprat was now in the front rank of French geology. The most eminent and influential men in the subject were falling over themselves to praise his work. He had apparently triumphed over the cliquishness and élitism of French intellectual society and stood on the threshold of entry into the inner circle of the great and the good. But none of this was going to happen. By the time the copies of this bulletin of the Société Géologique arrived in Hanoi, Deprat stood accused of fraud and the future had been changed for ever.

Part Two

The Affair

4 *Indo-China, February–October 1917*

On 27 February 1917 Jacques Deprat went down to the docks at Haiphong to meet the steamer bringing his old boss Honoré Lantenois from France. Umberto Margheriti, Deprat's junior colleague from the Service Géologique, accompanied him. Despite their previous outward cordiality, Deprat cannot have been overjoyed at Lantenois's return. André Lochard, Lantenois's interim successor, had been a model superior, taking care of administration and leaving Deprat totally free to do his scientific work. But now there was the prospect of Lantenois's intrusions and interest beginning all over again. He had interfered too much for Deprat's taste and there was no reason to think he would not do so again. In his own account of this first meeting for three years, Deprat mocks Lantenois's appearance and manner. He says that Lantenois was heavier than before, and his features more pale and swollen. As a mark of his status, in place of an officer's sabre he had brought a case of umbrellas and canes. He wore a rosette of the Légion d'Honneur, given to those of his military rank.

But once Deprat had accompanied Lantenois back to Hanoi, he then saw almost nothing of him for the next three weeks. This was curious, but was no hardship for Deprat, who continued to prepare for his next expedition. He was due to leave on a trip to Annam, the central part of present-day

Vietnam, the next month. In *Les Chiens aboient* Deprat notes that in this period he also saw very little of his colleague Henri Mansuy, who remained shut away in his laboratory. He writes that he did bump into Mansuy once in the laboratory, and that Mansuy answered him only in monosyllables and avoided looking at him. Deprat was worried by this reaction and went to Mansuy's home later in the day. But he was not invited in. Deprat had no notion of what this meant. After that Mansuy was hardly seen in the laboratories of the Service Géologique.

On 20 March, three weeks after Lantenois's return, Deprat received a message via Umberto Margheriti that Lantenois wanted to see him urgently on an important matter. Deprat immediately went to his superior's office, where he found Lantenois in an unusually agitated state. After some beating about the bush Lantenois managed to get to the point of their meeting. He had, he said, a painful duty to perform, which was to inform him that Henri Mansuy believed him guilty of prolonged and systematic scientific fraud. The specific accusation was that Deprat had placed fossils that were from Europe among those that he had gathered on his expeditions in Indo-China. According to Deprat's account, Lantenois related Mansuy's accusations and added, 'This is very serious is it not?'

Deprat was first stunned, then extremely angry. He demanded to know from Lantenois to which species the accusations referred. Lantenois produced a list, which had presumably been given to him by Mansuy. There were six specimens on this original list, though the final total of suspect fossils was ten. Deprat writes that he found the whole thing ridiculous and asked Lantenois to consider the stupidity of his accusations. Lantenois became a little defensive when faced with what amounted to outright abuse and declared, 'It is not me, it is Mansuy who is making the accusations.'

We obviously have no independent account of the meeting, but there seems no reason to doubt the essentials of Deprat's own version. He may have exaggerated Lantenois's hesitation and eagerness to distance himself personally from the accusations. But there is circumstantial evidence that Lantenois was initially not overkeen to confront Deprat. What is certain is that Deprat was accused of placing fossil specimens brought from Europe among those he claimed to have found in the field in Indo-China over a number of years. The seriousness of the charge would have been immediately apparent to Deprat, as it was to Lantenois, and no doubt had been to Henri Mansuy. We know, too, that Mansuy had informed Lantenois of his belief in Deprat's fraud as soon as Lantenois returned to Hanoi. The three-week delay before Lantenois confronted Deprat may have resulted from Lantenois's simple reluctance to take action, or from his lack of conviction that the charges were true.

It is fair to ask why the accusation of taking fossils found in one location and claiming to have found them in another should be such a serious matter. After all, as Deprat himself said (though with conscious irony) they were only six fossils out of several thousands he had collected in Indo-China. There is, of course, the simple matter of honesty. It is clear that to be accused of deliberate and sustained dishonesty in any form of work is a grave matter. Whatever claims science might make about uncovering the truth, it differs not at all from other forms of activity in its requirement for honesty.

From this follows the matter of trust and, in particular, the trust which colleagues place in each other's work. Again this is a universal quality within any human activity, but in science this trust is more formalised and extended than in other fields, mainly through the publication of scientific information. When one scientist reads the published paper of another, he or she may not agree with any interpretation of data made by the author, but will take for granted that the data itself is accurate and honestly gained. This formalisation of trust is one of the things that makes science such a powerful tool for increasing particular types of knowledge. The use to which such dishonesty might be put increases the seriousness of the accusations. Scientific frauds are not perpetrated simply to falsify information – i.e. to get things wrong – they are carried out in order to present an invented version of the truth, and one the 'discovery' of which will bring some credit to the perpetrator.

The three men involved at the outset of the affair were aware that these were grave matters. They were living at a time, and in a society, where the concept of honour was potent. To be accused of dishonesty and betrayal of trust at any time would be serious enough – here it was a metaphorical death sentence. A man's reputation was at stake, and if that fell then so would his career, his work, his livelihood, his future and, it soon became apparent, his past. And what if the accusations were not true, what would that mean for the accusers? They could scarcely carry on as before. To have unjustly impugned a man's honour was in itself a dishonourable action. They would be subject to the opprobrium of their colleagues, the sanctions of their superiors and the disapproval of the world. For them too, everything was at stake.

The first unusual aspect of this case was Lantenois's immediate anxiety to distance himself from the accusations. Although we have only Deprat's account of that first meeting, Lantenois later repeated his 'neutrality' in an effort to seem even-handed. This distancing by Lantenois was a curious and, it must be said, hypocritical act. In his position as the superior of both men he could not have simply passed on Mansuy's accusations to Deprat without deciding for himself whether they had some basis. He must have known that by stating the accusations, he was in fact making them. He seemed to want to have this both ways – to satisfy Mansuy by taking some sort of action, and Deprat by not taking sides. But if Lantenois was less convinced than Mansuy, Jacques Deprat singularly failed to take advantage of any difference between the two men. This may have been understandable in the heat of that first encounter, but over the coming months Deprat unwisely antagonised his superior, when a more careful handling of the situation might have persuaded Lantenois to let the whole thing subside. Deprat, it seems, could not separate the bringer of the accusations from the accuser. But, as we have seen, Deprat had always shown signs of resenting Lantenois's assumed superiority over him. In all their dealings, he treated Lantenois as an equal and in scientific matters as a definite inferior. To have this man impugn his scientific work was beyond endurance. After years of quiet resentment, Deprat may have seen these trumped-up charges as his chance to destroy the men who seemed intent on destroying him. Over the coming months he seemed to want Lantenois and Mansuy to be exposed, and to pay for their effrontery in accusing him. But his desire for revenge was to cost him dear.

The suspect fossils were all trilobite species known from Europe – no one had made any secret of this – which had not previously been found in Indo-China. But while the species themselves were known from Europe, the specimens were, of course, thought to have been discovered in Indo-China. Since the term 'European fossil' is used frequently in documents concerning the affair, it is best to be clear about the distinction between European species and European specimens. The former simply means species that are known to have been found in abundance in Europe, but could, in theory, occur in other places. The latter indicates actual fossils that have been found in rocks in Europe. The suspect fossils were therefore European species, which was possibly legitimate, and suspected of being European specimens, which would be fraudulent.

According to Mansuy, Deprat had systematically introduced European specimens into the samples he sent or brought back from his expeditions, over the whole of his time in Indo-China. Since Mansuy never commented on the affair, we do not know what he thought Deprat's motive for such a fraud might be. But from the fossils themselves, and Mansuy's original descriptions, we can discern a pattern, if not in Deprat's behaviour, then at least in Mansuy's suspicions. The European fossils allowed Deprat to date certain rock strata with great precision, and in particular the Bohemian stage of the Ordovician period, from which at least three of the contested fossils came. Deprat had also proposed that the presence of these European marine creatures in Indo-China was proof of the existence of an ocean linking the two continents in Ordovician times, and in the Cambrian and Silurian periods. Each new 'European' Ordovician fossil discovery in Indo-China re-inforced the legitimacy of this theory.

Mansuy had harboured his suspicions since 1915 – though they applied to fossils gathered from 1910 onwards. In a paper written in 1916 Mansuy had quite suddenly decided that the way in which he had matched up the data from fossils gathered by Deprat with the stratigraphic observations that Deprat was making in the field just did not make sense. Up until now he had been able to shoehorn different strata, using evidence of their ages from fossils and from their spatial inter-relationships, into a coherent stratigraphic structure, but he no longer believed this structure to be accurate. Most worryingly, the structure would work much better if the proposed existence of Ordovician and Silurian rocks in certain areas was dismissed:

> . . . most of the fauna in Tonkin considered up to now, on the basis of stratigraphic observations, as being of Gothlandian [i.e. Silurian] age, sometimes even Ordovician, undoubtedly combines all the traits, all the characteristics of Devonian fauna. All of these facts, all of these certainties are in complete contradiction to the observations made on the ground. Taking into account hesitations, incorrect interpretations, inevitable errors and relying on the most convincing palaeontological data, one is brought to the conclusion that a general revision of the principal stratigraphic data is needed, in particular that of the lower Palaeozoic of northern Indo-China. (Mansuy, 1916)

Mansuy's work had been based mostly on information gathered in the field by Deprat. If Mansuy's assessment was correct and the Ordovician and Gothlandian beds were really much younger Devonian strata, then Deprat's finds of Ordovician European fossil species stood out like a sore thumb. Mansuy does not mention any suspicion of fraud, or even anomaly, in this paper, but there is little doubt that his mind was moving in that direction. He had presumably seen the return of his old and trusted boss Lantenois as a chance to air his suspicions, and to make a formal accusation.

Initially Honoré Lantenois seems not to have threatened Deprat with disciplinary action, or even exposure of his alleged fraud. He simply confronted Deprat with the accusations, presumably expecting either an admission of guilt or a demonstration of innocence. Either way, the ball was now firmly in Deprat's court. If this were a legal case, it would be up to Lantenois or Mansuy to prove Deprat's guilt. But here the situation was reversed – Deprat must show why the suspect fossils were genuine. In any case, Deprat was eager to prove the absurdity of the charges as quickly as possible, though his impulsiveness was not his best suit in this situation.

It is a curious fact that, after the initial accusations, the progress of the affair was marked by long periods when nothing much happened, punctuated by sudden bursts of activity. It was as if the authorities in the colony (including Lantenois himself at the outset) could not really be bothered with the whole messy business. They would have preferred it to fade away and therefore had to be kicked into action every so often, before being gripped once more by bureaucratic inertia. The provocations to action were generally initiated by Deprat himself, for whom the lulls in the affair must have been agonising. Once the accusations had been made, he was unable to let the matter subside. He was now in an impossible situation which must be resolved one way or the other. Indeed for Deprat there was no middle way in this affair. Once it began he raised the stakes at every opportunity. As we have seen, he was unwilling, or simply unable, to play a tactical game which might end up with the charges being dropped. Once the game was on, either Lantenois and Mansuy must be destroyed, or he must be. At various times Deprat was offered compromises, but there was never a chance that he would consider them. While we may, in the interests of history, wish to add moral complexity to the question of guilt or innocence in this affair, the man at the centre rejected this outright. For Deprat, this was a Manichean struggle of right against wrong, of good against evil. He played it like a Greek tragedy, calling on the world to judge him, and when it did, he deliberately brought everything crashing in on top of him. In Deprat's moral universe there was no possibility of compromise. So, from time to time, he did or said or wrote something which forced Lantenois into action against him. Under these provocations Lantenois's assumption of neutrality could not last, and the affair became a desperate and vicious struggle between the two men. They were, depending on your viewpoint, like Conrad's 'two mastiffs fighting over a marrowy bone' or they were engaged in 'a quarrel of Titans – a battle of the gods'.

Jacques Deprat stormed out of his meeting with Honoré Lantenois on 20 March 1917, taking the list of suspect fossils with him. He immediately told his wife of Mansuy's accusations, and that evening he told his trusted colleague Umberto Margheriti. He then decided, with his wife's and Margheriti's encouragement, that he should act immediately to clear his name. The simplest way to do this would be to find another fossil of a suspect species at the same site as the original. He resolved to find another matching specimen, and deliver it to Lantenois. It does not seem to have occurred to him that this should be done in the company of an independent witness.

He had, in any case, been planning a three-week trip to the north of Annam. So the site he chose to revisit was Nui Nga Ma in northern Annam, close to the Hanoi–Saigon highway. Deprat travelled to Annam in late March 1917, a few days after his meeting with Lantenois. According to his own account, a letter from Lantenois was waiting for him at Ha Tinh, the nearest town to Nui Nga Ma. This is a curious letter, which we may feel was an invention by Deprat, but contemporary evidence for its existence comes from a letter from Deprat to Lacroix in France, and from the later official report by Habert (see page 98). In the letter, Lantenois ordered Deprat to go to the rock exposure at

Nui Nga Ma, 'at the place where you previously found the two fossil fragments. If you find another specimen of the same species, I will consider the affair, of which we spoke the other day, closed. Go there, this is an *official order* [original italics].'

If this is genuine, then Deprat had presumably told him of his intention to visit the site, and Lantenois agreed that this was an easy way either to resolve or confirm the 'affair'. Deprat's understanding was that Lantenois was not overkeen to pursue matters further at this stage, but was being prompted by Henri Mansuy, who, he believed, had his own motives for seeing him brought down.

But now a confusion arises between Deprat's own account of events and his previous research papers, which is extremely curious and which was central to the case against him. In his autobiography, *Les Chiens aboient*, he writes: 'Dorpat [Deprat] remembered having picked up the fragments in question in a piece of pebble lying on the ground, and resembling the neighbouring rocks. "He [Lantenois] knows that a piece of conglomerate could have been transported from far away, and that I have only a chance in a million of finding the same fossil [thought Deprat]. He wants the worst outcome."'

But in fact the original fossils had been found, according to Deprat's own 1912 report (see page 62), not in a pebble of the conglomerate, but in the quartzite bed underneath (Deprat, 1912b). Indeed this was the whole point of the importance of their discovery. Deprat was right to say that a fossil found in a conglomerate pebble could have been transported from a distance away. Conglomerates are rocks made up of rounded fragments, pebbles, boulders of previously formed rocks, set into a sand or silt matrix which binds them together like cement. They are formed when banks of beach or river pebbles are buried beneath sand or silt. And, like beach pebbles, the pebbles in a conglomerate will have originally come from elsewhere. The stratigraphic value of such a find is restricted because of this – a fossil can only tell you something about the age of the rock in which it was originally formed. Pebbles in conglomerates will necessarily be older and probably from other locations than the conglomerate itself. Fossils found in conglomerate pebbles tell you about the pebble's origin, but not much about the location where you find it.

The quartzite bed in which the original specimens of *Trinucleus ornatus* and *Dalmanites* were found was definitively fixed by Deprat in his original description (Deprat, 1913c):

> Probably the oldest horizon we actually know of in Indo-China is the one I have discovered at Nui-nga-ma in Annam, in the region of Vinh, south of Ben Thuy. These are very hard quartzites, of a pale yellowish colour, from which I have recovered:
>
> *Trinucleus ornatus* Sterb.
> *Dalmanites* cf. *caudata* Emerich.

In the report to the Académie des Sciences (Deprat 1912b), *Trinucleus* was described as being discovered in a pale grey or yellowish quartzite. The stratigraphic succession was given as:

> 5. Poudingues triasiques transgressifs [Triassic marine conglomerates]
> 4. Quartzites à *Trinucleus ornatus*, *Dalmanites* aff. *caudata*
> 3. Quartzites sans fossiles

The conglomerates above the quartzites are not only unreliable as stratigraphic indicators, they are from a much later date than the rocks underneath (Triassic compared to Ordovician). If the original fossil came from the conglomerate, then Deprat's claim that the quartzites were the oldest datable rocks in Indo-China was wrong.

In *Les Chiens aboient* he describes his 1917 visit, referring initially to his 1912 paper:

> In a work published five years previously, he indicated exactly the place where he made his find: a partially exposed surface,

near to a small pagoda. He returned there, to relieve his conscience, convinced that he would not find anything similar. He was surprised to see among the pieces of loose rock, (a disparate collection rolled by the tidal currents of a disappeared ocean) a piece of hard sandstone near the place where he had found the fossil previously. At the edge of a crack an imprint appeared. He saw that it was a fragment of a species which seemed, at first sight, to bear similarities to the first one.

Deprat says that he thought this a strange coincidence, but then decided that this was probably a piece left from the stone that he had previously broken up, which had been lying in this remote location ever since. Then: 'To make sure, he broke open the other pebbles that were lying around. He found nothing similar.' There is some ambiguity in the terminology used here. Sometimes the source is one of several '*morceaux de roche*' and sometimes a '*galet*'. But Deprat's description of the rock fragments being '*entraînés par les courants littoraux d'une mer disparue*' makes it clear that these were pebbles, and therefore from the conglomerate bed, rather than fragments of quartzite.

The fossil he had found this time was actually the tail segment, or pygidium, of a trilobite species from the family *Dalmanites* called *Dalmanitina (Dalmanitina) socialis*. This was another species known from the Ordovician of Europe, and which therefore made the presence of the fossils which Deprat had claimed to find there in 1912 (*Trinucleus ornatus* and *Dalmanites* cf. *caudata*), less anomalous.

Deprat might have been confused or forgetful about the bed in which he had found the suspect fossils five years earlier – after all he had, as he said, recovered thousands of specimens in Indo-China. But, on the other hand, he might have taken the trouble to check the record on such a vital matter. What is more likely, from what we know now, is that when he returned to the site at Nui Nga Ma he could not find a bed of quartzite. The existence of such a bed became, and has remained, a matter of hot dispute. But, from later information, it is certain that at the site which Deprat visited in March 1917 there was no quartzite bed. He could not therefore repeat his find of 1912, and instead, found a specimen in a pebble – which may have been a pebble of quartzite.

This was the first example of Deprat's behaviour increasing the appearance of his guilt. It was also the most serious, since however much Deprat might subsequently disown the other suspect fossils, there was no question that the fossil he brought back from Nui Nga Ma in March 1917 was collected by him, and not substituted by anyone else. This became a key element in the case against him. In fact there is a possible explanation for Deprat's error. He might possibly have returned to the wrong site at Nui Nga Ma. He had not been there for five years, and the only detailed maps of the area were the ones he had drawn himself. Geologists working in the field in the tropics often write up their notes at the end of the day because of the midday heat. Since they are no longer at the exact places they are mapping, this gives greater possibilities of plotting locations inaccurately. Deprat may have gone to the site, found no quartzite, been panicked into thinking he had been mistaken in his earlier work, and looked for fossils in pebbles of quartzite, instead of a bed of quartzite.

Later in *Les Chiens aboient*, Deprat maintains that Lantenois was seen in Ha Tinh, the nearest town to Nui Nga Ma, the day before he arrived, and might well have planted the specimen of *Dalmanitina socialis* where he knew Deprat was bound to find it. While implausibility must not be dismissed as fantasy, this does seem an incredibly far-fetched scenario, invented once the 1917 find was also shown to be a specimen from Europe as well as a European species. But even without the notion of Lantenois's involvement, the visit to Nui Nga Ma and the 'find' of *Dalmanitina socialis* was Deprat's biggest error of judgement. In his eagerness to clear his name, he simply offered more evidence of his possible guilt. After all, once he found the new specimen, he himself, as a scientist, should have checked that it was from the same bed as the earlier fossils, as a check on himself and on his own stratigraphic interpretation. Instead he seemed only to want to squash any further suspicions about him. This might be understandable in the circumstances, but in the long term it was unwise.

Deprat returned to the nearby town of Ha tinh with his new specimen, and immediately wrote to Lantenois in Hanoi: 'I have discovered another specimen. But as this is all to do with pebbles, I do not attach any importance to the find. However, by the terms of your letter I can avail myself of this. In any case, I take the incident to be closed.'

And that, Jacques Deprat assumed and hoped, was that.

Immediately on his return to Hanoi in early April, Deprat was called up to the French army to help combat an uprising by local Tonkinois nationalists. He remained in the army until the end of May, when he seems to have fallen ill. At the beginning of June, when he was stood down, Lantenois refused him permission to go on an expedition *de vérification* to Haut-Tonkin because of his ill health. This is the first indication that Deprat's discovery of another Ordovician trilobite at Nui Nga Ma, and his letter to Lantenois, had not killed off the affair, as he had hoped. It had merely been in suspension while Deprat did his military service. It appears that Lantenois was not prepared to concede that Deprat was in the clear, but neither, once again, was he eager to push the affair forward.

This awkward and uneasy truce continued into June. Deprat avoided going to the laboratories for fear of meeting Mansuy, but began to feel increasingly bored and frustrated as his health returned. The unresolved affair was restricting his ability to work – Lantenois was reluctant to let him go back to the field, but seemed unable to decide what to do next. Deprat was in an extremely uncomfortable limbo. Only a few people knew about the accusations against him, which must have made this enforced idleness even stranger to endure, never mind explain. Then a small but significant act by Deprat set things going again.

Deprat was preparing a paper for publication as a *Mémoire du*

Service Géologique de l'Indochine on the 'Palaeozoic formations of Haut-Tonkin and Yunnan'. In the text of this review of his previous work, Deprat inserted a phrase which deliberately minimised the scientific contribution that Mansuy had made to the geological work on the region. The *mémoire* was never distributed, so we have only Deprat's version from *Les Chiens aboient* to go on, as follows: 'It is important to emphasise how much the work of M. Henderson [Walcott] on the Silurian formations, has made the identification of most of the specimens which we have recovered, so simple. The beautiful definition of his photographs allows anyone to rapidly identify similar species. We must give this homage to the great specialist of the Silurian.'

The 'Henderson' in question was in fact Charles Walcott, later to find scientific immortality as the discoverer of the Burgess Shale. Walcott was a specialist on the early Palaeozoic period, and had worked his way up to become director of the US Geological Survey, and then in 1907 head of the Smithsonian Institute.

Deprat's generous praise of another scientist could hardly have done more to denigrate the work of Henri Mansuy. Mansuy's principal task, after all, was the identification of species which others, mainly Deprat, had gathered. The Silurian, in particular, had been fertile ground for Mansuy as it apparently had good exposures in northern Indo-China and Yunnan. The skill that Mansuy had exerted was nothing more, Deprat implied, than a matching of specimens to Walcott's photographs which 'anyone' could have carried out. This was a calculated attack, and admittedly rather a clever one, and it provoked a counter-reaction. Lantenois saw the proofs of the *mémoire*, and immediately insisted that the passage be altered.* Deprat

*This *mémoire*, which should have appeared in the 1916 volume of the *Mémoires de la Service Géologique de l'Indochine*, was never officially published, and remains one of the mysteries of the affair. It is thought have been printed and then removed from circulation by Lantenois. The Geological Society library in London has a note on the contents page of the relevant volume that this paper was never produced. It is, however, referred to in the 1955 *Lexique Stratigraphie International*, see page 188.

responded to this threat by lodging an official complaint against Lantenois for searching his office, but in the hierarchy of the colony, complaints to the Governor-General could only be made through the correct channels. Deprat had to send his complaint via Lantenois, who simply failed to pass it on. Deprat's action had pushed Lantenois further into Mansuy's camp and into further action.

On 18 July 1917 Deprat received a letter from Lantenois, which was in effect a reply to Deprat's letter from Ha Tinh back in April. Deprat's return from the army and hospital, and the 'Walcott incident' required a response. Deprat reproduces part of this letter in *Les Chiens aboient*. Lantenois states his own position as he sees it, which is as neutral referee between the accusations of Mansuy and the denials of Deprat – though this neutrality, if it ever existed, was under strain.

> M. Mansuy's statements have caused me great sorrow. They seemed incredible to me. However, I asked M. Mansuy to clarify them. I examined the specimens. This examination made an impression on me. There is a misunderstanding. I have by no means incriminated your work. I solemnly ask you if, in order to fix the ages of these formations, you sent M. Mansuy fossils which were not from these places. You mention your own competence which you claim to be superior to mine. I do not dispute this point. It is simply a question of morality. I propose therefore to go with you to the field. You will search in my presence, and if you find the same fossils, I will certify them. I will take them myself and submit them to M. Mansuy's inspection.
>
> I cannot allow you to refuse to carry out these excavations in front of me. I am your superior. You threaten to take the affair to Paris, in front of your colleagues. I accept this arbitration and I consent to submitting to them, if you judge it necessary, the question of whether you can refuse to accompany me.

Although we do not have Deprat's letter from Ha Tinh, it seems that Deprat had tried to head off Lantenois's intention to go with him to the suspect sites, by threatening to expose such a ridiculous notion to the opinion of their august colleagues back in France. Deprat had suggested that three of the most eminent French geologists – Pierre Termier, Albert Lacroix and Henri Douvillé – should be asked to judge whether he should be forced to do as Lantenois had asked. We should remember, in view of the events to come, just how high Deprat's stock stood among the geologists in Paris. He was their *jeune homme de grand avenir*, their young man with a great future. He was *the* expert on the geology of Indo-China. Lantenois, on the other hand, while an old friend of some of them, was a mere *fonctionnaire*, whose scientific views counted for very little. Deprat obviously felt that Lantenois would not risk being shown up as a fool in front of the great men of French geology. But here, it seems, he miscalculated. Lantenois not only felt secure enough to call this bluff, but the threat itself probably added to his sense of grievance against Deprat. It is worth noting something that Deprat may not have known or thought important, but which Lantenois certainly did – that two of the three eminent men were members of the Corps.

In his letter of 18 July 1917 Lantenois put forward the three arguments that made the fossils suspect, and invited Deprat's responses. The arguments were recorded in the Habert report, compiled later in 1918:*

1. Palaeontological facts: Until now no one has found species from the Cambrian of Europe in the Cambrian of Asia. The discovery in Asia of two European Cambrian trilobite species is in contradiction to all the facts known to date,

*The official investigation of the scientific aspects of the affair, as a prelude to a formal Commission of Inquiry, was carried out by a man called Habert in 1918. His report, which is now in the archive of the Académie des Sciences in Paris, gives a reliable history of the events from March 1918 to November 1918.

and is, at the least, unlikely.*

2. Lithological facts: The rocks which constitute the matrix of the incriminated fossils are lithologically identical to the rocks which contain these same species in the European formations.
3. Material facts: The incriminated specimens are each a unique example [i.e. the only one found]. All except two are of complete individuals, in a superb state of preservation, in which the matrix is not altered (metamorphosed), though trilobites of local provenance are generally found in fragments and are altered – their aspect is very different. This series of unique and perfect pieces, all European species, is truly an extraordinary thing.

Deprat answered each point, according to the Habert report, in a letter to Lantenois sent on 19 July 1917 – i.e. the day after Lantenois's letter arrived:

1. Palaeontological facts. From the fact that, until now no one has found European species in the Cambrian of Indo-China, it is not correct to conclude that no one ever will find any. This argument is therefore anti-scientific.
2. Lithological facts. This second argument has no more strength than the first: one can find all the European lithological facies in Indo-China, they are all represented here.
3. Material facts. Many other complete and well-preserved specimens have been found in Tonkin and in Yunnan. Why would the trilobites of Europe have the exclusive privilege of being in a good state of conservation?

At this time the affair remained a private matter between Lantenois and Deprat with Henri Mansuy in the background. In

*The Cambrian trilobites referred to are those from Lang Chiet. This argument also applies to the Ordovician trilobites.

Les Chiens aboient Deprat invents conversations between Lantenois and Mansuy, in which the latter is scathing about Lantenois's reluctance to force the issue. Mansuy was, in this view, pulling all the strings. It is impossible for us to know how closely this reflected reality, rather than Deprat's gut feeling. Mansuy did provide scientific information to Lantenois on a regular basis and could have been the motivating force behind the affair at the beginning – either through his own indignation at being duped by Deprat, or because of personal grievances against him (as Deprat implied). But as the affair progressed Lantenois certainly took complete control of the 'prosecution' himself. However, at this stage Lantenois was really telling Deprat that, if he did certain things, he would satisfy Lantenois's disquiet, and that would be the end of the matter. Deprat, for his part, resented any interference in his scientific work by Lantenois in particular, whom he regarded as an amateur geologist. He continued to treat Lantenois as an official equal and a scientific inferior. He felt instinctively that he could force Lantenois to back down through the weight of his own scientific authority.

Deprat was particularly incensed by the implied accusation of immoral behaviour. He in turn accused Mansuy of a lack of morality. He had letters and notes from Mansuy dated as recently as November 1916, in which the palaeontologist praised Deprat's work and his character. This, Deprat pointed out, was morally questionable behaviour if he believed Deprat to be a fraud. Deprat also implied that Mansuy himself had had the opportunity to commit fraud, since he was the only person who had made a detailed study of these fossils. He quotes part of his response to Lantenois in *Les Chiens aboient*:

> I regret having to give these explanations at the moment when my medical condition prevents me from having full intellectual strength – as you well know. You say that it was five years ago that M. Mihiel [Mansuy] began to have doubts about the first incriminated specimens. Well, I possess a file of letters from M. Mihiel himself written over the course of

several years, from that date [i.e. five years ago] *up to the month before your return*, all overflowing with admiration for my work, and affection for me personally. To take up the expression 'morality' of which you are so fond, here is a bundle of very troubling evidence against M. Mihiel. I am not passing comment. I write this to shed light on, if the case arises, the faith of others. You say also that this accusation causes you great pain? . . . No sir! There was always something between us, from the beginning of my time here.

Deprat saw motives for Lantenois's harrying of him in their past relationship. He referred cryptically in the letter to events soon after he arrived in Indo-China – probably the arguments over Deprat's publication rights, and over Captain Zeil, both of which Deprat won. In the letter he also belittled Lantenois and once again failed to respect his superior rank. He struck back fiercely, accusing Lantenois of being morally responsible for the affair, and for the damage it would cause to the Service Géologique. Battle had been well and truly joined. Deprat also raised the crucial point of whether and when any 'suspect' fossils should be sent to France for examination by experts: 'I naturally demand that I am informed when the suspect specimens that you have impounded are to be sent to France. I will exercise my rights to enclose specimens which I myself designate.'

But the issue which propelled the affair from an argument between three men into a public scandal, was Lantenois's official instruction to Deprat. Deprat refused point-blank to follow the order to accompany Lantenois to the sites where the suspect fossils were first found. He declared that this would be a humiliation for him and that he was, in any case, too ill to travel.

After a three-month stalemate from April to July 1917, the momentum of the affair had picked up dramatically. Lantenois replied to Deprat's letter the next day. Deprat had pointed out that one of the fossils was unarguably local, since a large block containing more samples was in the laboratory of the Service

Géologique. Lantenois had to back down on this one, but only this one: 'we [i.e. he and Mansuy] hasten to agree that the argument is in your favour and that the specimen is undoubtedly of Asiatic origin. All the same, the business of the other specimens must be cleared up.'

Lantenois renewed his proposition that they go to the sites, and that Deprat dig out the fossils in his presence. This time Lantenois wrote, 'If we find a single one of the other incriminated specimens, the affair will have taken a great step forward, and perhaps could even be completely resolved.' He added that, 'I am writing to the senior geologists that you spoke of previously [i.e. Termier, Lacroix and Douvillé]. I am asking them if they are of the opinion that you might be justified in ignoring what you call an insulting injunction.'

According to Deprat, and this is confirmed by the official inquiry, the letter ends with the confirmation of a crucial agreement between the parties: 'It does not seem to me to be appropriate to send the incriminated fossils to Paris. I give you my word of honour that, if we come to that, you will assist in the packing and enclose all that you consider suitable.' Deprat records that Lantenois renewed this guarantee two weeks later, on 6 August.

Several different strands of the affair now began to run in parallel, and in retrospect it seems that Deprat was to be a victim of bad timing, as well as of his own bad judgement. On the surface, and with the agreement of Deprat, Lantenois wrote to the three savants in Paris, asking their opinion about his order to Deprat to accompany him to the suspect fossil sites. Having agreed to do this, it would have seemed sensible for Lantenois to wait for their reply before pressing this point. If this had happened, the affair might never have erupted. But other things forced Lantenois's hand, and in the meantime he himself was secretly pushing matters forward.

Unbeknown to Deprat, Lantenois began to send material to Paris. This questionable behaviour is not in dispute – it forms part of the official Habert report into the affair. The following is a quote from the report: 'At intervals from the month of August 1917, M. Lantenois sent to MM. Lacroix, Douvillé and Termier, of the Académie des Sciences in Paris, photographs of the contested trilobites, M. Mansuy's determinations, some samples for comparison [*quelques pièces de comparaison*], and some specimens of rock taken from 4 of the suspect fossils.'

Mansuy's determinations (i.e. his descriptions of the specimens and the species to which they had been allocated, together with the reasons), were his original ones, but he also included some revisions formed in the light of his suspicions about the provenance of the fossils. The photographs would have been the plates from the published *mémoires* in which the fossils were first described.

According to Michel Durand-Delga's research:

> The first parcel arrived in Paris before 18 September 1917. We know this because of a letter from Henri Douvillé to Alfred Lacroix on that day. 'I am coming [to Paris] to take receipt of all the Lantenois–Deprat material. I am broken-hearted, why is it that the French in the colonies inevitably tear themselves to pieces. It is truly sad for the geology of Indo-China which appeared to be working so well. It was too good to last!' By estimating the time of transit, we can conclude that this package must have left Hanoi no later than 10 August.

Up to this point, it appears that Lantenois was sticking to the letter, though definitely not the spirit, of his agreement with Deprat by not sending the suspect fossils themselves, but this was shortly to alter. On the basis of this first batch the three geologists in Paris suspected that these fossil specimens were from Europe. Lantenois now decided to break his agreement with Deprat, as the Habert report makes clear: 'The case against M. Deprat became clear. The affair had become serious. Before pushing it to the limit, M. Lantenois wanted *to be sure*; he decided to send the fossils themselves for the savants to examine – and sent them with December's courier.'

The second batch was sent in two lots, on 6 and 12 December 1917. According to Michel Durand-Delga, the August package probably contained actual fossil specimens too – the enigmatically worded '*quelques pièces de comparaison*'. The Habert report, which was generally pro-Lantenois, did not duck the matter of his deception:

> The two packages, August's and December's, were sent without M. Deprat's knowledge and without M. Deprat being given the opportunity to dispute the specimens and documents sent to France. This was an error on the part of M. Lantenois, or at least a serious imprudence, since it now allows M. Deprat to suspect the nature of these packages and to accuse M. Lantenois of falsifying their contents.

In hindsight, Habert's criticism of Lantenois is mild. Deprat had come to an agreement that no material would be sent to France without his and Lantenois's assent. Lantenois knew that the identification of the fossils themselves was a crucial point in the case, so that it mattered greatly that both sides agreed on which specimens were placed in evidence. At this point the affair had not become a legal matter, which might excuse Lantenois's rashness (though not the breaking of his word). It is an axiom of jurisprudence, however, that the defence should see all the evidence being used by the prosecution. Lantenois's deliberate flouting of this golden rule put in danger any future legal measures against Deprat, and puts another layer into our historical judgement of the case – whatever Deprat's guilt or innocence, would any properly constituted court have convicted him after such a breach of his legal rights? It is moot to remember that Lantenois had said that the affair was a matter of morality. Deprat was right to point out that this flowed both ways. Dishonesty, it seems, could be acceptable in some situations, but not others.

In his own account in *Les Chiens aboient*, Deprat highlights Lantenois's duplicity. He relates a later conversation between his own solicitor and Lantenois, in which the solicitor asks how Lantenois can explain his actions. Lantenois replies, 'Convinced of M. Deprat's guilt, I believed it necessary to force the judgement.'

As far as Deprat knew, from early August 1917 he and Lantenois were waiting for a reply from Termier, Lacroix and Douvillé to the question of whether it was reasonable for Lantenois to ask him to return to the suspect sites, and to search for more fossils with Lantenois looking over his shoulder. He was not to find out about the secret packages being sent to France until March 1918.

But Deprat did not sit idly by and wait for his fate to unfold. His strategy over the next few months was to make the trilobite affair into a scientific argument. After the 'Walcott incident' he made more successful attempts to denigrate Lantenois's scientific reputation, and to reinforce his own. He wrote letters to influential geologists in France, mentioning his disappointment at Lantenois's return to Indo-China. Then, in the summer of 1917, he sent three short papers to the Académie des Sciences and a substantial review paper to the Société Géologique in Paris. He used these notes variously to deride and criticise Lantenois's earlier work, to signal his intention to return to Yunnan, and to put the scientific case for his innocence. It is fascinating to see these apparently disinterested scientific papers being used as weapons in Deprat's struggle for survival. In the first paper, presented to the Académie des Sciences on 6 August by Pierre Termier, Deprat specifically cited Lantenois's earlier work: 'All of the mylonitic formations of Tonkin have been reported before my own researches as metamorphic (Lantenois, Zeil), despite the absence of contact minerals. This prevents a real understanding of the structure of Tonkin, for which reason I stress this point' (Deprat, 1917c).

A mylonitic rock is one which has been pulverised by outside forces to the point where it has become granulated. The chemical composition of the rock remains the same. Its presence is a sign of intense geological activity, usually faulting and shearing. Metamorphism, on the other hand, is generally taken to mean the chemical alteration of a rock through heat, pressure or the gradual percolation of groundwaters. Metamorphism can be a sign of igneous or volcanic activity in the region. Deprat was presumably saying that the mistaken reporting of the presence of metamorphic rocks by Lantenois and Zeil was an obstruction to understanding the tectonic history of the region. It implied igneous, rather than tectonic activity. Though dressed in the passive language of scientific discourse, this was a calculated dismissal of Lantenois's work. This might not have mattered so much if Lantenois had been a prolific scientist – after all, every scientist's work is subject to re-interpretation and updating – but Lantenois had published very few geological papers and would have been sensitive to their criticism by anyone. The wording of Deprat's comments was also clearly designed to belittle Lantenois's work, where in earlier years he had been generous to all his predecessors.

In a second paper sent to Paris in 1917, on the Cambrian of west Yunnan, Deprat announced that he wished to return to Yunnan that summer. The paper, which was presented to the Académie by Henri Douvillé on 22 October, demonstrates that there is interesting work still to be done, and implies that Deprat is the man to do it (Deprat, 1917d).

By now Lantenois had either read or been told of Deprat's August paper in which his work was criticised, and realised that two could play this game. Lantenois himself put pen to paper and wrote his first scientific report for ten years. Entitled 'Crush zones and nappes in the Chapa region, near Laokay (Tonkin)' (Lantenois, 1917) its purpose was presumably to re-establish his own credentials as a practising geologist. But if this was intended to be at the expense of Jacques Deprat, then it was an embarrassing failure, and had entirely the opposite effect.

The one-page note was presented to a meeting of the Société Géologique de France on 19 November 1917. The presentation was again made by Pierre Termier. The journal *Comptes-Rendus de la Société Géologique de France* carries the text of the paper followed by Termier's comments. Termier begins his response to the paper in a way that is scarcely flattering to Lantenois:

> The phenomena that M. Lantenois has demonstrated to us, confirm in the most pleasing manner the previous observations of M. J. Deprat, and the deductions which followed from them. We already know that the area of nappes called by M. Deprat *nappes preyunnanaises* stretch to the south-west as far as the valley of the Fleuve Rouge, even if it does not go further.

Termier continues to map out the geology of the region as described by Jacques Deprat, including his discovery that the 'preyunnanaise nappes' are aligned from north-west to south-east, and that their fading out or drift towards the south-east uncovers little by little an almost exclusively crystalline region. After this lengthy discussion of Deprat's work, in which his name is mentioned four times, Termier gets round to mentioning the author of the paper on which he is passing comment: 'The mylonite nappe, discovered to the south-west of Laokay by M. Lantenois, forms part of this vast system of preyunnanaise nappes.'

In other words Lantenois's discovery, while a decent piece of work, is merely a footnote to the conceptual work done by Deprat. Indeed Lantenois has merely drawn attention to Deprat's work and given Termier – the kingpin of French geology – another opportunity to express his own keen interest in the younger man's tectonic studies. Reading Termier's comments, there is little question about who is the important geologist in Indo-China.

The flood of papers from Indo-China continued. It is important to take account of the time delay between these papers being written in Hanoi and presented in Paris. Even though this time was remarkably short by today's standards of scientific publication, it was nevertheless significant. The protagonists in Indo-China were deliberately not showing their work to each other, so the first that each knew of the other's remarks was when the papers arrived in Paris, and possibly not until they were formally presented. Deprat wrote his third report for the Académie des Sciences in the first part of September 1917, and this was presented to the academy on 5 November 1917, again by Pierre Termier (Deprat, 1917e). The writing of this paper was to precipitate the beginning of Deprat's defeat.

With most of his other actions designed to help his defence, we can see with hindsight that Deprat would have done better to hesitate, and contemplate their consequences a little more than he did. In this case even he himself admitted that he made a blunder. If the first paper Deprat had sent to the academy had been a mild provocation to Lantenois, this was a red rag to a bull. It is perhaps understandable that Deprat should want to kill off the affair as quickly as possible – he was, after all, in an unenviable position, accused by a colleague and his superior, and unable to continue his work. But in trying to force some kind of resolution, as he had done by revisiting Nui Nga Ma in March, he made another serious misjudgement.

In *Les Chiens* he writes that Lantenois had, some time previously, indicated some fossils in a geological formation where they could never have existed, because the age of the rocks was very different from the known age of the fossils. Knowing, Deprat writes, that Lantenois had lied and kept the evidence himself, Deprat sent him an official request for an explanation. The matter was important, says Deprat, because it concerned a geological formation stretching over 200 kilometres. The error referred to by Deprat occurs in Lantenois's 1907 paper 'Note sur la géologie de l'Indochine'. Deprat makes a reference to this in his paper presented to the Académie des Sciences on 5 November 1917. The paper concerns the Permian and Triassic rocks of the area around Ha Long Bay (known to Deprat as baie d'Along), and on the continental shelf of Tonkin. The bay is famous for its beautiful limestone islands which lend it the name Ha Long, which means dragon's teeth in

Vietnamese. Deprat gives his own view of the way in which the important Rhetian formation (the Rhetian is the uppermost stage of the Triassic period) lies on the older sediments, and contrasts his conclusions with Lantenois's earlier work:

> The Rhetian is in contact, throughout the coastal region, with the Ouralo-Permian limestones of Ha Long Bay and of Fai Tsi Long. It has been accepted [there is reference here to Lantenois's 1907 paper] that the southern margin of the Rhetian coincides with a large fault, the *continental shelf fault*, which would have signified a large-scale tectonic event. My observations oblige me to renounce this view and to consider this margin as other than a fault; in fact everywhere that I have studied the contact between the Rhetian and the Palaeozoic region of the islands, I have seen the Rhetian lying transgressively on the Palaeozoic rocks immediately underneath.

Both Lantenois and Deprat had seen Permian limestones overlain by Rhetian rocks, with nothing in between. Either the deposition of sediment had been interrupted – so that there were no rocks of lower Triassic or middle Triassic age formed in the region – and then resumed again in the Rhetian period; or something had happened to the region's rocks afterwards to give this appearance. Lantenois chose the latter option, Deprat the former. It is generally recognised that the Rhetian saw a worldwide rise in sea levels after the generally dry conditions of much of the Triassic period. Many shelf areas had therefore been above sea level and generally either not accumulating sediment, or even being subjected to erosion, until the great marine flooding or transgression of the Rhetian. This explains the gap in sediment that both Deprat and Lantenois had seen, and Deprat was the one who seems to have been proved right. He goes on:

> The line of contact [between the Rhetian and the Permian] has been, thanks to erosion, regularly exposed, simulating a

great circular arc with a slightly convex curvature, turned towards the south, and passing through Hongay [now Hon Gai], and a great fault line has been placed across this trace of the plan of the transgression [another reference to Lantenois's work here]. I can show a number of sections which do not leave room for such an interpretation and which show the Rhetian sandstones lying on the Ouralian limestones, which dip underneath them.

Although this is an effective critique of Lantenois's work, there is no mention of Lantenois using 'false' fossil evidence to support his theory. Either Lantenois had mentioned privately that he had certain fossils, or this was an extrapolation of Lantenois's error by Deprat. It may have been during the preparation of this paper, in late September 1917, that he came across Lantenois's error. Or it may be that he had known about this error for some time, and now pressed it into use in his fight for scientific advantage over Lantenois. But in his letter to Lantenois, he went too far: 'If these things are made public, the affair would become a little embarrassing.'

We can read this charitably as meaning 'we all make mistakes, and you too could be made to look a fool'. But really the implied threat of exposure was close to blackmail – and Deprat seemed to realise this afterwards, when it was too late. Lantenois's response was immediate and furious. His letter to Deprat dated 1 October is quoted by Deprat in *Les Chiens*: 'I have given you an order to follow me to the field to find the fossils incriminated by M. Mihiel [Mansuy] in front of me. Answer immediately *yes* or *no*. If it is "no", I will ask that you be put in front of a disciplinary hearing, for refusing to obey.'

For Lantenois there was now no question of waiting for the advice of geologists in distant Paris. This had become a matter of his personal authority. In fact Lantenois said he acted on 1 October 1917 because he had visited the site at Nui Nga Ma himself, and did not find the band of quartzite. But Deprat's account of his own folly is a more obvious reason. Deprat sent back his refusal on 2 October. He stated that a visit to Nui Nga Ma would serve no purpose. He reminded Lantenois that he had, in March 1917, discovered a third Ordovician fossil on the site, which confirmed the authenticity of the two others.

The next day Deprat in turn received a reply from Lantenois: 'I am placing before the Governor your refusal to obey, and your letter of common insults, and asking for disciplinary action to be taken.'

Deprat's career was suddenly in danger, not because the fossils had been proved fraudulent, but because of a simple refusal to obey orders. As he himself recounts in *Les Chiens aboient*, 'Five days later [Deprat] received notification of his suspension as Head of the Service Geologique . . .'

The golden edifice of Jacques Deprat's future was beginning to crumble and everything he did to try to shore it up simply made matters worse.

5 *Indo-China, October 1917–February 1919*

There is little doubt that his suspension was a terrible blow to Deprat. It was also a great surprise. Up to this point he had seemed to regard the affair as an internal argument between himself and Lantenois, with Mansuy prompting his opponent from the wings. He had convinced himself that if he could simply defeat Lantenois's arguments on his own terms, then he would be in the clear. He had forgotten about the real world in which people may be called to account for their actions, and the world of the French government machine in which orders were made to be obeyed. His status was not God-given, but conferred by the state. It could be, and now was, taken away as easily as it had been granted.

Deprat was allowed an interview with the Governor-General of the colony, Albert Sarraut, to plead his case. Sarraut had been Governor-General of Indo-China from 1911 to 1914, had served as a Minister in the French government for the first two years of the war, and had returned to Indo-China in January 1917. He was later Premier of France for short periods in 1933 and 1936. Far from being a third-rate official sent off to moulder away in the colonies, Sarraut was a powerful figure in French politics. Indeed the high-flying careers of several Governors-General of Indo-China show how important the colony was to governments in Paris.

Sarraut listened courteously to Deprat's case, but he did not rescind the decision. Deprat remained suspended from his job and Henri Mansuy was made temporary head of the service. Deprat's suspension began on 7 October 1917, but for the time being no further action was taken against him. He was once again in limbo, having no official position but not having been formally disciplined.

In late 1917 events in France also began to go badly for Deprat. Pierre Termier's comments about Lantenois's paper, and his presentation of Deprat's paper on 5 November (pages 107 and 108), are even more striking than they first appear. In fact, on 1 November, just four days before he presented Deprat's paper, Termier had telegraphed Lantenois in Hanoi informing him of the probable fraudulence of Deprat's trilobites. The Habert report summarily describes this turning point: 'On 1 November M. Termier told M. Lantenois by telegram that the matrix of the suspect species was lithologically identical to the matrix of the same species in Europe.' Lantenois kept this information to himself and Mansuy and, as we have seen, secretly sent more samples for confirmation in December.

On the same day, 5 November 1917, as his note on the Triassic rocks of Ha Long Bay had been presented to the Académie des Sciences, Deprat's extensive review paper was read at a meeting of the Société Géologique in Paris. The paper, which was officially published in 1918, aims to reinforce his earlier arguments for a marine connection between Europe and south Asia during the Palaeozoic period, and is therefore an attempt to establish a scientific basis for his own innocence. It remains Deprat's final contribution to the science of geology, and is a measured assessment of the tectonics of the region. The title of the paper is 'The trend lines of south-east Asia, and their relations to ancient elements and geosynclines'. It is worth pausing to see what exactly this title signifies, and how it relates to geological knowledge in the early twentieth century. At that time the powerful tectonic forces in the Earth's crust were seen to operate in certain directions which could be mapped out using '*lignes directrices*' or 'trend lines' – nowadays these would be related to continental movements, but this idea had not yet become widely accepted. Geologists had figured out that in many regions of the Earth there were ancient blocks which were geologically inactive, and which were fringed by more recently active zones. These active zones were characterised by rapid building of mountain chains and parallel trenches and by the almost equally rapid erosion of the mountains into the trenches. These trenches are called geosynclines. This type of process is now happening on the western fringe of South America, where the Andes are still being built up by volcanic activity, but are also being eroded, with most of the debris ending up in the Peru–Chile ocean trench.

Geologists interested in tectonics learn to recognise stable blocks, mountain chains and geosynclines. This would be easy enough if we were only interested in the present phase of the Earth's history. The tricky part lies in recognising preserved forms of these elements from hundreds of millions of years ago and using them to figure out the story of each particular episode in the overall history of a region. In the title of his final paper, Deprat was signalling that this was what he was setting out to do. He was applying the latest ideas in tectonics (itself the most innovative area in geology) to a part of the Earth which he had studied in detail for the previous eight years. This was a serious and considered attempt to shore up his reputation against any attacks that might come from Lantenois and Mansuy – and in the short term it worked. Deprat also used the paper to reinforce a proposition which would remove any suspicion from the 'European' trilobites:

> There is, all in all, very frequently a striking correspondence, over enormous distances, between sediments of the same age containing the same faunas. This phenomenon is well known and the facts which I cite only confirm it. It is probably a biological effect. In any case, these numerous examples of biological correlation between regions as diverse as China and

> northern Indo-China, the Shan states [i.e. Thailand and Burma] and northern Europe clearly show the strong relationships across the vast depression formed by the enlargement of the north Tethys [Sea], between the great barrier of ancient elements in the south and the Mongolian element and the Palaeozoic facies [i.e. rock formations] of northern Europe. This relationship was already established in the mid-Cambrian as shown by the appearance of the genera *Conocephalites*, *Conoryphe*, in the south of China. (Deprat, 1918)

The Tethys, in Deprat's view, had enlarged during the mid-Cambrian period and remained a vast body of water stretching from Europe to southern Asia and as far east as Mongolia. Fossil remains from the mid-Cambrian period had already shown this, so the continuation of this situation into the Ordovician and Silurian periods was certainly possible. If Europe and Asia were linked by one sea – i.e. the Tethys – then finding European trilobites in southern Asia would be a natural consequence. Any attempt to incriminate Deprat for finding just such fossils would be likely to be dismissed as ridiculous. As Michel Durand-Delga writes, 'In a moderate tone, this paper constitutes a preventive defence, aimed at geologists in France, who remained unaware of the existence of the "affair".'

Lantenois, meanwhile, set about persuading the Governor-General that a Commission of Inquiry should be convened to examine the charge against Deprat – disobedience to a superior official – and exonerate or discipline him accordingly. On 1 November, as we have seen, Lantenois received the telegram from Termier confirming the similarity of the fossil matrix to European rock types. In early December he sent more fossils, photographs and notes to the three savants in France.

Events in Paris and Hanoi continued to run in parallel, and messages, which were often contradictory in their import, began to cross in the post – not surprising when a steamer from France to Indo-China would take four to five weeks, even in peacetime. On 10 December 1917, two months after Deprat's suspension, a letter from the three eminent geologists in Paris arrived in Hanoi. This was their response to Lantenois's request for advice on whether Deprat should return to the suspect fossil sites in Lantenois's company. It must have seemed a very long time since this request had been made; both Lantenois's and Deprat's worlds had changed beyond recognition since August. Nevertheless it was an important message, with copies sent to both Deprat and Lantenois. On the point of whether Deprat should have complied with Lantenois's request, and subsequent order, to return to the field, the savants were, perhaps surprisingly, equivocal. We have only Deprat's account of their verdict but this has never been challenged by the other participants. In *Les Chiens aboient* he writes that the three agreed with him that 'such an expedition would be impossible'. We are to take it that this opinion was based on a scientific and personal assessment. They presumably believed that asking a geologist to return to a location and recover an identical fossil species, while under the pressure of being watched, was unreasonable and unlikely to produce any results. Finding another specimen of the same fossil species in the same place would not necessarily be easy and failure to do so would prove little. Instead they naïvely recommended sending Deprat to repeat his explorations. 'It is possible that you will find the disputed fossils,' Deprat quotes them as saying, 'with the advantage of making new discoveries of the same order as those which have placed your name in the first rank of world experts.'

The last sentence might seem to have been over-egged by Deprat, but we must not forget the high esteem in which he was held in France at the time. Deprat was relieved and overjoyed at the message. He quotes himself as saying to his friends '*Tout est sauvé*.' All is saved. His optimism was premature and short-lived.

The affair had now become an official matter because of Deprat's suspension and, more seriously, Lantenois's position

Jacques Deprat as a young man in France.

INDICATIONS OF THE LAVISH COLONIAL LIFE IN INDO-CHINA. The photograph on the left shows Jacques Deprat's wife Marguerite with their two daughters and his parents; below are Jacques Deprat with his two daughters. Both photographs were taken outside the family mansion in Hanoi.

INDO-CHINA AND YUNNAN.
The classical and sterile splendour of the French University of Indo-China in Hanoi (*top*) contrasts with the busy streets of Yunnan-fou (*bottom*).

Henri Mansuy pictured in 1932.

Honoré Lantenois in 1913.

Pierre Termier.

Alfred Lacroix.

Henri Douvillé.

Emmanuel de Margerie.

Herbert Wild in the Pyrenees.
This page: Wild on the northern face of the Pic de Coutchès, photographed by Robert Ollivier (*left*); Herbert Wild and his daughter Alice above Lac d'Arriel in 1930 (*bottom*).
Opposite page: the Club Pyrénéen on a winter outing in 1934 or early 1935, *left to right* Herbert Wild, Albert Tachot, Pierre Verdenal, Bernard Bernis, Gaston Santé (*top*); the high Pyrenees at Vignemale, east of the Ansabère massif (*centre*); Lescun, the last village in France before the Ansabère massif and the Col de Petragème (*bottom*).

Jacques Deprat at fifty, Pau 1930.

had changed noticeably. No longer willing or needing to play the role of neutral arbiter, Lantenois was fully opposed to Deprat, convinced of his guilt and determined to see his career destroyed. The opinion of the three wise men in France, coolly detached from the tensions of Hanoi, and presumably aimed at calming the situation, might have done just that had it arrived in late September. Now, in December, it was too late. By raising the stakes so dramatically in October, Deprat had made the experts' views on his conduct marginal, if not irrelevant. But Deprat was not solely responsible for the downward turn in his fortunes. Lantenois had, after all, been sending material to France in order, as he said, 'to force a judgement'. Indeed the most striking aspect of this period is the mixed messages coming from France. On the one hand, Termier, Lacroix and Douvillé were saying that Deprat should be allowed back to the field, where he might be able to rediscover the suspect fossil species; on the other, they were saying that the specimens that Lantenois had sent were definitely of European provenance. This confusion was to be compounded just one day after Deprat's hopes had been so dramatically raised.

On 11 December 1917 Deprat was summoned to a meeting with Louis Constantin, whose administrative empire included the Service des Mines and therefore the Service Géologique. Deprat had met Constantin as soon as he arrived in Indo-China and describes him in *Les Chiens aboient* as an archetypal bureaucrat. Honoré Lantenois was waiting in Constantin's office when Deprat arrived. On the same boat as the message from Termier, Lacroix and Douvillé, was another letter from Pierre Termier addressed to Lantenois. At the meeting Lantenois proceeded to read from this letter. Once again Deprat's description of the letter's contents is the only one we have: 'He [Termier]wrote at length that for nine years he had been convinced of Deprat's scientific "improbity". He continued on this subject for three pages, with expressions of contempt.'

At this point we might feel reason to question, not Deprat's factual account, but his impression of the letter being read to him. It is noticeable that he did not quote from Termier's letter and it is certainly possible that he was not given a copy. His account therefore probably relies on his immediate impressions of what was being read. It is difficult to understand why Pierre Termier, a man with a reputation for extraordinary politeness and sensitivity and a public admirer of Deprat's work, would go out of his way to pour scorn on Deprat in this way.

The explanation for Deprat's version of Termier's letter may lie in the real reason for the meeting with Constantin. In his letter Pierre Termier made an extraordinary offer. If Deprat signed a confession admitting scientific fraud, Termier would find him a position in France in recognition of his past services. The offer would have had to be agreed by Lantenois and by Constantin before it was relayed to Deprat. Deprat immediately turned it down. We should remember that at this time he was unaware that suspect fossils had been sent to France and unaware in particular of Termier's 1 November telegram to Lantenois in which their European provenance had been confirmed. The offer from Termier is likely therefore to have come as a considerable shock to Deprat – he suddenly discovered that the leader of the French geological world considered him a fraud – and may explain Deprat's later memory of the content of Termier's letter. Deprat was highly sensitive to the slightest hint that anyone did not believe him and so regarded Termier, who may simply have been trying to find a way out of the situation, as a traitor to his cause. Once again through Deprat's eyes we see the world as black and white.

From Deprat's point of view, Termier had praised his work publicly, and now refused to support him in his hour of need. As for Termier, it seems likely that while he retained respect for Deprat and his work, he felt from his discussions with Henri Douvillé and from his own long-term friendship with Lantenois, that Deprat must be guilty of some degree of scientific fraud. It is not clear what the status of the letter from Termier was. It may have been a private message to Lantenois assuring *him* of support, while trying to resolve the situation.

The offer was obviously intended to be put to Deprat, but Termier may have wished the rest of the letter to remain private.

Deprat may have felt justified in turning down Termier's offer, but things could not remain as they were. His suspension from his official job as head of the Service Géologique was an interim measure. Once he had refused the compromise, an official Commission of Inquiry became inevitable. Some time in early December Governor-General Sarraut agreed – the Commission to decide on Deprat's disobedience was to meet in January 1918.

The system of justice which has existed in France since the Napoleonic Empire applies not only to criminal and civil courts, but also to government administrative matters. As in the criminal courts, an investigator or *rapporteur* is appointed to gather evidence, and to present a summary of the case to a committee of 'judges'. This *rapporteur* is free to make limited recommendations, but his role is theoretically neutral – although it is easy to see that his presentation of the case is likely to be influential. The *rapporteur* appointed for the first Commission of Inquiry into the Deprat affair was a legal official called Thermes. He began his work in December 1917, interviewing Deprat, Lantenois and other witnesses. His inquiries were concerned solely with the matter of disobedience and insults to a superior, and not with the question of whether the trilobite fossils were genuine. Thermes's report to the commission is recorded by Deprat in *Les Chiens aboient* as saying, 'the subject's response to his superior was made a little *vivement*, but he [Thermes] let it be understood that the provocation was sufficient to motivate this response, and the conclusions were really a reprimand to the accuser'.

Thermes confided to Deprat before the commission met that he did not think he would be harshly treated and that he was unlikely to be demoted. If we accept the view from Paris that Deprat's return to the sites with Lantenois was not a good idea, then Deprat's case was at least arguable. On the day of the inquiry itself, in late January 1918, Deprat was therefore full of misplaced confidence. The commission was chaired by Louis Constantin himself. In addition there were two other engineers – Albert Normandin, a 33-year-old 'Ingénieur ordinaire', and Bernard Denain, a 45-year-old 'Ingénieur en chef'. The five-man committee was completed by a 'Resident First Class', Pierre Pasquier, and the *rapporteur*, Thermes. Deprat should have known, from the presence of the 'Ingénieurs', that the odds were stacked against him. In addition, Lantenois had already circulated Termier's letter to all the members of the commission: he was leaving nothing to chance.

Despite Thermes's optimism and his generally neutral report, the outcome of the commission was a crushing defeat for Deprat. By three votes to two he was demoted to geologist third class, the lowest grade in the Colonial Service. To add insult to injury, the Service Géologique was placed under the direct command of Honoré Lantenois. A further proposal to sack Deprat from the service altogether was defeated by three votes to two. According to Michel Durand-Delga, Constantin probably drew back from that ultimate sanction. Though there is no official record of the voting, from later indications it is safe to assume that Pasquier and Thermes voted against demotion and sacking, and the three engineers therefore voted in favour. The *esprit de corps* was showing its potency. This guess is supported by Pasquier's later behaviour: he was to become Governor-General of Indo-China in 1929, and made attempts then to get Deprat to return to the colony.

As soon as the verdict was announced Jacques Deprat was forced to sign a piece of paper agreeing to his demotion. It was now brought home to him that he would be under the command of his accuser and tormentor, Henri Mansuy, who was to remain as temporary head of the Service Géologique, though the service was now under Lantenois's direct command. Immediately after the commission's verdict, Deprat had some sort of nervous breakdown and spent the next two weeks in the psychiatric department of Hanoi hospital, in the care of a Dr Ortolan.

The verdict of the disciplinary Commission of Inquiry, while a humiliating defeat for Jacques Deprat, was only a partial victory for Honoré Lantenois. The question of the contested trilobites had not been settled – indeed it had not yet been addressed – and, worse still, Deprat remained in the Service Géologique de l'Indochine. This was, to say the least, an uncomfortable and unsatisfactory situation for both men. It was clear that Deprat was not going to resign his position; in fact he began proceedings immediately for an appeal against his demotion. It was up to Lantenois, therefore, to act.

Lantenois went back to Louis Constantin within days of the commission's verdict, and persuaded him to approach the Governor-General. On 22 February 1918, Governor Sarraut, at Lantenois's and Constantin's prompting, ordered that an investigative visit to the site at Nui Nga Ma be made, as a 'preliminary measure' to a new Commission of Inquiry – this one to investigate the question of Deprat's alleged fraud rather than his disobedience. The visit was to take place whenever Lantenois ordered. This time Deprat, on advice from his friends, decided to accept the order – to have refused would have almost certainly have seen his dismissal from government service. Nevertheless, Deprat felt impelled to write to the Governor-General, arguing that any results of such a visit would have very little significance.

The official visit to Nui Nga Ma, in late February 1918, was a touch farcical. This site, easily reachable from Hanoi, had now become the focus of the questions about Deprat's scientific and personal integrity. To date, Deprat had claimed to have found three Ordovician trilobite fossils at this site – all belonging to species known from Ordovician strata in Europe. The first two had been found in 1912 in a bed of quartzite, and the third in March 1917 in a pebble from a bed of conglomerate. The group which made the 1918 visit was led by Louis Conrandy, Inspector of the Civil Service. Though there were no other geologists present, Deprat himself was able to nominate Léon Autigeon, Professor of Natural Sciences at Hanoi Lycée, and an archaeologist, Chassigneux. There was also one engineer, Charles Hoppe, director of public works in the city of Vinh, and a man called Gollion, a director of the coal-mining industry in the colony. Deprat and Lantenois were also in the party.

In Deprat's account of the visit in *Les Chiens aboient*, he describes the whole affair as ridiculous. He writes that his doctor had advised him not to go on the trip, but that he thought he should. His wife accompanied him to the only hotel in Ha Tinh, the nearest town to Nui Nga Ma. Lantenois was already there, bustling about and looking pleased with himself. Lantenois gave the other members of the party a short course in the rudiments of geology. Deprat says that only Autigeon and Gollion had any knowledge of the subject at all. Lantenois led the group up to the area of Ben Thuy. 'They wandered over the pebble [conglomerate] formations. Naturally they found nothing. Dorpat [Deprat] then directed them to the place where he had previously found the fossil specimen.'

Deprat, by his own account, displayed his lack of interest in the visit to the others and explained the futility of trying to find another of the incriminated species. He says that Autigeon replied that they should look anyway, although he had obviously begun to grasp the absurdity of the situation himself. A bizarre exchange between Deprat and Lantenois is then related in *Les Chiens*. Deprat makes a short speech to the group saying that it is over five years since he came to this place and it is impossible for him to know exactly where the fossil came from, so the whole exercise is therefore nonsensical. Lantenois then intervenes and reminds Deprat and the others that he recovered another fossil from this site the previous year (March 1917). Deprat confirms this, and shows the fossil, at which Lantenois gives only the briefest glance. Deprat also says that he has asked Lantenois if he might see the original fossils, found in 1912, so that he might compare the two, but that Lantenois has refused this request. This 1917 fossil had also, Lantenois tells the group, been found to be 'suspect'.

There is a little confusion over why Deprat still had the fossil that he collected in 1917. We might assume that Deprat handed it over to Lantenois for inspection by Mansuy and others once Deprat brought it back from Nui Nga Ma – otherwise how would Lantenois have known it to be 'suspect'? But Deprat's account seems to suggest that he only handed it over to Louis Conrandy, the leader of the 1918 trip to Nui Nga Ma, when they were actually standing on the site. So either Lantenois had given the fossil back to Deprat after it had been 'determined', or, more likely, Deprat, being suspicious of the possibility of substitutions, had kept back this specimen. Lantenois's declaration of this as 'suspect' would then be on the basis that it was another European trilobite species that had been found by Deprat alone.

The visit could not, of course, prove Deprat wrong. The fact that it would be impossible to prove a negative was part of Deprat's argument – but it did not prove him right either. The question of the absence of quartzite beds (page 93) is not mentioned in Deprat's account of the visit, but it is likely that Lantenois went back to Deprat's original 1912 paper, and raised the matter during the trip. The party returned to Hanoi and presented a report to Louis Constantin, who presumably passed it on to the Governor-General. Deprat writes that apart from Autigeon, who realised the absurdity of the visit, the others simply went along with whatever Lantenois told them. Though he describes their motive as fear of Lantenois, no doubt they had in mind Deprat's recent demotion, and Lantenois's seniority, as well as his influence in the colony. The report of this group has never been found, but seems not to have been decisive or condemnatory enough to goad the higher authorities into action. Honoré Lantenois was now keen for things to proceed quickly, but Constantin was, it seems, increasingly bored by the affair, and increasingly reluctant to raise it with the Governor-General. The site visit had really been a way of keeping Lantenois happy, and appearing to do something. Deprat had, after all, already been severely disciplined. For the colony's administrators there would have been little point in exposing the fraud to the world, simply in order to dismiss him from the service – something which Constantin had had the opportunity to do already, and declined. For them the affair had been 'solved', whereas for Lantenois and Deprat it had simply put them into an impossible situation.

News of Deprat's demotion and of the 'trilobite affair' had of course spread through Hanoi, but only at the level of gossip. Deprat writes in *Les Chiens aboient* that in early 1918 the word 'fraud' was heard for the first time in the salons of Hanoi – and once whispered it could neither be traced nor erased. The affair, though, remained a local matter. In February and early March 1918, with Constantin in no hurry to set up another commission, the affair might have ground to a halt, but then, as so often before, another event revived the momentum.

On 4 March 1918, five days after the visit to Nui Nga Ma, a letter from Alfred Lacroix, Henri Douvillé and Pierre Termier arrived in Hanoi, having been sent from Paris on 3 December 1917. The inordinate delay in the letter's arrival was due to hostilities in the Mediterranean, which were either holding up shipping bound for southern Asia via the Suez Canal or forcing it to go around Africa. The letter was addressed to Honoré Lantenois with a copy to Jacques Deprat. Its content is described and partially quoted in the Habert report.

First, the letter confirms that the twelve contested trilobites* that Deprat claimed to have found in the field and which were figured (i.e. drawn or photographed) by Mansuy are those which Lantenois has sent for them to judge. Second, to quote from the report, in the letter 'the three experts . . . affirm their absolute certainty of the European provenance of the incriminated fossils' after comparison of the matrix of the fossils with the matrix of European trilobites of the same age. Third, according to Jacques Deprat, they also said, 'It is obvious that we cannot say whether this is an accidental occurrence or an imposture.'

★

*The number of suspect specimens varied over time. Deprat writes in *Les Chiens aboient* that the original list contained six, the Habert report does not mention an exact figure, and the total is now taken to be ten.

This was another severe shock for Deprat. It was only when this letter arrived in Hanoi that Deprat knew that any of the fossils had been sent to Paris – in contravention of a specific commitment from Lantenois that they would not be. Even worse, the three experts did not, as Deprat might have expected, allow for the possibility that even if the fossils were of European species, they might have legitimately occurred in beds in Indo-China.

It is here, in the story of an apparent fraud, that we can come to understand a little more of the negotiation involved in the growth of scientific knowledge. The fact that the trilobites which subsequently came under suspicion were of European species had not been concealed at the time of their discovery – in fact it was highlighted in the original papers. The acceptance of these original papers by the French geological world meant that the possibility of finding European trilobite species from the lower Palaeozoic era in southern Asia, however apparently unlikely, had already been faced. It is important to bear in mind that science carries within it a discernible tension. The likelihood of certain facts being true is used in what we might call scientific argument (which would include deduction, induction, hypothesising) or theorising. In other words a scientist will persuade him or herself first, and others second, of the validity of an idea on the basis of the likelihood of its being true. This principle is a slight corruption of Occam's Razor, where the best theory makes the fewest assumptions. But the facts which any theory is intended to explain cannot be judged on their likelihood, only on the validity of their discovery or expression. So the 'idea' of finding European fossil species in Indo-China was far-fetched until one was found, but once one was found, the 'fact' – and therefore the idea – was entirely accepted. Once this 'fact' became suspect, the unlikelihood of the idea once again took hold. In one sense Deprat had been quite right to say (page 99) that the argument, 'because no European fossil species have ever been found in Indo-China, none ever will be found' was 'anti-scientific'. But it was the suspicion of fraud that tilted the balance back towards this conservative and more plausible position. In science radical theories must be based on extremely solid facts.

So now the match between the matrixes of the suspect fossils and of fossils of the same species from European sites was close enough for the experts to state categorically that they could not have occurred 'naturally' in Indo-China, as Deprat had argued. The specimens must have come from Europe. This was a double blow for Deprat, since these were the experts whom he had himself chosen as arbitrators in the affair. Honoré Lantenois immediately took the letter from the three experts to Louis Constantin, to make him move on a new Commission of Inquiry into the suspected scientific fraud. The name of Pierre Termier, in particular, should have had an effect on the administration (though we should allow that important men in one field will often count for nothing in another). Lantenois, in any case, began to bombard the administration with memos and messages calling for a resolution to the affair.

In *Les Chiens aboient* Deprat mentions that his wife Marguerite also went to see Louis Constantin at this time. According to this account, she told the Engineer-in-Chief that there had been a substitution of the suspect fossils, that Mansuy and Lantenois had together plotted against her husband, and that action should be taken against them. This is the first indication of a radical change in Deprat's defence, who up to now had argued that the fossils were genuine. Once the experts in Paris had ruled that they were fakes, the onus was on Deprat to come up with an explanation as to how that might have happened. The most obvious one was that fake fossils had been substituted sometime between Deprat's sending them back to Hanoi after his first discovery of them, and their arrival in Paris. The prime suspect in Deprat's eyes was Henri Mansuy, aided and abetted by Honoré Lantenois. The affair suddenly changed from being an examination of Jacques Deprat's guilt or innocence, into an argument between two competing accusations – either Deprat carried out the fraud or Mansuy and Lantenois did. Constantin was now under pressure from both sides to do *something*, even though it seems he would have preferred to do nothing. He decided that he must raise the matter again with the Governor-General.

In April 1918, therefore, Governor-General Sarraut ordered a second Commission of Inquiry, this time to look specifically into the question of the trilobites. Up to this point Deprat had been disciplined only for his disobedience to Lantenois. His suspension in October 1917 and subsequent demotion in January 1918 had both been for disobedience. Now, for the first time, science itself became the centrepiece of the affair. It is extremely rare for disputed cases of scientific fraud to be tested in a legal, or even quasi-legal setting. The Deprat affair was setting out on an unusual and difficult path, where two forms of truth – scientific and legal – must be tested against each other. Once again a *rapporteur* was appointed to gather evidence about the affair and to compile a report which would then be presented to a Commission of Inquiry. The growing importance of the affair was reflected in the seniority of the *rapporteur*. His name was Habert and, as well as being Counsel to the Court of Appeal in Hanoi (as Thermes had been), he was Director of Judicial Affairs in the government of the colony. This stage of the inquiry was, as Habert was soon to learn, far more complicated than the earlier inquiry into Deprat's disobedience. Habert began his investigations in April, and did not submit his report until September 1918. Fortunately, Habert felt it necessary to summarise the history of the affair, before giving his own views and conclusions. His report is an important guide to the events in Indo-China.

Deprat now knew that he was fighting for his reputation and his life as a geologist. Habert's investigation and the subsequent Commission of Inquiry were to be an important part of this, but it was now clear that in matters scientific, the administrators in Indo-China were taking their cue from the eminent geologists in Paris. So Deprat worked on two fronts, attempting to persuade Habert of his innocence while simultaneously sending letters and yet more scientific papers to France. Deprat believed that Habert was against him from the start. This may have been true, but the ineptitude and implausibility of Deprat's defence seems to have made Habert genuinely believe that he was guilty. Indeed Deprat's defence was to become the focus of the affair. From our standpoint its incoherence gives, at first sight, the appearance of guilt, but on closer examination it appears simply desperate. Whether this was the desperation of a guilty man looking for a way out, or an innocent man caught in a nightmarish situation which he simply could not explain, is not necessarily so simple to decide. On reflection we begin to understand that desperation and incoherence are not products of guilt or innocence, but of the denial of meaning. The fact that people sometimes act against their own best interests tells us that actions and motives are not to be explained by each other like a clockwork mechanism, or like a scientific theory. The Deprat affair happened just as European culture was rebelling against received notions of coherence of character, and beginning to explore the idea that irrationality had meaning. The affair and Jacques Deprat himself at least deserve an understanding which shares in this embrace of complexity and uncertainty.

Once he had time to study the letter from Lacroix, Douvillé and Termier, Deprat became absolutely convinced that they must be right, and that the fossils that the trio had examined and reported on were indeed of European origin. His task now was to convince those who were to judge him that the fossils which had been sent to Paris were not, could not be, the ones he had found in the field. He first had to explain to Habert how this might have come about. Habert's report contains a summary of Deprat's argument:

> M. Mansuy, who wished to incriminate him in order to take his place as head of the service, fraudulently slipped into his collections, without him knowing, fossils of European provenance. 'This was' he [Deprat] says, 'easy for him to do.

> He alone worked on the fossils. In the field, when I found them, I scarcely looked at them, they were immediately packed up and sent to M. Mansuy, who alone unpacked and identified them. They did not concern me any more, I did not look at them again. Later M. Mansuy sent me his determinations, I accepted them with closed eyes since I had absolute confidence in him, and it is on these determinations that I based my work. In these conditions, it was easy for M. Mansuy to make all the substitutions that he wanted, and one can see that he could have imputed the apocryphal fossils to me, and I would not have known about it. That explains why, to this day, I have asserted the authenticity of the incriminated specimens, believing in good faith, that these were the fossils found by me.'

As well as making his case to Habert, Deprat wrote to Lacroix later that year (15 November 1918), 'I have become confident that the fossils are not mine.'

Deprat also set out his case in a letter to the Governor-General on 4 April 1918. The reason for writing was, once again, to shift the emphasis of the inquiry from focusing on his own guilt or innocence to an investigation of competing claims. Deprat's letter to Sarraut prompted the Governor-General to send a telegram to Alfred Lacroix, via the Ministry for the Colonies in Paris, on 29 April. The content shows that the progress of the Deprat affair had now become a common talking point in Hanoi:

> Geologist Deprat accused of scientific fraud challenges all suspect trilobites. Suggests Geologist Mansuy has, for reasons of self-interest, substituted each time trilobites of European provenance for trilobites of local provenance sent to him by Deprat, who, too trusting, was unaware of the substitution. A moral debate is going on throughout the Colony. You offered to continue to lend me your assistance. Send an official cable via the Minister for Colonies. Give your

> assessment. Confirm the European provenance of the eight suspect trilobites sent to Douvillé by Lantenois August–December 1917 and the identification of the trilobites with plates in the Memoirs of the Service published or in preparation.

Sarraut was concerned that the disciplining of Deprat might not be such a simple matter, and might turn into an irresolvable scientific argument, with Deprat's word against Mansuy's. He wanted Lacroix to confirm that the fossils were from Europe, but he also wanted to know that the fossils they were inspecting were the same fossils which were described in the original papers. This could be checked by comparing the specimens with the photographs. Lacroix consulted Henri Douvillé, who found the suggestion of a conspiracy by Mansuy against Deprat incredible. Pierre Termier was away from Paris when the telegram arrived, but Douvillé suggested to Lacroix that they reply to the Governor-General immediately:

> The eight trilobites sent in August–December to Douvillé are incontestably those which are figured in the publications of the Service. We are persuaded of the perfect honesty of M. Mansuy and believe him incapable of having committed the fraud of which he is accused. Moreover we consider it impossible that Mansuy had to hand precisely those European species cited by Deprat as being discovered in Indo-China.

The letter was sent from the geologists to the Minister on 23 May, and on to Governor-General Sarraut, by telegram on 31 May 1918.

The response by Lacroix and Douvillé is curious in two ways. First, if it was Mansuy who identified the specimens that were sent back from the field by Deprat, it would not have been necessary for him to 'have to hand precisely those species cited by M. Deprat'. Deprat's argument, though they may not have realised this, was that this was precisely what happened. Indeed the theoretical method of substitution which they propose, only to knock down, is clearly preposterous. It would involve Deprat finding and naming European species, and Mansuy then substituting actual European specimens for Deprat's Indo-Chinese ones. Deprat never suggested such a thing, and if this is what Douvillé and Lacroix thought he had suggested, then it is no wonder they dismissed it. But more likely, they either deliberately misinterpreted his argument to make it appear ridiculous, or they believed that Deprat must have identified the species himself while in the field. Deprat argued that he did not, and that therefore all Mansuy needed were some European specimens to put in with his field samples when they were sent back to the laboratory.

The second curiosity in the telegram is Lacroix and Douvillé's assertion that they 'are persuaded of the perfect honesty of M. Mansuy and believe him incapable of having committed the fraud of which he is accused'. What happens if we substitute 'Deprat' for 'Mansuy' in this sentence? Why was Deprat thought capable of fraud but Mansuy not? This is not an attempt to pick holes in a throwaway remark. On the contrary, here we are approaching one of the dark undercurrents of the affair. Just as the European species, once suspect, became unlikely to be genuine; so Deprat, once accused, became 'capable' of being guilty.

Deprat put his arguments for substitution by Mansuy into a 'Note concernant les Trilobites' which he prepared for Habert. As well as the opportunities available to Mansuy, there was, according to Deprat, other evidence of substitution. The matrix of the fossils as described by Henri Mansuy in his memorandum, which was sent with the samples to France, did not match the original descriptions in scientific papers by Deprat. Deprat also cited Mansuy's change of mind about the identification of some specimens as evidence of substitution. Unfortunately for his own defence (although it is not certain that this had any bearing at the time) these accusations were accompanied by inaccuracies about the fossils themselves. For example, in his note to Habert he wrote that the trinucleus found at Nui Nga Ma in 1912 was found in 'bright white quartzite, rich in shiny fragments of white mica'. But in his 1913 paper he had described the rock as a quartzite sandstone 'yellow, very distinct and entirely lacking in mica' (Deprat, 1913b). The specimen is in fact in a grey (or dull) micaceous sandstone.

Deprat writes in *Les Chiens aboient* that, during the long-drawn-out compilation of Habert's report, he received a totally unexpected visit from Jean-Baptiste Counillon, his predecessor, who had also been chased from office by Honoré Lantenois. According to Deprat, Counillon told him that his collection of European fossils had gone missing from the laboratories of the Service Géologique when he worked there. This is a rather obvious attempt by Deprat to implicate Mansuy, who was the palaeontologist in charge of the service's collection – it would have given Mansuy a cache of European specimens to place among Deprat's finds – and perhaps should not be taken too seriously. Deprat told Counillon that, when the commission sat, he would call him as a witness on his behalf.

Despite Deprat's vigorous defence of his own position, there is no doubt that he felt trapped and became extremely depressed by the affair. His own account refers to the impossibility of overcoming the '*Corps sacré*' when one of their own is under threat. Lantenois, being an Ingénieur au Corps, was using all his contacts to denigrate Deprat, often defaming him in official correspondence. It was this more than anything which seemed to enrage and depress Deprat. He thought Lantenois's behaviour beyond the pale: 'In France a single one of these messages would be enough to break the career of an official.'

Deprat had accused Mansuy and Lantenois of conspiring against him, and even though this was said in response to the accusation against him, he could hardly have expected Lantenois to do anything other than fight his corner. It so happened that Lantenois was extremely well connected – through his attendance at an élite college – at a time when to be well connected meant everything. Deprat had staked all on his ability as a superior and highly renowned scientist to face down Lantenois, but now he was learning that a brilliant mind is of little consequence against an entire social order. The history of human moral authority has shown that it is not the principle that has mattered but to whom we decide it applies. Being outside the fold, as Deprat in some ways liked to be, gives certain advantages and disadvantages, but when it comes to the dispensation of justice it is a dangerous place to be.

Deprat writes in *Les Chiens aboient* that he went on a fishing trip at this time to one of Hanoi's lakes. While out on the water in a small boat, totally alone, he contemplated taking his own life. He had seen his noble stance against the world's insults gradually corrode, first into a messy dogfight with a man who would not let go, and now into a nightmarish unrelenting process which he barely understood, and over which he had no control. He and Lantenois may have begun as Titans battling like gods, but they had rapidly become no better than those bristling, snarling mastiffs. By now there was little nobility left in the business – he was the outsider and as such he was destined to lose. The main thing that persuaded him from suicide, he writes, was the thought that he would be deserting his wife and children. He thought in particular of how courageous and supportive his wife Marguerite had been throughout his troubles. He decided then that whatever happened, he could accept his fate. He had begun to see that there would be a life beyond the end of this affair, whatever that end might be.

In the next passage in *Les Chiens* Deprat mentions that he was increasingly taking solace in writing music. This, as with the names of the characters in the book, is a code. In fact Deprat was practising his literary skills, as if in preparation for the time when they would become vital to him. The two themes of being an outsider in a world controlled by others, and of being an artist in a world which does not recognise such a thing, begin to dominate the telling of his own story.

★

During the summer of 1918, while Habert did his work, Deprat decided to continue using scientific journals as a way of putting his case. On 24 August 1918 he formally submitted a dossier (presumably the 'Note concernant les Trilobites') to Habert. On the same date he sent two notes for publication to the Bulletin of the Société Géologique in Paris. He enclosed copies of the notes with his submission to Habert. These notes had the dramatic effect of making the affair public in France for the first time. Up until now only the Minister for the Colonies, together with Lacroix, Douvillé and Termier, officially knew anything about what was going on. Now Deprat, perhaps unwittingly, drew the Société Géologique, and thereby the scientific community in France, into the affair. In the two notes Deprat called into question the origin of certain fossils determined by Mansuy and supposedly collected by himself. The titles of these notes were 'On the subject of the mid-Cambrian of southern Yunnan' and 'Erratum in post-Cambrian Palaeozoic rocks in Indo-China and southern China'.

Deprat had either consciously devised a strategy which would shift the focus of the inquiry, or was acting instinctively in the face of changing facts. Now that he believed the fossils were fakes, he continued to argue that they must have been substituted. These papers were either an honest attempt to alert the geological world to the 'errors' in his past papers, or a clever ploy in which he would appear to the outside world to be uncovering a fraud. He could then hardly be held to be the perpetrator.

The notes were offered for publication in the society's regular journal, *Bulletins de la Société Géologique de France*, the outlet for several of Deprat's previous papers. The Bulletin Committee of the society met on 4 November 1918 and, no doubt warned by one of the three savants, Lacroix, Douvillé or Termier, decided to turn Deprat's papers over to Pierre Termier. He advised the committee not to publish. This advice was formally adopted at their next meeting on 18 November, after the society had received a letter from Lantenois and further advice from Lacroix, Douvillé and Termier. On 9 December 1918 the full Council of the Société Géologique de France met. The minutes record: 'The President [Léon Bertrand] opened a discussion on the documents relating to the Deprat affair, transmitted to the Council by the Bulletin Committee. After discussion it was decided by 8 votes to 3 abstentions not to include in any of our publications the three notes sent by M. Deprat.'

Deprat sent another note before he knew of this decision. The council of 13 January 1919 again decided not to print this last note, but to wait for the affair to run its course. The content of the first two notes has been preserved in the archives of the Académie des Sciences and remains unpublished. In addition on 24 February 1919, the President revealed to the Council that 'MM. Lantenois and Mansuy have undertaken not to present anything to the Société Géologique, as long as the affair is under way.'

This refusal of Deprat's 1918 papers was in contrast to the reception given to his work twelve months earlier. Then, even though the trio of experts had begun to develop strong suspicions about the trilobites, Deprat's work had still been considered legitimate. Now the geologists in France had become more strongly convinced of his guilt, and it seems that the society did not wish to let itself be used by either side in what was becoming an increasingly public and bitter affair.

Habert's report was compiled and eventually presented to Governor-General Sarraut on 8 September 1918. The *rapporteur* carefully laid out the history of the affair and the arguments on each side. He gave full space to Lantenois's three main points against Deprat and to Deprat's responses (pages 98–9). He also detailed the views of the three savants, and Deprat's 'radical change of argument', in which he denied that the fossils were his. As we have seen, he gave Deprat's view of how and why Mansuy could have made the necessary substitutions.

Habert then gave his own view of the affair. His main

conclusion was that Deprat's version of events did not bear close examination. Indeed, the second half of the thirteen-page report is given over to evidence and opinion as to why substitutions by Mansuy were not possible. The principal reasons were as follows.

Contrary to his statements, Deprat did study in great detail, and in the field, the fossils he recovered. He continued to show a great interest in them – it was not true that he sent them in bulk and then never looked at them again. Once or twice fossils were sent to Mansuy, who unpacked them in the absence of Deprat, but this did not happen in the case of the suspect fossils. Deprat examined the fossils with Mansuy and the two men engaged in long discussions about them. Perhaps sensitive to the charge that this would have been Mansuy's word against Deprat's, Habert said that there were witnesses to this.

He also pointed out that each of the suspect fossils was the subject of a note to the Académie des Sciences, in which Deprat signalled their importance. They were also described in the *mémoires* of the Service Géologique de l'Indochine.

> Is it possible [asked Habert] that he would have written these papers for the Académie des Sciences, that he would have based these works on the simple lists which M. Mansuy had given him, without ever having had the curiosity to look at these fossils which he spoke of, and to which he gave such importance?
>
> Moreover M. Deprat himself photographed some of the trilobites. The others were photographed by the photographer attached to the service, but M. Deprat saw the prints. He saw the proofs imposed on the paste-ups sent to the printer in France, he saw these photos in the plates of the *mémoires*. Finally, he inevitably saw the fossils themselves which remained in the glass cabinets of the collections of the service, with labels indicating their provenance, until December 1917.
>
> It is very difficult in these circumstances, to believe that M. Deprat's attention was never drawn to these specimens: and if

he really did not bring them to the service himself, it is reasonable to say that he could not have avoided seeing, at first glance, that there had been a substitution.

Deprat's claim was that, having recovered thousands of fossils while in the field in Indo-China, he would not remember them all, and therefore any substitution by Mansuy would go unnoticed by him. Habert disputed this point. He said that trilobite specimens were scarce, and that the European species had such a different appearance that Mansuy had described them as 'like a new penny in a handful of old medals'.

Habert recorded three points made by Deprat as evidence of a conspiracy against him. First, the secret sending of material from Hanoi to Paris by Lantenois in 1917. Having already said that this was an error of judgement by Lantenois, Habert turned this episode against Deprat. He wrote that Deprat initially said that the substitutions were made at that stage – i.e. fake specimens were packed and sent to France. But when it became clear that the specimens received in France matched the photographs in the original papers describing the fossils, Deprat changed his tune and said that the substitutions must have been carried out when he first handed the specimens over to Mansuy. Habert was clearly unimpressed by Deprat's shifting defence.

The second point made by Deprat was that the identifications of some of the fossils sent to France did not match the original attributions. The *Trinucleus ornatus* recovered from Nui Nga Ma in 1912, had been renamed *Trinucleus goldfussi.* Similarly a *Dalmanites longicaudatus var. orientalis* found at Lang-Chiet was now classified as a 'European species' of *Dalmanites longicaudatus*. Habert said that such changes in determinations were common and dismissed this as being wholly beside the point.

Deprat's third point was that at least one of the fossils was described in Mansuy's notes accompanying the package to France as composed of a different matrix to his own original description. The fossils from Lang-Chiet were described in 1913 as being in a fine greenish sandstone, though now they were described as being in a blue calcareous schist. Deprat said that they must therefore be different fossils. Habert had consulted Mansuy about this and discovered that Mansuy's original description was based on Deprat's notes. The description seemed right so he had not investigated further, but before sending the packages to France he had tested the matrix with acid, and found it to be definitely calcareous. Furthermore, Lantenois had told Deprat about this in his letter of 18 July 1917 and Deprat had not protested. Habert concluded that this argument was also weak and beside the point.

Habert also commented on Mansuy's supposed motive for conspiring against Deprat. He found that there was no reason to believe that Mansuy had ever had the ambition to be Chef de la Service Géologique. Mansuy was sixty-two years old in 1918. If Deprat was to be believed, then he had been making substitutions of fossils since 1910. Habert found it unbelievable that Mansuy would have waited so long before bringing about the scandal that he had plotted, when he had enough ammunition to do it earlier.

On the question of Deprat's possible motive, Habert was more convinced.

> The savants have mentioned the scientific importance of the suspect fossils. For my part I cannot help remarking that M. Deprat reported these fossils to the Académie des Sciences, thereby bringing out their importance, and that he emphasised this in his work where he gave them a predominant role. I conclude from this that their discovery served a certain self-interest, which drew the attention of the scientific world to the author.

Overall, the Habert report made a powerful case against Deprat. It is worth noting, however, that the whole of Habert's case rested on the assumption, then accepted by everyone including Deprat, that the fossils were fakes. All in all Habert concluded that there was enough evidence for Jacques Deprat to appear before a disciplinary Commission of Inquiry under the accusation of 'scientific fraud constituting grave professional misconduct', but this recommendation introduced a problem which Habert himself identified. The composition of such a commission was strictly laid down in the regulations governing the Public Service and could not be varied. Effectively Deprat would be judged by a panel selected from the senior grades of the Colonial Service. Habert was aware, however, that some direct involvement by expert geologists was necessary in this case. Arguments and counter-arguments over scientific points in front of a panel of *fonctionnaires* would not be satisfactory. As well as that, if this process was carried out in Indo-China the composition of such a commission would itself present difficulties. As Habert pointed out, a committee 'composed of officials not having any competence in geology, or of Engineers having more or less a connection to the Engineer-in-Chief M. Lantenois, would not offer him [Deprat] all the necessary guarantees [of impartiality]'.

Here we see an open acknowledgement of the pervasiveness and influence of the 'Engineers' in the government of the colony. To get round these two problems, Habert suggested that the scientific aspects of the affair should be placed before a committee of geologists in France, who could advise the authorities as to whether his conclusions on the scientific points were sound and give their thoughts on any other scientific matters which might arise. If they supported Habert's interpretation of the science then Deprat could be sent to face a formal Commission of Inquiry: 'I suggest that, in order to obtain this result it would not be sufficient to send the documents to the experts in Paris, and get them to give their advice on the affair. It is absolutely necessary, in my view, that the experts hear the contradictory explanations of MM. Deprat, Lantenois and Mansuy for themselves.'

This was a neat way of solving both difficulties. Jacques Deprat, Honoré Lantenois and Henri Mansuy would be sent to France to argue their case in front of their fellow geologists. If the committee of geologists concurred with Habert, Jacques Deprat could then face a Commission of Inquiry in France, rather than on Lantenois's home turf of Indo-China. In his paper on the Deprat affair, Michel Durand-Delga suggests that this proposal was not simply thought up by Habert, but that the Governor-General or his advisers had decided that this was an opportunity to pass a very delicate matter out of their hands. The implication is that the Governor-General told Habert to advise him to send the problem back home to Paris.

Between the delivery of the report on 8 September 1918 and the final decision to send the protagonists to France, there were three months of comings and goings in Hanoi. On 7 October Governor-General Sarraut met Deprat and put to him the proposal for arbitration in France, where he would be paid a salary equivalent to his colonial pay. It seems that Deprat was initially reluctant to accept, believing that his lawyer in Hanoi had very good grounds for an appeal against his original demotion. He was still fighting this cause, although the tide of events was threatening to engulf him. He probably realised that once he was sent to France he would never be allowed to return to Indo-China. It is not clear, though, that he had any real choice in the matter, and it could be that Sarraut was simply being polite, or legalistically watertight, by consulting him. Deprat accepted the proposal in a letter on 20 October 1918, but with the condition that he could nominate half the members of the Commission of Inquiry. Ten days later Sarraut replied that the Minister for the Colonies alone had the authority to set the commission's membership. On 2 November Sarraut wrote again, insisting on an unconditional reply, which Deprat duly gave on 14 November.

So, in November 1918, Jacques Deprat was a geologist third class in the French government service. He had been demoted twenty months previously by a Commission of Inquiry into his disobedience of a superior. He was still processing an appeal against that decision through a lawyer based in Hanoi. Now under investigation for scientific fraud, he was the subject of an unfavourable report by the *rapporteur*, Habert. He was to appear before an 'Expert Committee' of geologists who were to be asked to advise on the scientific aspects of the case. The matter would then go forward to a second Commission of Inquiry which would rule on the question of 'scientific fraud amounting to professional misconduct', and either acquit Deprat or hand down some form of discipline. It is worth remembering that, although both the Governor-General of Indo-China and the Minister for the Colonies had become involved in the affair, Deprat was not up for trial on a criminal charge. Indeed we might ask, as Louis Constantin probably had, whether the alleged scientific fraud amounted to a more serious offence in the eyes of the government service than Deprat's disobedience of, and insulting behaviour towards, his superior, Lantenois. In that case, as we have seen, Deprat could have been sacked from the service, but Constantin had declined that course of action. How had a matter of professional misconduct become, since then, such a *cause célèbre*? The answer must lie with Deprat and Lantenois. Each of them was determined, once the affair began, to see it through to a proper conclusion. Neither of them was satisfied with the unstable situation that the first commission had produced, and each saw the destruction of the other's career and reputation as the only solution. With neither of them willing to turn away, the seriousness of the affair inevitably snowballed, until the country's most prestigious scientific institutions and highest government officials became entangled.

On 19 October Deprat introduced another element into the already convoluted affair. He wrote to Alfred Lacroix in Paris, expressing his contempt for Lantenois in very strong terms and mentioning a potential scandal that had threatened Lantenois's position. Deprat was threatening to write to a Member of Parliament in order to get him to ask the Minister:

> why a man involved in a disgraceful personal affair, as

> repugnant as one could imagine, indeed a perversion, found committing a flagrant offence in a 'Eulembourg' affair with a coolie of the lowest type, has not been pursued to the end, and why despite the flagrant offence and the verbal warning given by a gendarme, a warning which is recorded in Hanoi, the affair has been hushed up.

Eulembourg (or Eulenburg) had been German Ambassador to Vienna. During his trial in 1907 he had revealed the homosexual activities of certain German officials and a senior French diplomat. The case was scandalous enough at the time for Eulenburg's name to be common currency for some years afterwards. According to Michel Durand-Delga, this type of behaviour by Deprat was a mistake, since Lacroix was a very stiff bourgeois who wanted things to be done in the right way. It was, in any case, beyond the pale to threaten Lantenois with revelations about his private life. Deprat was clearly becoming desperate, but it seems that, apart from this one instance, he did not refer to Lantenois's homosexuality.

Given Lacroix's verdict on the fossils, and on Deprat's accusations of a conspiracy (though Deprat might not have known about the telegram of 31 May 1918, see page 130), Deprat's letter of 19 October was an odd tactic. The trio of savants had already condemned him, but he was still writing to them as if they were neutrals in the affair. He presumably wanted Lacroix, Douvillé and Termier to feel that he was still with them and that they had all been fooled by Mansuy and Lantenois. On 15 November 1918 Deprat wrote again to Lacroix from Hanoi. In a six-page, 4,000 word letter, Deprat wrote that he would produce 'letters and samples' showing 'a Mansuy who, made by me, wrote letters to me overflowing with friendliness and admiration for my work, flattering me as well and asking me for promotion, eight days before the announcement of Lantenois's return'. If Deprat thought that this might help his cause he was to be disillusioned.

★

This long, rambling letter was sent four days after the signing of the Armistice which ended the First World War – a war in which the existence of France had been at stake and in which millions of her young men had been killed or severely wounded. The momentous news had been immediately telegrammed to Indo-China, but, as Michel Durand-Delga points out, the actors in the drama of the trilobites continued to behave as if they had not noticed. Many of the older generation of geologists back in France had lost sons, nephews, cousins or friends during the war. For some of them, the mere hint that a young man like Deprat, insulated from the conflict, surviving unscathed and untroubled, could have perpetrated such dishonesty was a betrayal of the ideals of the generation who had died for their country. And at a time of national grieving for lost heroes, the least suspicion of arrogance or self-assertion would be viscerally unwelcome.

In late 1918 Honoré Lantenois intervened in the affair much more effectively than Deprat. He wrote to the Governor-General and 'asked that M. Mansuy is not called to Paris unless the Expert Committee formally asks him. This eventuality seems unlikely, since M. Mansuy has placed all his thoughts from a scientific viewpoint, in some very detailed Notes, which are attached to the dossier.'

We can surmise that Lantenois realised that Mansuy's fawning behaviour towards Deprat right up to Lantenois's return in February 1917 would be called into question. If it came to cross-examination, Mansuy could be made to appear hypocritical at the least. Lantenois's request was successful, despite being diametrically opposed to Habert's recommendation – 'it would not be sufficient to send the documents to the savants in Paris, and get them to give their advice on the affair. It is absolutely necessary, in my view, that the savants hear the contradictory explanations of MM. Deprat, Lantenois and Mansuy for themselves.' Henri Mansuy, the most important witness in the whole affair, was excused from appearing before the only bodies which were to look formally into the scientific aspects of the case. This remarkable decision seemed to pass without comment at the time.

It is unlikely that Deprat still harboured any illusions that he might come through the disciplinary process in France with enough credit to be restored to his post as head of the Service Géologique de l'Indochine. But if he did, then these would have been dissolved when, in January 1919, a newly appointed head of the service arrived from France. Charles Jacob had been Professor of Geology at Toulouse University both before and after the war. He had, like Deprat, been recruited on Lantenois's behalf by Pierre Termier. He told Jacob in the spring of 1918 that this was a golden opportunity, that good groundwork had been done, and that it was a magnificent place to study, particularly for someone of '*un esprit original et hardi comme vôtre*'. Termier also warned, though, that the Deprat affair was not settled – at this time Deprat had simply been demoted and Lantenois was recruiting a replacement: 'Deprat is fiercely defending himself by counter-attacking and accusing Mansuy of having sent us European fossils in order to make us believe that he, Deprat, is an impostor. This does not deceive anyone, but it no doubt obliges the Governor to be prudent.' Jacob arrived a matter of days before Lantenois and Deprat left for France.

On 31 January 1919 Governor-General Sarraut wrote a long letter to his superior, the Minister for the Colonies, outlining the affair and advising on how it should be handled. In Michel Durand-Delga's opinion this letter reads as if it had been drawn up by Honoré Lantenois. In effect, he says, Lantenois became the Governor-General's agent in Paris, and was sent there to put the agreed plan into action. The same boat from Haiphong that took this letter and two crates of documents concerning the affair also carried the Deprat family back to France. They left Haiphong on 2 February 1919 on board the *Sphinx*, almost exactly ten years after their arrival. Ten years earlier Indo-China had offered intriguing possibilities to the young geologist. It might be a scientific backwater where he would use up his days serving the administration and producing nothing of interest to anyone in the outside world, or it might provide the chance to show what he could achieve. Deprat had, through enormous energy, determination and skill, manufactured a worldwide reputation for the Service Géologique de l'Indochine and a glittering career for himself. Two years before, the future had been limited only by his own imagination; he seemed able to do almost anything. Now, as he looked at Haiphong harbour disappearing from view, he knew that whatever happened in France his dreams were dust.

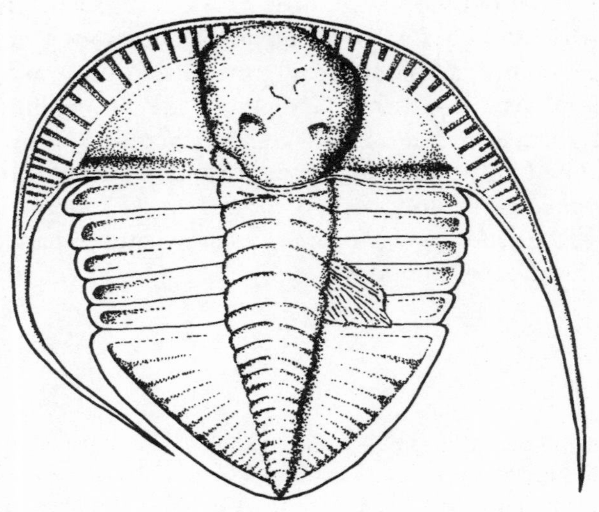

This single specimen of the trilobite *Dionide formosa* (Fossil no. 1)* was found by Deprat working alone in the col de Tsin Chouéi in the Chinese province of Yunnan between December 1909 and April 1910. It is first mentioned in Deprat and Mansuy (1910), and then discussed more fully in Deprat (1912a) and described in Mansuy (1912). This illustration (magnified × 3.5) is from the photograph in Mansuy's paper. This drawing and those on the following three pages are for illustration only – they are drawn from photographs, not from the original specimens, and are not to be taken as scientific figures. In his description Deprat says that *Dionide formosa* indicated the age of one of the beds as Ordovician. He included the beds immediately underneath as Ordovician on the basis that they graded into the *Dionide formosa* bed. Mansuy includes the fossil in the Silurian section of his paper, while acknowledging that it is known from the Ordovician of Europe, and shows a southern extension of the Ordovician into this region. This specimen was taken to France by Henri Mansuy in 1910 and placed in the collection of the Ecole des Mines by Henri Douvillé. It is now lost.

* The ten suspect fossils were originally numbered by Honoré Lantenois in order of their supposed discovery. This numbering was followed by Michel Durand-Delga in his 1990 paper, and is adhered to here.

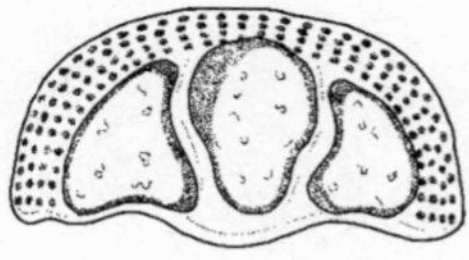

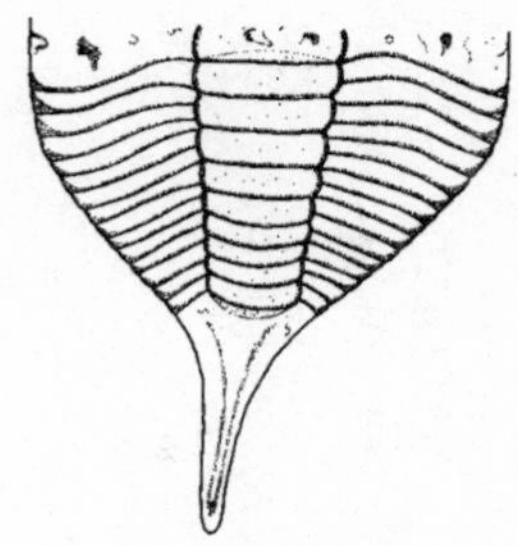

Three of the suspect fossils (Fossils 2, 3, 3a) were recovered by Deprat from Nui Nga Ma in north Annam, the central narrow strip of present-day Vietnam. This was to be the most contentious site during the affair. The first two, identified by Mansuy as *Trinucleus ornatus* and *Dalmanites* cf. *caudata*★ (Fossils 2 & 3) were found in March or early April 1912. They were first mentioned in Deprat (1912b) and more fully described in Deprat (1913c) and Mansuy (1913a). Mansuy later changed the attribution of *Trinucleus ornatus* to *T. goldfussi*, now classified as *Deanaspis goldfussi*. This specimen was rediscovered in the Collège de France in 1989. The precise species of the *Dalmanitina* fossil was not immediately identified, though from the illustration in Mansuy (1913a) it is thought to be (Henry, 1994) *Dalmanites socialis*. The specimen is now lost. The third specimen from Nui Nga Ma was retrieved by Deprat in March 1917. It has been identified by Henry (1994) as the pygidium also of *Dalmanitina (Dalmanitina) socialis*. This specimen (Fossil 3a) was also rediscovered in the archives of the Collège de France in 1989. The illustrations here are of Fossil 2 (× 2) on the left, drawn from a photograph in Henry (1994), and Fossil 3 (× 1.1) drawn from a photograph in Mansuy (1913a).

★ The designation 'cf.' indicates that the species is not precisely known, but is similar to the species named, and awaits confirmation.

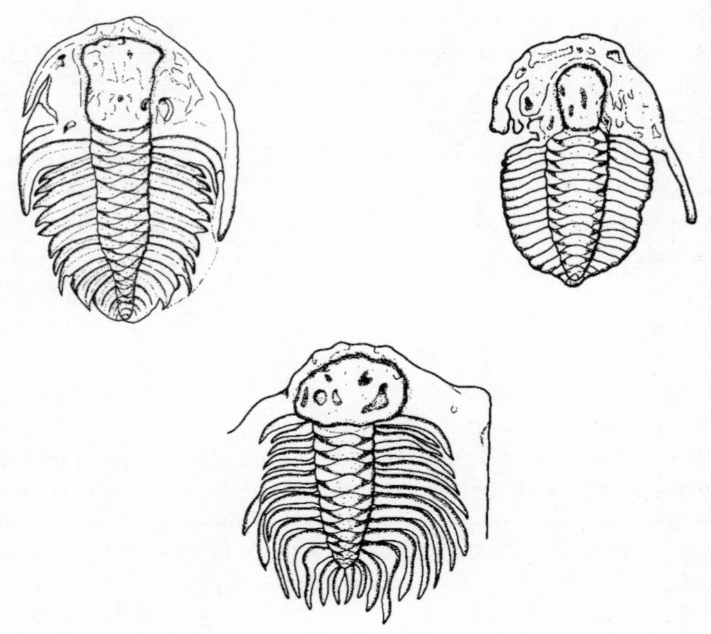

Three Gothlandian or Silurian trilobites (Fossils 4, 5, 6, left to right, above) were said by Deprat to have been found in a small valley known as Lang-Chiet in the basin of the Rivière Noire in the south-west of Tonkin, in June 1912. They are first mentioned in Deprat (1913a), discussed in Deprat (1913c) and identified, described and figured in Mansuy (1913b) as *Dalmanites longicaudatus* 'var. *orientalis*', *Acidaspis quadrimucronata*, and *Cyphasis* cf. *convexa*. These drawings (magnifications: fossil 4 × 1, fossil 5 × 1.4, fossil 6 × 3) are from photographs taken by Deprat and published in Mansuy (1913b). Deprat also immediately sent copies of the photographs to Douvillé in Paris. Douvillé confirmed that they were European species, but at the time (1913) expressed no surprise at them being found in Indo-China. Having, in 1913, described it as identical to specimens found in Burma by Cowper Reed, Mansuy later changed his attribution of *Dalmanites longicaudatus* to a European variety. The specimens of these fossils have not been found since the affair.

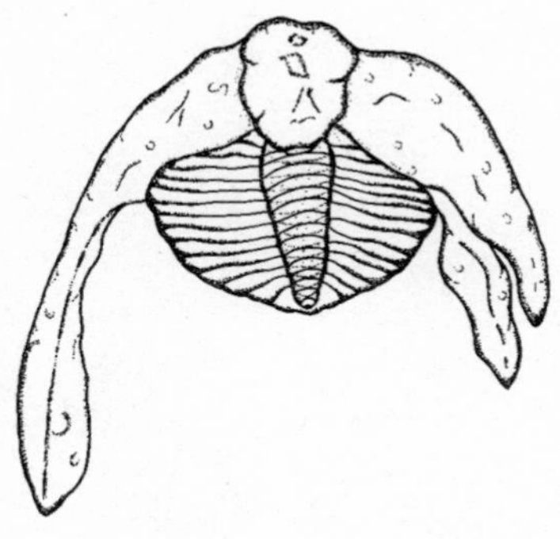

Another specimen of *Trinucleus ornatus* (Fossil 7, shown magnified × 1.3) was brought back from Haut-Tonkin by Deprat in the summer of 1915. The site is described in Deprat (1915d), and the fossil described and figured in Mansuy (1915b). The provenance of this fossil and the dating of the section where it was found are discussed on pages 197–202. The specimen has not been recovered since the affair. Deprat brought back another trilobite specimen, this time *Calymene* cf. *aragoi* (Fossil 8), from the same area in late 1916. It is mentioned only in Deprat (1917b). It was to have been described in a later *mémoire* by Mansuy, but the affair broke, and all mention of it was deleted. The specimen has now disappeared.

Deprat returned from south-east Yunnan in 1916 with specimens recovered from a mid-Cambrian formation at Tien-fong. Among the 'enormous quantities of Cambrian trilobites', he found single specimens of *Ptychoparia striata* and *Ellipsocephalus hoffi* (Fossils 9, 10), both known from Europe. Deprat described his find in a note sent to the Académie des Sciences (Deprat, 1917b). There is no further mention of these fossils in published papers, as Deprat's later *mémoire* was suppressed. They appeared in the proofs of Mansuy (1916a), but not in the final version. The precise location of the site is not known and the specimens have disappeared. A third 'European' specimen found with the other two, *Conocephalus emmrichi*, was initially found suspect by Mansuy, who later admitted that this was a genuine Asian fossil.

6 *France, March 1919–November 1920*

The Deprats arrived back in France in March 1919. They must have been struck by the changes in their country in the ten years of their absence. Above all, the effects of the First World War on France were profound. The unprecedented slaughter of the Western Front had literally decimated a generation – 10 per cent of the active male population had been killed or permanently disabled. Every town, every village and every family in France was bereft. For many in France, as in Britain, the war was a signal that the old order had failed and must be swept away. A spirit of newness spread through the cultural life of the country and Paris rapidly became the most exciting city in Europe and the cultural centre of the world. Paradoxically, though, French politics stagnated. The trauma of a mechanised war produced a nostalgia for some pre-existing France and a reaction against modern political ideas. In addition the death of so many young men gave old politicians and old ideas a new lease of life. Post-war France was dominated by conservative governments, a hegemony made easier by the refusal of the socialist parties to take part in government. And if government remained conservative, then the apparatus and instincts of the French state stayed even more so. While Montmartre and the Left Bank challenged all notions of artistic and cultural correctness, French administration remained bureaucratic, stiff, bourgeois, élitist.

On their arrival in France, Marguerite Deprat and her two daughters went to stay with her cousins in Nevers, a provincial town three hours' train ride from Paris. Jacques Deprat went to Paris to bustle – to visit influential people and persuade them of his innocence, and of the conspiracy against him by Mansuy and Lantenois. But everywhere he went he found that Honoré Lantenois had got there before him. First Deprat went to the Ministry for the Colonies. Lantenois had already been there and, as a senior civil servant, had gained access to the highest levels. Deprat writes that he was received with politeness by officials and told that his rights would be protected. He nevertheless felt that the bureaucracy of government was ranged against him. 'When he was there, he felt like he was lost in a horrifying and hostile desert.' Reading his account, the overwhelming quality of Deprat's experience in Paris was a kind of desperate paranoia. The 'ministry' seems now to us the archetypal location for such fears. But we are living in a different psychological world from Deprat's. We live after Kafka, and after the emergence of the omnipotently oppressive state. Deprat seemed to experience and articulate the twentieth-century touchstone of alienation at its outset.

Things got better temporarily for Deprat (just as they seemed to from time to time for Joseph K.) when he went to see Lucien Cayeux, now Professor of Geology at the prestigious Collège de France. Deprat knew Cayeux well and knew that he did not think much of Lantenois. Cayeux was, like Deprat, an 'outsider' in that he was not one of the Corps. He was, by Deprat's account, friendly and open, to the degree that on 22 March Deprat wrote to the Ministry asking that Cayeux be put on the committee which was, in his words, to arbitrate between Lantenois and himself. He also nominated two other committee members, probably his old teachers Fournier and Besson from Besançon. None of this had any effect, because in the end the Minister did not decide on the make-up of the Expert Committee. Instead he handed responsibility to the profession itself and to the 'learned members' of the Société Géologique de France.

Lantenois had arrived back in France on 12 March, seven days before Deprat, and had used that week energetically and judiciously. He had written to Henri Douvillé on 10 January 1919 that when in Paris he would take care not to see any geologists except Douvillé, Termier and Lacroix, who were already part of the affair. This was presumably a demonstration of his understanding of the need to keep everything above board. But then in a letter to Charles Jacob in Hanoi he revealed that he had also seen Emmanuel de Margerie, 'with whom I have a long relationship'. Lantenois in fact met de Margerie on 13 and 20 March. This was not simply a get-together of old friends. Lantenois knew the contents of the letter from Governor-General Sarraut. In that letter Sarraut suggested using the Société Géologique and its President-elect to examine the science of the 'trilobite affair'. Emmanuel de Margerie was the President-elect, and was to become the central figure in the destruction of Deprat's career in France.

Once the Minister for the Colonies, J. Simon, had Sarraut's letter, he proceeded to follow its recommendations. On 28 March 1919 he wrote to Emmanuel de Margerie enclosing a copy of Habert's report. De Margerie was, no doubt, expecting this letter after his conversations with his old friend Lantenois. The Minister first outlined the current state of the case:

> M. le Président I have the honour of informing you that M. Deprat, Dr. of Sciences, Geologist in the Service Géologique de l'Indochine, has been accused of serious professional misconduct by his Chef de Service, M. Lantenois . . . the so-called trilobite affair – the facts if they are confirmed could warrant bringing M. Deprat in front of a Commission of Inquiry.

The Minister requested that, at the forthcoming society council meeting, de Margerie designate members of an Expert Committee to follow M. Habert's recommendations and 'examine the numerous scientific matters which arise from the discussion of the facts'. He included the terms of reference for such a Committee:

> This Committee is in no way to be bound by the report and conclusions of M. Habert. It will determine those things which should be the objects of its enquiries, as touching on scientific matters. It will interview MM. Lantenois and Deprat, call up all statements and testimonies that it judges to be useful in the demonstration of the truth, and propose to the Minister those measures for which the case appears to be established, but which it could not take itself. In a word it will set itself to cast the most complete light possible, from a scientific point of view, on the so-called trilobite affair, and will give its findings in a final report to the Minister.

Ten days later, on 8 April 1919, 14 members of the 23-strong Council of the Société Géologique de France attended a regular session. This was to be an historic meeting, and one which remains controversial. Among those present were Pierre Termier, Henri Douvillé, Léon Bertrand, Emile Haug, General Jourdy and, of course, Emmanuel de Margerie. These were the eminent geologists who had been so eager to praise Deprat and his work at the Toronto Congress in 1913, and at the society's annual meeting in January 1917. How different it all was now. De Margerie outlined the Minister's request and set out to persuade the council members that the society should take on the role that the Minister requested. This is all neatly recorded in the council minutes, where there is also a record of some dissent. De Margerie read the Minister's letter, and circulated copies of the Habert report, together with a copy of Lantenois's charges against Deprat, and a letter from Deprat in which he expressed his own views about the make-up of any committee of experts. The council members discussed whether they should accept or reject the principle of such an inquiry by the society. The minutes record that: 'MM. Dollfus and Raymond stated that neither the Society nor the Council had the capacity or authority [*qualité* in the original] to take part in an administrative and disciplinary matter concerning one of its members.'

De Margerie as President of the society replied, as the minutes state:

> The President said that the Minister did not want to rule on questions which touched on scientific matters, without having the advice of experts . . . it is not a matter for us of taking legal decisions, but solely of passing comment on the special materials which are the object of our studies. The State, far from involving itself in our internal affairs, is asking us to give it some degree of technical explanation. We will not shirk from the honour which this brings us, because of the fear of exposing some disagreements among us.

If anyone else spoke in favour, this was not recorded. The principle of the council setting up such a committee was put to the vote and accepted. The minutes record:

> The President proposes to limit the number of members of the committee to five. It is recognised that MM. Douvillé, Lacroix and Termier have already given testimony [in the affair], and been previously invoked by M. Lantenois, and cannot take part. In order to avoid too much discussion, the President proposes that there are represented on the Committee – with the exception of the Ecole des Mines as already understood – the great educational institutions of Paris: Collège de France, Ecole Centrale, Muséum d'Histoire Naturelle, Sorbonne, etc. etc. The function of Chairman [of the Expert Committee] will be exercised by M. Emm. de Margerie.

The make-up of the committee was agreed, and the minutes state, 'It is decided that the first meeting will be around 6 May. M. Cayeux has kindly placed the geology laboratory of the Collège de France at the Council's disposal.'

The full committee was to be:

Emmanuel de Margerie, President-elect of the Geological Society
Lucien Cayeux, secretary to the committee, Professor of Geology at the Collège de France
Léon Bertrand, Professor of Structural and Applied Geology at the Sorbonne
Jules Bergeron, Professor of Geology at the Ecole Centrale
René Chudeau

While the others were selected from the élite of the subject, the choice of Chudeau was curious, since he himself had been involved in a scandal in which he was forced to leave his job in Besançon, Deprat's home town. Although the whole council of the Société Géologique de France acceded to the Minister's request, one is struck, reading the minutes, by de Margerie's enthusiasm for what was a precipitate step. Dollfus and Raymond were surely right to argue that the Société Géologique de France was and is a learned society, and should not allow itself to be used *by others* to judge its own members. For de Margerie, the request made to him personally by the Minister was probably a considerable honour which he would have been reluctant to throw back. And there is also the matter of his relationship with Honoré Lantenois. De Margerie had no formal qualifications in geology. He was, in essence, a rich amateur, who made up for lack of diplomas by prodigious energy. Lantenois, a man from a relatively modest family background, seems to have revered the wealthy and powerful de Margerie (despite the presence of the tell-tale 'de' in his name, the Margeries were not an aristocratic family, just wealthy). If Lantenois was, as Michel Durand-Delga claims, putting the Governor-General's plan into action, then part of his role was to persuade de Margerie of the need for his enthusiastic assistance.

As so often happens, those who do not agree with a course of action will prefer, if given the choice, not to be involved in its execution. The dissenters Dollfus and Raymond did not volunteer to be placed on the committee – which thereby became entirely composed of those who agreed with de Margerie that the society was justified in being part of a disciplinary process. Some may have had pure motives – believing it was their duty to give their colleague the benefit of being judged in scientific matters by his fellow scientists. Nevertheless, those who felt that Deprat was somehow being treated wrongly did not have their say on the committee.

Jacques Deprat was duly informed of the committee's existence and make-up and given notice that he would be required to appear before it. He writes in *Les Chiens aboient* that the composition of the committee concerned him – the only member he approved of was Lucien Cayeux. The committee held a total of twelve sessions between 6 and 26 May 1919, in the geology laboratory of the Collège de France. Its method of operation was to study all the relevant documents, and then to question Lantenois and Deprat in person. It seems that this was done separately at first, but that both men were sometimes in a session together. Deprat's account of the committee's proceedings is nightmarish. The sessions he describes are reminiscent of Kafka's evocations of alienation and paranoia, in which every statement or gesture of the accused makes him appear more guilty. The questions which can be asked, the statements which can be made, the terms of reference of the committee, the rights of the accused, who can speak when, who can be questioned or criticised, what is a reasonable question and what is not, are all decided by the chairman, whose sole aim is to find him guilty.

The fact that Deprat's defence depended entirely on proving another man guilty was the first of his difficulties. It was obvious that the committee did not believe in Mansuy's guilt, and therefore deeply resented this attempt to impugn an innocent man's reputation. As the sessions went on things got worse for Deprat. As well as accusing Mansuy of fraud, he called Lantenois's competence into question. As proof of this he referred at one point to a letter he had received some time before from Lucien Cayeux, in which Cayeux wrote of 'Lantenois's lack of knowledge'. This tactic did not, it seems, endear him to the committee members, and only served to alienate Cayeux – the one member he thought was on his side – from Deprat's cause. Deprat also raised the question of the fossil which had been brought to France by Mansuy in 1910. It had been thought to be genuine by no less an authority than Henri Douvillé, so why was it thought to be suspect now? Did Douvillé not know his palaeontology?

Criticism of Mansuy, Lantenois and Douvillé was the only way that Deprat could demonstrate his innocence, and yet it was the worst possible strategy for his defence. Douvillé, in particular, was an eminent scientist whose actions were beyond reproach. For Deprat to cite Douvillé's incompetence made him appear ridiculous and pathetic in the eyes of the committee members. Questioning the judgement of 'superior' scientists was simply not allowed by de Margerie, who repeatedly shouted Deprat down. At the last session, physically and mentally wearied by the whole process, Deprat understood that nothing he could say would make any difference. In *Les Chiens aboient* he relates his feelings:

> He sensed something unspeakable come over him. The horror of one of the victims of the diabolic inventions of the Inquisition. He opened his mouth to give an explanation. He kept silent. The faces in front of him, except for Cayeux and Bergeron, had a closed expression, very private. He understood that they knew what was coming. What good would it do to talk? So, at this decisive moment he made a firm resolution. He would accept everything.

Deprat is a skilful writer, and his evocation of the proceedings shows him as an innocent victim of a vengeful establishment. This may be a partial account, but evidence from Lantenois's letters and de Margerie's later behaviour show that the outcome of the Expert Committee was decided before it met. Lantenois was confident enough to be able to write to Charles Jacob on 11 May, 'The final result is absolutely not in doubt.' Deprat was not merely to be found guilty of fraudulently planting the suspect fossils, his character and by implication the whole of his scientific work was to be called into question. It was the beginning of a campaign to have all trace of Jacques Deprat removed from the scientific record.

The report of the Expert Committee is only just over four pages long, and deals briskly with the scientific points raised by Habert, before adding some of its own. First, the fossils themselves:

> As regards the incriminated fossils, the Committee was, firstly, unfavourably impressed by the fact that all these fossils are first-class, museum-quality specimens, found as single unique specimens, their matrix presenting an appearance very different from the other specimens of regional provenance.
>
> This unfavourable impression was heightened by the systematic refusal of M. Deprat to return to the field . . . the Committee finds the reasons invoked by him to be unacceptable . . . the only case where M. Deprat consented to return to the field (Nui Nga Ma) did not confirm his reasons. (Société Géologique, 1919)

Most damaging of all perhaps, and something not raised by Habert, was Deprat's inability, or refusal, to hand over his field notebooks to the committee. Habert, not being a scientist, would perhaps not have understood the vital part that field or laboratory notes play in any analysis of a scientist's work. The geologists on the Expert Committee certainly did. These would have formed a crucial part of the evidence in the case since they would have carried Deprat's recordings of the recovery of each specimen, *as he found it*. This would have helped to clear up the question of whether the specimens were substituted later by Mansuy, or anyone else. Deprat told the committee that his notebooks had not survived, having been destroyed or rotted by termites and humidity. The committee found this hard to accept, particularly since the letters filed in M. Deprat's dossier were in a 'perfect state of conservation'.

The Expert Committee agreed with Habert that Deprat would had seen the fossils after any supposed substitution by Mansuy, and would have noticed their peculiar nature. The report cites Deprat's expertise in palaeontology, as demonstrated by his work on fusulinids, as evidence that Mansuy would not have been able to get away with such a fraud.

The Committee had another criticism of Deprat's work, which was not made by Habert and which reinforced their doubts about the suspect fossils. They found, after studying the work that Deprat had carried out and published in his time in Indo-China, that the precision of his papers was not matched by the amount of time he spent in the field. The amount of detail that he supplied was too great to have been recovered in the time available. This led them to suspect that much of his work in Indo-China was fabricated.

The fossils found at Nui Nga Ma in north Annam were, once again, the focus of the investigations. The site had been first visited by Jacques Deprat in 1912, when he reported finding Ordovician trilobites in a bed of quartzite. He returned to the site in March 1917, on his own, in order to prove his innocence. On that visit he found another Ordovician trilobite of a 'European' species, this time in a loose pebble of quartzite from a conglomerate bed. In 1918 an organised party had gone to the site and found no fossils.

The report of the Expert Committee lists five specific points concerning the Nui Nga Ma fossils:

1. The part of the section of Nui Nga Ma relating to the supposed quartzites, claimed to be fossiliferous (Deprat 1912b), was entirely invented by M. Deprat, just as he confessed to the Committee.
2. The specimens taken from Nui Nga Ma by witnesses in the

presence of M. Deprat [this must mean pieces of conglomerate pebble picked up on the March 1918 visit] do not in any way resemble the matrix of the fossils brought back from these deposits, including the third fossil given by M. Deprat to M. Corandi [this should read 'M. Conrandy', see p. 123] on his return from his second trip.

3. Neither researches by the witness [i.e. Lantenois] nor by the other people who accompanied them, found the least fossiliferous debris during several hours at the site.
4. M. Deprat judged it ridiculous, and this without the slightest plausible reason, that the visit would increase the chances of discovering new fossils.
5. Finally, the matrix of the third fossil brought back from Nui Nga Ma by M. Deprat was shown under the microscope to have an absolutely exceptional character, similar on all points to the quartzite of *Dalmanites socialis* of Mount Drabow (Bohemian), and that this third fossil is, in all probability, of Bohemian origin.

The *coup de grâce* in the report, ironically since he was the one member favoured by Deprat, came from Lucien Cayeux. He was asked by de Margerie to carry out a detailed mineralogical analysis of the matrix of the third fossil from Nui Nga Ma (point 5 above). This was the only fossil which Deprat agreed that he had, without question, found himself – it was the only one whose 'source' was above dispute. Cayeux produced a separate report to the committee, which went into great technical detail about the mineralogy of several specimens that had been given to him. He looked at the third fossil itself; some other small samples of the rock in which this fossil was embedded; and some quartzite samples from Mt Drabow, the place where *Dalmanites socialis* is found in Europe. The main report blandly states Cayeux's opinion, but fortunately his own report to the Expert Committee has also survived, allowing us to follow how Cayeux came to this conclusion. We can therefore see how this crucial piece of expert testimony, which ended any hopes

Deprat had of showing his innocence, was deeply flawed. The first major surprise in Cayeux's report is his comment on the two separate samples taken from the *Dalmanites* fossil itself.

> Before passing to the description of the mineral content of the second group, it is important to underline the fact that the two fragments studied, although taken from a single and unique specimen broken by M. Deprat, differ noticeably from each other. One is poor in iron oxide while the other is notably ferruginous. There are equally differences in the rutile [a mineral] content. (Cayeux, 1919)

Cayeux explains that 'even a small specimen is far from identical in all its parts. But the differences which it shows are purely quantitative.'

His analysis of the second group of samples (i.e. those from Europe) shows that there are similarities with the first group (from Nui Nga Ma), but, 'All things considered, the specimens from the Ecole des Mines are not identical to the two fragments of quartzite sandstone from Nui Nga Ma, with which I compared them.'

Despite this difference, Cayeux reminds the Expert Committee of his earlier point, that two samples from the same place need not be mineralogically identical.

> To conclude, I remind you that the quartzite sandstone of Nui Nga Ma is of an exceptional type, that the material for comparison, originating in Mt Drabow [in Bohemia] and furnished by the Ecole des Mines, appears to be of the same exceptional type. The analogies between the two rocks are so numerous and so close, and their differences so negligible that I cannot see how to avoid the conclusion that they are all of the same origin.
>
> The truth obliges me to declare, without reservation, that the least that one can say about the quartzite sandstone of *Dalmanites*, brought back from Nui Nga Ma in 1917 – and

without intervening in the world of palaeontology – is that there is every probability that it came from Bohemia.

At first glance Cayeux's reasoning may seem sound. The rocks were not identical, but they had plenty of similarities, and since rocks from the same place were not necessarily mineralogically identical, then that was no barrier to saying these were from the same location. But there was nothing in Cayeux's analysis and reasoning that would not allow the opposite conclusion – i.e. that these rocks were from entirely different locations. His argument that the rocks were of the same exceptional type (though slightly different from each other), and therefore must be from the same place, is not conclusive. The rock was 'exceptional' only because Cayeux had not seen others like it. His opinion was limited by his experience and perhaps by prejudice. We should also note that he took care to say that 'there is every possibility that it [the suspect fossil] came from Bohemia', not that it certainly did. The weakness of Cayeux's reasoning was passed over by the other members of the Expert Committee, who simply took his conclusions on board. It is not clear whether Deprat had the opportunity to see Cayeux's report or to question him about it. It is likely that, being an eminent man (like Termier, Lacroix and Douvillé), Cayeux's competence was beyond examination, especially by a man like Deprat who had become deeply suspect.

The committee had received letters from a string of people whom Deprat had criticised (mostly with good reason) in the past, which were probably solicited by Lantenois. Included in this list were Captain Zeil, whom Deprat had forced out of the Service Géologique de l'Indochine in 1910, and Jean-Louis Giraud, the young geologist who had joined the service in 1915, and then had a severe falling out with Deprat. Giraud's role in the affair is not easy to quantify, though Michel Durand-Delga feels that his great personal antipathy to Deprat (this was mutual) may have been the catalyst that gave Mansuy the confidence to act. In any case these letters, though hardly adding to the evidence, impugned Deprat's character.

On 4 June 1919, ten days after the last session, the report of the Expert Committee was sent to the Minister for the Colonies. The final paragraph reads: 'The Committee could not accept the charge that M. Mansuy had any presumption of guilt in the so-called trilobite affair. It affirms its conviction that M. Mansuy had nothing to do with the scientific fraud that is imputed to him by M. Deprat. On the contrary, the Committee unanimously concludes that M. Deprat is guilty.'

The Expert Committee had gone further than it needed. It had simply been asked to confirm the scientific questions raised by the Habert report, not to judge whether Deprat was 'guilty' of any particular offence. This was to be decided by a further tribunal, which would take the committee's findings into account. Why did they decide to declare their belief in Deprat's guilt? It is likely that de Margerie, under the prompting of his old friend Honoré Lantenois, pushed for out and out condemnation. Deprat might have hoped that his fellow geologists would see that there were complexities in the case, and that it was impossible to say for certain what had happened. De Margerie had ensured that the conclusion was unequivocal.

For Jacques Deprat his experience at the hands of the Expert Committee was deeply demoralising. He can't have been surprised at its findings, but nevertheless they came as yet another blow. Michel Durand-Delga comments, 'Deprat returned to Nevers with his wife, a morally and physically broken man.' There is an intriguing postscript to the meetings of the Expert Committee. In his own account Deprat writes that the committee proffered the idea that the placement of the fossils was the result of a misunderstanding, an unfortunate mix-up in his collections, for which he would take responsibility. But Deprat says that he refused this offer of a get-out, probably realising that, in the eyes of the geological world, it would be tantamount to admitting his guilt. Whether the compromise offer was indeed made is impossible to know for sure. It was certainly not within the remit of the committee, as put in writing by the Minister, but on the other hand it would have been a convenient way for the government to be rid of an irritating problem. The Minister for the Colonies had neatly passed the affair on to the Société Géologique. Now they, in a matter of just a few weeks, had passed it back again. Having received an unequivocal verdict from the geological profession, the Minister seemed reluctant to proceed further. Both the Habert report and the report of the Expert Committee were to be used as information to be fed into an official government Commission of Inquiry into Deprat's 'scientific fraud constituting serious professional misconduct'. This commission would have the power to act on its findings by, for example, sacking Deprat from the Colonial Service. Deprat went back to Nevers and waited for the next stage of the process to unfold.

Both Deprat and Lantenois were keen for this tribunal to go ahead as quickly as possible. Lantenois hoped to get Deprat finally sacked from the Colonial Service, while Deprat believed that in this forum, where he would have the right to be represented by a lawyer, he could mount a coherent defence, and get the chance to attack Mansuy's and Lantenois's positions – something neither Habert nor the Expert Committee had allowed him to do. He would, after more than two years of being under suspicion, finally have his day in court.

The setting up of a final Commission of Inquiry was a laborious process. By 22 and 23 September 1919, three and a half months after the Expert Committee had submitted their report, the administration was still not ready. The commission was to be presided over by the Inspector General of Public Works, Bouteville, an old friend and colleague of Honoré Lantenois, but on those dates it was discovered that certain documents were still missing and so the tribunal was postponed. Deprat's solicitor called at the Ministry to enquire about the reasons for the delay. Deprat wrote that the civil servants seemed embarrassed, and it is again likely that they were not keen to continue or to have their hand forced. In view of what was about to happen, this might have been due to a political decision to slow things down. Lantenois also complained at the slowness of the Ministry. He feared that there would be backsliding and manoeuvring at the last moment. Nevertheless, on 19 October Lantenois felt able to write to Jacob in Hanoi, 'The sacking of Deprat is no longer in question. I say: Phew! because I have had a moment of doubt.' Lantenois's confidence was based either on the knowledge that the Commission of Inquiry was to go ahead, or additionally on information from Bouteville that Deprat would be found guilty. Either way, Lantenois's optimism was about to be rudely shattered, as the Deprat affair went through yet another extraordinary twist. The next event seems to have been totally unexpected by any of the people involved, except perhaps the senior civil servants in the Ministry for the Colonies – and even they may have been unaware of the bombshell that was about to be dropped.

On 30 October 1919 Lantenois was sent the following message by the Minister for the Colonies, J. Simon:

> The facts against M. Deprat, geologist in the Indo-China Service, falling under the cases envisaged by the Amnesty law of 26 [October], the disciplinary inquiry is henceforth halted. I believe I should however express to you my satisfaction for the firmness and energy which you have employed to bring to term a delicate affair, in the course of which you have kept in mind the honour and good of the Service entrusted to your care.

France has a long tradition of granting amnesties. Usually this happens when a new President is elected, or at some other significant time in the life of the nation. The 1919 amnesty introduced by Clemenceau's government was actually brought in just before the first post-war elections in November. The amnesties usually extend to only very minor offences, but in October 1919 there was good reason for making it wider than usual. France had lost a large proportion of its young men in the war. The 1919 amnesty, as well as being part of the healing process of the nation, was a way of ensuring that as many men as possible were available for work, and for government service.

Deprat received news that the amnesty applied to him within a few days. And with this brief message the Deprat affair was officially over as suddenly as it had begun. Deprat was now formally free to return to Indo-China and take up his old position in the colonial service, though he would still be a geologist third class. Nevertheless he could continue to advance his appeal against his previous demotion – a matter he was still pursuing through a lawyer in Hanoi. But during the course of the affair Deprat had made a lot of enemies, and these men were determined to see that he never returned to the colony.

Despite the dropping of all charges against him, Deprat was bitterly disappointed by the amnesty. Up until now every report and tribunal had, he felt, been loaded against him. While the original Thermes report back in January 1918 had been favourable or at least neutral, the first commission had an inbuilt majority of Lantenois's fellow engineers, who simply voted along party lines, while the two 'neutral' committee members both voted against disciplining Deprat. His ongoing appeal against this decision had a strong legal basis. Habert had also, Deprat felt, been against him from the start – though there is no firm or circumstantial evidence for this. And the final Expert Committee of the Société Géologique was, in Deprat's view, a nightmarish farce, with de Margerie shouting him down at every session, determined to confirm his guilt. Now, at last, he had been looking forward to a commission where his rights would be protected, where his advocate would be able to challenge the evidence of others without fear of being silenced and where, therefore, the double-dealing and dishonesty of both Mansuy and Lantenois would be exposed.

Deprat wrote to the Minister, asking that the second Commission of Inquiry be allowed to go ahead. He was refused. After verifying that there was no chance of a change in this decision, Deprat wrote again to the Minister: 'I intend, when I return to the colony, to ask other colleagues to come and verify my work. I will then take complete control over the measures which I intend to take.' In other words, Deprat was not content simply to let the question of his guilt or innocence be put to one side. He would prove his innocence and then, he implied, take action against those who had accused him. This bravado was a step too far. It was now clear to the Minister and his officials that the awkward situation which they had inherited from Indo-China would not be resolved by simply returning Deprat to Hanoi. And if it was not obvious to him, then it was soon to become so. Even if he did not see the contents of Deprat's letter to the Minister, the prospect of Deprat's return obviously alarmed Honoré Lantenois. After his two-year fight with Deprat, he must have been devastated by the news of the amnesty. Having done everything to demonstrate Deprat's guilt, and having worked tirelessly to have him removed from the Colonial Service, having suffered every kind of insult at the hands of his junior colleague, Lantenois had seen the outcome he so dearly hoped for snatched from his grasp at the last possible moment. Nevertheless he swung quickly into action. First, he contacted Emmanuel de Margerie. Up to this point the Société Géologique de France had been involved in the affair in an advisory capacity, now its role was to be taken a step further.

The Council of the Société Géologique met at 28 rue Serpente in Paris on 4 November 1919 – just four days after the Minister's letter announcing the amnesty was sent to Lantenois. It was to be another historic meeting. The minutes record:

> The President made known the results of the Inquiry for which he was given responsibility by the Council, in conjunction with MM. Bergeron, L. Bertrand, Cayeux and Chudeau, on the subject of the so-called 'affair of the Trilobites'. Following this communication, the Council, by unanimity of those members present, declared that M. Deprat be struck off the membership of the Society (Art. 6, paragr. 2

of the new regulations; 'The Council can strike off [a member] for bringing disrepute [to the society].')

Raymond and Dollfus were again present at the council meeting, but this time did not raise any objection. There is no record of any discussion of this decision, though there may well have been one. In hindsight, though, the council's behaviour does seem questionable, at the very least. The work of the Expert Committee had been carried out for a specific purpose as part, but only part, of a quasi-legal process. In order, as Habert had put it, for Deprat's rights to be guaranteed, this would precede a full Commission of Inquiry. In effect it would be feeding information and evidence into that commission. Once this process was cut short, it is doubtful whether the council of the society was within its rights to consider the matter fully explored. Deprat was not given the opportunity to give a statement, argument or justification in front of the council that threw him out of the society. He was effectively punished without having been found guilty. In fact Deprat's ejection had been decided in advance. In a letter to Jacob dated 17 July 1919, Lantenois had written, 'Deprat will be sacked, then thrown out of the Société Géologique.'

There is evidence that some Swiss members of the society later objected to this use of the council's powers. Nevertheless, if the council's legal right was questionable, their power was not. Deprat was expelled – the first and only individual member of the Société Géologique de France to whom this has happened.* De Margerie wrote to Deprat advising him of the council's decision. Despite being thrown out of the society, Deprat still remained a part of the Colonial Service, and was still pardoned of all charges relating to the trilobites. By now Lantenois had been officially retired from the Indo-China service, and therefore had no official capacity in the colony. Nevertheless he was

*After the First World War the society controversially expelled all of its German and Austrian members.

hell-bent on ensuring that Deprat did not return to Indo-China. He turned to the Académie des Sciences for help.

On 8 November 1919 Lantenois brought Alfred Lacroix, Henri Douvillé and Pierre Termier back into the affair. He asked them to use their considerable influence as members of the Académie des Sciences to put pressure on the Minister for the Colonies and on the Governor-General in Hanoi. Lantenois pointed out that Deprat could not possibly work together with his former colleagues, and that his return would mar the good name of the Service Géologique de l'Indochine, leading to its total collapse. Something must be done. The three senior geologists duly wrote to the Minister and Governor-General on 17 November:

> There is not, we believe, a single geologist, a single palaeontologist, a single mineralogist, in France or in the French colonies, who has not heard about the facts and who has not sought to form an opinion on the basis of the affair. You know as well that the opinion that has thus been formed has been unanimous and that between the two men, one of whom must without question have committed a fraud, no one could hesitate for long. M. Mansuy has been exonerated by everyone . . . M. Deprat is, in the scientific world, condemned by everyone.

They went on to argue that Deprat's return to Hanoi would be a catastrophe. According to Michel Durand-Delga, the text reads as if Lantenois had drawn it up, which he probably did.

On 8 December all six members of the mineralogy section of the Académie des Sciences wrote to the Minister and the Governor-General in support of their three colleagues: 'It seems to us that it would be regrettable to re-establish M. Deprat in the geological service in Hanoi, as he has been convicted of serious scientific fraud and improbity.'

Emmanuel de Margerie took matters a stage further. He also wrote to the Minister for the Colonies on 25 November in a letter co-signed by René Chudeau, Léon Bertrand and Lucien Cayeux. 'You will allow my colleagues and their President, Minister, to protest with all their energy against the return of this civil servant to Indo-China . . . My honest conscience is turned against the criminal acts of an individual that we all consider an impostor and a fraud, and who henceforth merits only being doomed to public contempt.'

It seems surprising that the Académie des Sciences should allow itself to get involved at this stage of the affair. It was not part of their responsibility to oversee the placement of scientists. No doubt they thought they were helping to protect the good name of French science. It is also likely, given de Margerie's extraordinary remarks (whatever Deprat might be guilty of, he was not a criminal!) that the Deprat affair had created quite a storm within the upper echelons of French geology, and French science in general. All through his own account, Deprat stresses his impatience with the hierarchy of the colonial life, and this went for the scientific world too. He did not defer to people like de Margerie and did little to hide his contempt for them. He regarded them as dull career scientists with nothing to contribute. This infuriated many who might otherwise have been favourable to him, and seems to have turned the scientific establishment thoroughly against him. It was, in any case, quite wrong of the academicians to state that Deprat had been convicted of scientific fraud. His case had, in fact, been dropped before it came to 'trial'.

Lantenois meanwhile was indefatigable; he did not just work against the return of Deprat to service, he still wanted him sacked. He wrote to the Governor-General in Hanoi on 4 and 8 December, and to Lochard, his successor, and to Jacob, Deprat's successor. The message was the same in all the letters; the colony and the Colonial Service must get rid of Deprat at all costs. It is as well to remind ourselves that Lantenois no longer had any official link to the colony.

Deprat remained in Nevers, released from all charges against him and legally free to return to work. But during the course of the enquiries against him his work had been found to be fraudulent. Though this only strictly applied to the suspect trilobites, it was clear that the Expert Committee of the Société Géologique considered that all of Deprat's work in Indo-China was suspect. Indeed any work that Deprat had done anywhere was now considered 'unsafe'. In addition, his colleagues in the Service Géologique de l'Indochine had been asked to give testimonies about Deprat, and had declared themselves to be untrusting of their former chief. There was now, in any case, a new head of the service. With all this history, how was Deprat to re-enter the service, let alone operate as a scientist? The problem of what to do with Jacques Deprat had no obvious solution, and neither was it obvious who should take responsibility for deciding his fate.

Unsurprisingly, there was now a good deal of administrative indecision. Under the pressure from the geological establishment, the Minister decided in January 1920 that it would be wise to keep Deprat in France for the time being. He then appears to have knocked the ball back into the Governor-General of Indo-China's court (who had, after all sent it to him in the first place). Maurice Long had succeeded Sarraut, and seemed determined to have nothing to do with the Deprat affair. We can gather this from a note sent to the colony some ten months later, as recorded by Durand-Delga:

> Inspector-General Bouteville sent a note to Hanoi on 4 October 1920:
>
> M. Long not having responded to this [earlier] communication, a first reminder was addressed to him by cable on 26 July 1920. I am sending him a second reminder today.

Deprat meanwhile wrote to the Minister asking for leave, having been in continuous service for ten years. This was spring 1920, and he was cut off from all contact with his employers, apart from his occasional pay cheques. According to Deprat, there were at least two farcical episodes when he was ordered to return to Indo-China – the orders arriving, deliberately it seems, a month after the stated date of embarkation.

The end of Deprat's service was a messy business. Eventually the resolution appeared in the form of a re-organisation of the Service Géologique de l'Indochine – so that there was no longer a place for Deprat in it. In other words, his job was to be made redundant. The official document, signed by Governor-General Long in November 1920, contains a list of every individual's new duties, including:

> M. Mansuy is named . . . as curator of the Museum of the Geological Service.
>
> M. Deprat, geologist third class of the permanent division of public works, is made redundant because of the phasing out of his job. M. Deprat will receive redundancy compensation equal to six months' pay in Europe.

Deprat's service officially ended in November 1920. Although it was formally agreed that he should receive full pay for the April to November 1920 period, it took him four years to recover this money from the French government. That, quite literally, was the end of the Deprat affair and the end of Jacques Deprat, geologist. The affair had stumbled and spurted along for three and a half years before it came to some kind of resolution. After such a drawn-out process, the end was bound to appear sudden and brutal. When the din of battle suddenly subsided, Deprat must have felt very alone and very unwanted. If we reckon Deprat to have been a proud man, at times arrogant, then he was surely shattered by the affair and by its ending. As long as it went on, he seemed to believe that he might be able to turn the proceedings his way, but in fact things just got worse and worse. As well as his own downfall, there was the bitterness he must have felt at the triumph of his hated adversary Honoré

Lantenois. The inferior geologist and puffed-up *fonctionnaire* had got everything he wanted – Deprat's dismissal, his expulsion from the geological world, his public disgrace, his impoverishment. From this disaster it would be hard for any man to recover. In 1920 Jacques Deprat disappeared completely and was apparently never heard from again.

Part Three

The Aftermath

7 *A Place in History*

In November 1920 Jacques Deprat, geologist, disappeared off the face of the Earth. Honoré Lantenois had succeeded in his misson to drive Deprat out of the government service and out of the world of science. His triumph seemed complete. But one difficulty remained. Jacques Deprat might have disappeared, but his legacy had not. Scientific papers by Deprat, published in a continuous stream since 1900, had become part of the database of the science of geology. The papers which touched on the incriminated fossils were obviously unsafe as sources of reference – steps must be taken to make geologists aware of their dubious nature. And what of Deprat's other work? What was the status of his studies of the tectonics of Yunnan and Indo-China, of his papers on fusulinid micro-fossils, and what about his earlier work on the geology of the Mediterranean? Could any of this be relied upon? And who was to decide?

The answer to this last question has occupied French geology on and off for eighty years. The ebb and flow that Deprat's reputation has endured since 1920 are an acute reminder that things are not always what they seem on the surface. There appears to be a need for a certain indeterminate time to elapse before events can become properly part of history – and thereby available for an analysis which, while never disengaged, might at least be impartial. The following chronological history is largely based on researches by the first serious historian of the affair and its aftermath, Michel Durand-Delga, whose work was published seventy years after Deprat's disgrace. It offers a picture of a community of scientists coming to terms with its own actions.

The key player in the immediate aftermath of the Deprat affair was not Honoré Lantenois, nor even Emmanuel de Margerie or Pierre Termier. Instead the tone for treatment of Deprat's work, and the recovery of the geology of Indo-China and its geological service, was set by Charles Jacob, Deprat's successor as head of the Service Géologique de l'Indochine. Jacob was the major figure in the years after the affair because he was the first geologist to go over the territory that Deprat had studied in Indo-China, and because he subsequently became Professor of Geology at the Sorbonne and one of the most powerful and respected figures in French geology.

Jacob arrived as the new Head of the Service Géologique in January 1919, just three days before Deprat left for France. Jacob found the service a difficult place to work in the aftermath of the affair. He wrote that Henri Mansuy and Madeleine Colani gave him little support, though he was better served by Deprat's erstwhile supporters, Dussault and Margheriti. Jacob decided that his best strategy was to publish papers which reviewed the work of the service to date, thereby allowing him to point out 'errors' that had been made in the past. This would be better than baldly listing 'facts' or papers which should be disregarded. Meanwhile he asked Mlle Colani to review Deprat's work on the micro-fossil fusulinids of Indo-China, Yunnan and Japan. Jacob set about visiting as much of the area of northern Indo-China as he could manage, reviewing the past work (most of which had been carried out by Deprat), and presenting his own results and interpretations.

In 1920 he published, together with his student Renée Bourret, a detailed report both on the geology of north Tonkin, and on Deprat's studies of the area. Though finding some agreement on the overall structure of the region, it is fair to say that throughout his paper Jacob is continually critical of particular observations or interpretations made by Deprat. But since this paper is explicitly a critique of Deprat's work, then it seems that Jacob took his task as being to highlight their differences. As for the suspect fossils themselves, in this paper Jacob gives a detailed interpretation of the area in which Deprat claimed to have found his second specimen of *Trinucleus ornatus* in 1915 (see pages 73–4), and demonstrates why this was impossible. Jacob's interpretation of this fossil has become the focus of interesting arguments in recent years (see pages 197–202).

A year later, in 1921, Jacob published a paper in the *Bulletins de la Service Géologique de l'Indochine* entitled 'Etudes Géologiques dans le Nord-Annam et le Tonkin'. The paper gives an outline of Deprat's ideas on the tectonic history of this large region of Indo-China, which Jacob estimated to have gone beyond the conclusions that could be drawn from his researches. Jacob then summarises his own and his colleagues' investigations of this region, made in the years 1919 to 1921, and concludes that, not only are Deprat's interpretations full of errors, but that he missed some things that he ought to have spotted. In summary Jacob writes:

> The structure of Tonkin emerges therefore, as Homogenous, as posing a single overall problem, for the whole expanse which stretches to the eastern frontier up to Trah Ninh and the Annam Cordillera, with elements and linkages, for the most part very different from those which were recognised or proposed by M. Deprat.

In the same year Jacob published a geological map of the north of Indo-China. This was substantially Deprat's work, though he was not credited. Many years later, after her husband's death, Mme Deprat was to write, 'The map of Indo-China was made by him and was published by his successors, without mentioning him, and by stealing his documents.'

Ever since 1918 Deprat had been pressing an appeal against his original demotion to geologist third class, through a Hanoi solicitor, Chabrol. This appeal continued even after Deprat was made redundant from the service in November 1920. Once again a *rapporteur* was appointed, and once again it seems that he found in Deprat's favour, but was then over-ruled by the committee which judged the case. Deprat's objections to his demotion were that the commission which had judged him was illegal, that he was not given the opportunity of having legal representation, and that material without direct bearing on the case (i.e. Termier's letter, see pages 117–20) was distributed to members of the commission. The appeal was finally heard in France in November 1921, nearly four years after the demotion took place, by the Conseil d'Etat, the highest administrative authority in the land. Deprat's appeal was rejected, though this was, the official record states, 'contrary to the conclusions given by M. le Commissaire du Gouvernement Corneille'.

It is fair to assume that the *rapporteur*, Corneille, had found in favour of Deprat, but that the consequences of this ruling being followed by the official commission would have been severely embarrassing. Michel Durand-Delga suggests that the Minister for the Colonies stepped in and made sure the right verdict was reached.

The following year Jacob published a short summary of his work to date in 'La Géologie de l'Indochine'. As Michel Durand-Delga reports, Jacob was generous enough to acknowledge Deprat as the geologist who had first talked of nappes in Indo-China, who had discovered Cambrian rocks in Haut-Tonkin, and whose geomorphological work remained important. But Durand-Delga quotes the eminent Swiss geologist, Emile Argand, as congratulating Jacob on his discovery of the nappes of Indo-China, while omitting the name of Deprat. Others, though, were not so easily swept along. A friend of Jacob wrote to him quoting the Scottish geologist Gregory, who was well up on the Deprat affair, as saying that 'your views [on the geological history of Indo-China] seem to be those of your predecessor'.

Honoré Lantenois, now back in Paris, wrote regularly on the

subject of Deprat to Charles Jacob in Hanoi in the early 1920s. Essentially Lantenois wanted the Service Géologique de l'Indochine to publicly disown *all* of Deprat's works – a step which Jacob resisted.

In 1924 Madeleine Colani published a review of Deprat's four major papers on the fusulinids of Indo-China, Yunnan and Japan, as requested by Jacob. Colani had been employed at Deprat's instigation. During the affair, however, she became close to Henri Mansuy and was highly critical of Deprat. Her 1924 fusulinid paper is a sustained attack on Deprat's earlier work: 'The results which are recorded here [i.e. in Deprat's papers] would have, if they were not inaccurate, a capital importance.'

Colani dismissed Deprat's claim, given in a 1914 paper, that fusulinid fossils have the same importance for the Palaeozoic era as nummulites, orthophragmines or lepidocyclines. She wrote that of the three new genera proposed by Deprat only one was perhaps worth conserving, and of fifty-two new species, only eleven species and eight forms were 'not to be dismissed'. According to Colani, Deprat's work in this area was, implicitly, inaccurate and almost worthless – though she did not go so far as to consider it fraudulent.

In 1926 Henri Mansuy retired to Paris and went to live in an apartment in Montparnasse, just round the corner from his old friend Lantenois. The same year Jacques Deprat, writing under a pseudonym, published his own version of the affair. *Les Chiens aboient* is a *roman-à-clef* – though in this case the characters are so little disguised that there is hardly a need for a 'key' to decode the book. The publication of the book caused something of a stir in Indo-China and among French geologists, and stimulated a response from Honoré Lantenois. Its main impact has been longer term though. The book is a partial, but essentially accurate, record (i.e. it cross-checks with other sources where they exist) of the events in Indo-China and Paris. It has the disadvantage of being written with hindsight, so that it is impossible to know from *Les Chiens aboient* what Deprat thought, for example, of the influence of the Corps in the colony before 1917. Nevertheless it is a fascinating document. But we might then ask why Deprat wrote it. He had left the world of geology in 1920 and had by 1926 begun a fruitful new life. We might have expected him to want to walk away from the affair, with the philosophical attitude he adopted at the end of the Expert Committee hearings. But he chose not to do this. He chose to re-engage with the past one more time, and we can easily understand that this was a painful process for him to go through – to relive his humiliation and the disintegration of his hopes and dreams. What did he gain in return? What does Deprat want us to see when we read *Les Chiens aboient*, and what do we really see in this wanting of his? Is it simply that he needed to have his say, to present his side of the story? Arthur Miller has said that the central requirement of every tragic hero is the willingness to make himself completely known. The fascination of Jacques Deprat is that his tragedy was played out in public. His hopes, fears, ambitions, triumphs, mistakes and judgements are recorded in the pages of scientific journals, reports and documents. Perhaps he felt once again that necessary illusion of shaping events through his own actions. *Les Chiens aboient* was his attempt to have the last word and to bring down the curtain on the tragedy of Jacques Deprat.

Honoré Lantenois's response to the publication of *Les Chiens aboient* was immediate, but ultimately futile. He drew up a paper which he intended to be published as a special bulletin of the Service Géologique de l'Indochine. Though he himself wrote it, it was his intention that the paper should be seen as coming from the service in general, and not from him personally. The reason for publication was given in the first paragraph, in Lantenois's strangled official prose:

> In the higher interest of the Truth and to stop short a campaign of rumour which has begun to be established under cover of anonymity [i.e. the publication of *Les Chiens aboient*], the Service Géologique de l'Indochine duly takes upon itself the imperative to publish the following Note which confirms

and completes the previous communications inserted in the Bulletins of the Service.

The Note summarised the 'facts' of the Deprat case, while emphasising two points. First, that the fossils allowed Deprat to date particular rocks with certainty; and, second, that they supported his 'hypothesis of supposed communication between the seas of Indo-China and Yunnan in the Ordovician period, and between the seas of Indo-China and Europe in the Cambrian, Ordovician and Gothlandian periods'. Lantenois showed how Deprat had used the ten incriminated fossils to build up a pattern of lower Palaeozoic stratigraphy across Yunnan and Indo-China that was, quite simply, false. Each new 'find' was effectively used to confirm the validity of previous questionable specimens. Lantenois also specifically mentioned the Ordovician quartzites at Nui Nga Ma as being an invention; a continuous section of Cambrian and Ordovician rocks, described by Deprat at Kwei-Tchéou as 'pure fiction'; and the existence of Ordovician rocks in north Tonkin as impossible because 'the Devonian rests directly on the Cambrian'.

Unfortunately for Lantenois, the appetite among other geologists for this review of the affair and the continuing degradation of Deprat was waning. The Head of the Service in Indo-China in 1927, Blondel, asked Charles Jacob, now at the Sorbonne, for advice. He counselled against publication of Lantenois's piece, believing it would simply bring the service into disrepute without providing any useful information. After all Jacob had already provided geologists with his own review of the work of the Service Géologique de l'Indochine, and of the geology of Indo-China in lengthy papers published in 1920, 1921 and 1922. The Deprat affair was something that French geology wanted to forget, not to explore. Lantenois was furious, but his influence was now limited. The paper was never published, but is preserved in the archives of the Muséum National d'Histoire Naturelle in Paris.

In 1927, having read *Les Chiens aboient*, Maurice Lugeon,

Professor of Geology at the University of Lausanne, and one of Europe's most distinguished scientists, wrote to Charles Jacob at the Sorbonne. Lugeon expressed his view that Deprat was a talented geologist, though there were undoubtedly faults in his work which could not have come about simply by accident. Lugeon also wrote, 'It remains the case that I still do not like Lantenois.' Durand-Delga reveals that Jacob had underlined this sentence on the letter he received, as if he agreed with it. At the very least, this letter shows that Lugeon had read *Les Chiens aboient* and that it was a matter of debate in the scientific community. In the same year a Captain Patte, working in north-east Tonkin, wrote to Jacob back in Paris that he had discovered a specimen of a trilobite from the trinucleus family (though since this specimen was never formally described, it must remain subject to some doubt). It was now conveniently forgotten that Mansuy and Douvillé had said that Deprat's discovery of trinucleus trilobites in the north of Tonkin was impossible.

Pierre Termier was now one of the great men of world geology. In 1929 he published his last book, which was a collection of papers given at recent conferences. One of the papers was from a conference held at Lausanne on 2 September 1928 – just eight years after the final act of the affair in which Termier had played a key role:

> This distinction of the two Corsicas was suggested more than thirty years ago. In 1896 Emile Haug proposed that the crystalline schists of the eastern region should be regarded as the extension of the schistes lustrés of Piedmont; and in 1905 Jacques Deprat put forward the hypothesis of a dragging of the eastern region over the western region, a hypothesis based on a curious fact, observed by him, of the existence between the two regions of a large crush zone, where the granite of western Corsica is crushed or laminated, and transformed in this granitic rock in a particular way that my friend Eusèbe Nantien called, a long time beforehand, *protogine*.

For Termier to cite Deprat's work in this way was a remarkable tribute from Termier to a geologist who was supposed to be in disgrace, and all of whose works were presumed to be considered 'unsafe'. This picking out of Deprat's contribution does not sit well with the supposed content of Termier's letter of December 1917 (see page 117) in which he denigrated all of Deprat's work – a fact which leads us to suspect Deprat's interpretation of the letter. Termier was expressing the growing view that, while Deprat was guilty of fraud, he had made valuable contributions to his science which should not be overlooked.

In 1930 Jacob noted: 'Lantenois is still dabbling in the Deprat story.' This, says Durand-Delga, was probably prompted by a letter Jacob received from Justin Fromaget, who was working in the Service Géologique de l'Indochine. Fromaget wrote to Jacob: 'M. Lantenois is unhappy that I do not wish to systematically denigrate the work of Deprat and hopes that I will not hesitate to do so.' Three years later Justin Fromaget, who was a strong believer in Deprat's mistreatment, if not innocence, was made head of the Service Géologique de l'Indochine.

In 1935 a palaeontologist named Jean Gubler published a work on fusulinids of the Permian period in Indo-China. Gubler's work strongly supported Madeleine Colani's 1924 view of Deprat's work on fusulinids. He cited Deprat's work extensively – there are seven papers by Deprat in the bibliography. But he followed Colani in rejecting Deprat's description of three new genera, and of most of the new species he had named. In his only mention of Deprat in the text Gubler says: 'Deprat attempted for the first time to establish a chronology. His attempt does not, it appears, correspond to reality.' He also implicitly criticised Deprat's view of the importance of fusulinids in the biostratigraphy of the Permian period: 'the importance of fusulinids has been over-estimated, at least as concerns the Permian period'.

Pierre Pasquier, the senior civil servant who sat on the original Commission of Inquiry into Deprat's disobedience of Lantenois in January 1918 (see page 120), and probably voted in favour of Deprat, became Governor-General of Indo-China in 1929.

There is a curious postscript to a letter from Justin Fromaget in Hanoi to Charles Jacob in Paris in November 1932: 'Pasquier is favourable to a return of Deprat as head of service, and his office is studying a request from Deprat proposing his re-integration.' Michel Durand-Delga says this may be true, or Fromaget may have been passing on a rumour – he never referred to the matter again, though Pasquier is generally considered to have thought Deprat innocent, or at least badly treated.

On 1 July 1936, following lobbying by Honoré Lantenois, Alfred Lacroix and Henri Douvillé, and a long letter of recommendation by his old mentor Professor Verneau, Henri Mansuy was made an Officer of the Légion d'Honneur. Deprat's account of Mansuy's somewhat hypocritical desire for this honour, published ten years earlier in *Les Chiens aboient*, had come to fruition. Mansuy died two years later. He had officially retired from government service in Indo-China in 1921, but then obtained another post in the colony studying prehistory, through Verneau's influence. He returned finally to France in 1926. His obituary was written by the faithful Madeleine Colani. The second spell in Indo-China, from 1922 to 1926, had not been a success, she wrote: 'His health had changed, he became highly nervous. Fortunately, a distraction helped him, he had taken into his house some young orphan children . . . He had the feelings of an affectionate grandfather for them.'

Then in 1940 Honoré Lantenois died, an event which had a profound effect on the way that Deprat's work was seen – or more likely on the willingness of geologists to express their views of his researches, his career and the affair which ruined him.

In 1941, Justin Fromaget, now head of the Service Géologique de l'Indochine, and a field geologist in the region for twenty years, published his magnum opus, 'L'Indochine française, sa structure géologique, ses roches, ses mines et leurs relations possibles avec la tectonique'. In his work and his correspondence Fromaget had shown an independence of mind, and in some ways saw himself as a kindred spirit to Deprat. He had cited Deprat's work in at least one of his papers, and in 1937, when he was having a lively disagreement with his superiors, he had written that 'A new Deprat affair will arise, I fear, as I am being pushed to the edge.' He apparently felt that Deprat had been got rid of, rather than that he had committed any offence. Now in 1941, with Lantenois dead, Fromaget had the chance to expand on his views.

At the start of his *mémoire* Fromaget gives this dedication:

> I dedicate this work, which summarises more than half a century of difficult and often dispiriting efforts and in which I give the principal results of twenty years of personal research, to all who gave the best part of their lives to the geology of Indo-China, H. Counillon, J. Deprat, H. Mansuy and L. Dussault.

Further dedicatees include Lantenois and Termier.

In the *mémoire* itself Fromaget praises Deprat's work on Yunnan, on the tectonic history and structure of north Tonkin, and on the general geology of Indo-China. He also singles out Deprat's four *mémoires* on fusulinids as being 'remarkable' – this in turn leads Fromaget to a criticism of Colani's 1924 *mémoire*, which he says 'was written with too much partiality'.

The inclusion of so much of Deprat's work in a review paper of this importance, quite apart from the specific praise given, was a signal to the geological world that the time had come to accept the name of Jacques Deprat back into the fold. Even more explicit recognition of Jacques Deprat, and of the wrong that had been done to him, was to follow.

R. Furon published an encyclopedic work in 1955 on *L'Histoire de la géologie de la France d'outre-mer*, i.e. the French Empire beyond France itself. The section on Indo-China has this heading: 'De 1900 à 1920: Deprat et Mansuy' and contains the following assessment:

> The great expansion began with the arrival of J. Deprat, who became Chef du Service Géologique from 1908 to 1918.

> Already known for his work on Corsica and Greece, J. Deprat became the great explorer of Indo-China (and of neighbouring Yunnan). He made several crucial discoveries: the Cambrian of southern Tonkin, the Devonian of the Rivière Noire, the *Gigantopteris* beds of Yunnan, etc. His great *Mémoires* on the geology of Tonkin and of Yunnan remain classics. Among all his palaeontological collections, he himself studied the fusulinids of the Ouralo-Permian.
>
> After an exhausting stay, nine years without being able to return home because of the war, J. Deprat, exposed to scandal-mongering, and to the jealousy of mediocrities, renounced geology.

In 1956 a standard reference volume, the *Lexique stratigraphie international*, included a chapter on Asia by E. Saurin. The section on Indo-China cites Deprat's work on many occasions, including the 1916 paper that was never published and cannot now be traced (see page 96). In the section on Ordovician strata in Indo-China, Saurin addresses the most controversial part of the Deprat affair – the fossils from Nui Nga Ma near Ben Thuy in north Annam. It was to here that Deprat had returned in March 1917 to find another 'European' trilobite, and it was here that the presence of quartzite beds became the centre of confusion and dispute. But according to Saurin:

> Near to Ben Thuy, in the Nghê-An province (north Annam), J. Deprat reported, at Nui Nga Ma, some yellowish-white quartzites containing *Trinucleus ornatus* and *Dalmanites* cf. *caudata*. The existence of these quartzites has been denied by H. Lantenois. However I have been able to personally observe, in the company of J. Fromaget, that sporadic quartzites certainly exist on the granite of Nui Nga Ma; we did not find any fossils there.

The quartzites which Deprat himself had been unable to find again did in fact exist.

A year later, in 1957, a new one-volume encyclopedia on the *History of Science* was published in Paris. A. Birembaut wrote the section on 'La Géologie' and felt compelled to include some comment on the Deprat affair, while comparing it to an earlier celebrated case:

> This progress [of geology], while it makes impossible the recurrence of the famous error to which Beringer fell victim at the start of the 18th century,* could not however prevent

*The Deprat affair is a peculiar echo of the Beringer case. In the early eighteenth century there was great discussion over whether fossils, in particular fossil shells, were the remnants of living beings, or were the product of entirely unrelated forces, which coincidentally made them appear similar to living things. Behringer's tragedy is related by Frank Dawson Adams – the man who, as President of the World Congress of 1913, sat next to Jacques Deprat on that Toronto lawn:

> Beringer was keenly interested in collecting the fossils which abounded in the Muschelkalk about Würzburg. Some sons of Belial among his students prepared a number of artificial fossils by moulding forms of various living or imaginary things in clay which was then baked hard and scattered in fragments about on the hillsides where Beringer was wont to search for fossils. These the Professor was delighted to find. He studied them with great care and their discovery stimulated him to continue his search with increased diligence, which was rewarded by the finding of other specimens, more and more remarkable in character, fishes were followed by many strange marine forms, insects, bees in their hives, or sucking honey from fossil plants, birds in flight or on their nests. To these followed even stranger forms, figures of the sun and moon, then weird letters, some evidently Hebrew characters, while others seemed to be related to Babylonian or other scripts. One of these which he describes and discusses with all due reverence actually presented the Divine name. He wrote a treatise concerning these discoveries illustrated by 21 folio plates. As certain persons had ventured to assert that these fossils had been made artificially, he devotes a chapter of the treatise to refuting such statements. The distressing climax was reached, however, when later he one day found a fragment bearing his own name upon it. So great was his chagrin and mortification in discovering that he had been made the subject of a cruel and silly hoax, that he endeavoured to buy up the whole edition of his work. In doing so he impoverished himself and it is said shortened his days. Unfortunately he did not destroy the copies which he purchased; they were found in his house after his death and bought by a publisher who provided them with a new title-page and issued them in 1767 as a second edition of his work. (Frank Dawson Adams, 1938)

Birembaut believed Deprat to be the victim, not of a cruel and silly hoax, but of a similarly fraudulent substitution, made to bring about his downfall.

> the malevolent acts, under which Jacques Deprat, then a geologist in Indo-China, suffered. Exposed to the combined jealousy of a high official and a subordinate, who placed in his collections some fossils of European provenance, Deprat was forced to abandon a scientific career which promised to be brilliant. He recounted his distressing tale in 1926 . . . in a *roman-à-clef, Les Chiens aboient.*

This chapter is a survey of the development of geology since the earliest times, so mention of the Deprat affair signals its continuing importance to at least some geologists in France.

During the 1960s the theory of continental drift, proposed by Alfred Wegener in the first decades of the twentieth century, received strong support from geophysicists working on the magnetisation of ocean-floor rocks. Within a few years continental drift, and its driving mechanism, plate tectonics, became generally accepted as the overarching explanation for the geological development of the Earth's crust. The implications of continental movement for palaeontology and, conversely, the usefulness of palaeontology in unravelling continental movements, rapidly became apparent. If the same species of fossil was found in widely separated places, but nowhere in between, might it not be because these places were at one time physically adjacent? The already extensive attempts to correlate fossils across continents were given fresh impetus by this new function that they served. The science of palaeobiogeography has become one of the most fertile disciplines within geology. The discovery of European fossils in Asia and vice versa began to be reported increasingly. In 1984 Raimund Feist and Robert Courtessole reported the discovery of trilobites of east Asian species from the Upper Cambrian period in the Montagne Noire region of Languedoc in southern France.

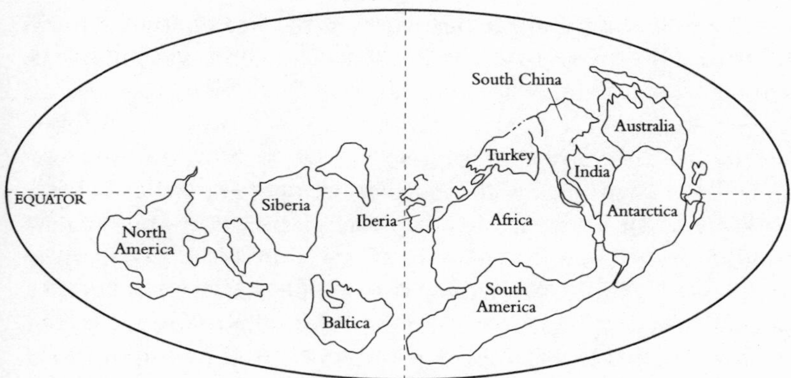

The position of the continents in the Early Cambrian period, as suggested by Pillola, 1990. Southern Europe and parts of South Asia share a formal province along the northern coastline of the super-continent Gondwanaland.

Then in 1989 a sensational discovery was made. A geologist named Jacques Sigal had been doing research into the Deprat affair. He was looking for some papers in the out-of-town site of the Collège de France at Meudon when he came across some drawers of specimens. Among the fossils contained in the drawers, Sigal realised to his astonishment, were some of the 'suspect' trilobites from the Deprat affair. These had been missing, believed lost, for nearly seventy years. And as well as the trilobites Sigal found a collection of Deprat's thin sections of fusulinids.

The following year further work on the links between fossils of Asia and Europe in the lower Palaeozoic era was published. In a report to the Académie des Sciences, Gian Luigi Pillola concluded, 'A lithological analysis and a revision of the trilobite faunas from the lower Cambrian of SW Sardinia permit good correlations with SW China; a palaeobiogeographical sketch is proposed.' In other words, a fresh classification of trilobite families, together with analysis of the matrixes of fossils from these two locations, had shown them to be closely related in two ways – first, as animal types, and second, in their rock types. The author included a sketch-map (previous page) showing how these things could be explained by the close proximity of the two continents in the lower Cambrian period.

Neither Pillola's nor Feist and Courtessole's papers confirmed that Deprat's European trilobite fossils were genuinely found in Indo-China (and it must be said that palaeogeographic maps of such an early geological period are highly speculative), but they appeared to dramatically increase the possibility that this might be the case. There was a growing consensus that, not only was there a marine link between Europe and southern Asia during the Lower Palaeozoic era, but that the two continental blocks were geographically close together. The 1917 ruling by Termier, Lacroix and Douvillé (confirmed by Cayeux's 1919 microscopic examinations) that the suspect trilobites were of European provenance, had never been questioned. The whole affair had been an argument about whether Deprat or someone else planted the fraudulent fossils. Now the most fundamental question of all began to be asked. Were the 'suspect' fossils actually genuine? Was there a fraud at all?

8 *Towards a Verdict?*

Over the years various geologists have given their views on Deprat's work, and on the justice or otherwise of his treatment. These views have mostly been based on an involvement in the case, or an emotional response to it, or on a study of a small part of the evidence. It was not until 1990 that a truly thorough investigation of the Deprat affair took place. Michel Durand-Delga, a retired Professor of Geology from the Universities of Paris and Toulouse and a member of the Académie des Sciences, published the results of his study of the affair in a paper that runs to over a hundred pages of detailed and closely argued text. This major piece of historical research was presented to a General Meeting of the Société Géologique de France on 10 June 1990. The paper and the wealth of factual material it contains is the source for much of the information on the affair presented in this book. But as well as giving the details of the case, Durand-Delga raised certain arguments which had not been discussed at the time of the affair, before giving his own considered conclusions. Although Durand-Delga points out various difficulties with the 'prosecution case' against Deprat, the main thrust of his paper is twofold – first, to show how the social structure and climate in France and Indo-China contributed to Deprat's downfall, and may have even precipitated it; and second, to challenge the previously accepted notion that the suspect fossils must be fake. If it were proven that they were genuine, or if a reasonable doubt were cast on the contention that they were fake, then all the difficulties of Deprat's tortuous defence would disappear.

On the first point, we have already been able to see the extent to which Deprat was an outsider in the world which he chose to inhabit. The degree of influence of the Corps, the importance of showing deference, the illusion of welcome followed by the closing of ranks, are all shown beyond dispute, and are supported by evidence from elsewhere. While Durand-Delga cannot show that there was a definite conspiracy against Deprat, he demonstrates that there was mutual antipathy between him and his accusers *before* the affair, and that his legal rights were subtly and systematically denied him because of the social milieu in which he lived and worked.

As far as the fossils are concerned, Durand-Delga's charge is that the savants and Expert Committee which gave rulings on these were either unqualified to do so, not scrupulous in their investigations and their thinking, or simply mistaken. First, they asserted that the matrix of the fossils did not match that of the local rock. This was, in fact, impossible to prove. None of the experts who ruled on the provenance of the fossils had ever visited the locations where the fossils were alleged to have been found. In some cases only Deprat himself had been there – they would have needed the defendant to give evidence for his own conviction. Second, they made the converse point that the matrix exactly matched that of the European fossil beds where these species were originally found. Here Durand-Delga returns to the illogicality of Professor Lucien Cayeux's mineralogical analysis (page 162). There is another point against Cayeux. He found the same mineralogical combination in Deprat's fossil as in some rocks from Bohemia supplied by Douvillé, which he said was '*tout à fait exceptionnel*', and was therefore driven to conclude that the fossil supposedly from Nui Nga Ma probably came from Bohemia. But Durand-Delga reports that modern petrologists have concluded that the elements which Cayeux thought exceptional are commonplace products of mild metamorphism, which occur in rocks all over the world. They are not at all exceptional. Also the similarity of rock types across Europe and south-east Asia in the lower Palaeozoic era is now well known. The dark or dark green schists of most of the contested fossils are common in lower Palaeozoic rocks from both Europe and Asia.

Once these two pieces of evidence – the dissimilarity of the fossils with local Indo-China matrix, and the identity with European rocks – are shown to be unsafe, then the case against Deprat rests on only one argument: that European trilobite species could not be found in Indo-China. Durand-Delga summarises some recent developments in the understanding of continental movements in the lower Palaeozoic era. Remember that Lantenois had emphasised in 1927 how the allegedly fake fossils were placed to prove Deprat's theory of 'marine communication' between Europe and Asia at this time. Durand-Delga cites recent work which shows that the northern shoreline of the ancient continent of Gondwanaland contained elements of Western Europe and south-east Asia. In the lower Palaeozoic era these now widely separated parts of the world were part of the same faunal province – i.e. the same genera and, in some cases, species of marine animals were living in each. Deprat anticipated this discovery when he wrote to Habert in 1917: 'Just because until today no one has ever found a European species in the Cambrian of Indo-China, we cannot conclude that no one will ever find any.' The absence of Ordovician rocks in northern Indo-China and Yunnan was cited by Lantenois and others as proof of Deprat's guilt, but Durand-Delga points out that in the years since Ordovician strata have indeed been found in these regions.

Deprat did not have the opportunity to reply to one particular charge laid against him both by the Expert Committee of the Société Géologique and by Jacob. Both reported that the time that Deprat had spent in the field was too short to have produced work of the accuracy which he claimed – the clear implication being that he was making things up. The overall charge is difficult to rule on, since it is entirely nebulous: who can say how much time is 'right' or 'wrong'? But Durand-Delga shows that Deprat averaged four months per year in the field during his time in Indo-China compared to Jacob's two, while producing roughly the same amount of published material per annum.

We have seen that some other charges were laid against Deprat after he had left the geological world. The most specific of these was Jacob's accusation, made in his 1921 paper, that one of Deprat's Ordovician trilobites came from a section of strata that does not contain rocks of Ordovician age (see page 179). Michel Durand-Delga comes to Deprat's defence over this fossil.

In his 1915 paper Deprat provided a cross-section through a rock formation in north Tonkin. The section was actually exposed along the side of a road running between two places called Dong Van and Chang Poung (Deprat, 1915d). Deprat stated in his paper that the section is made up of rocks of Cambrian and of Ordovician age. Cambrian rocks are the oldest in the Palaeozoic era and Ordovician are the next oldest. In this formation the boundary between the two is impossible to place exactly since the rocks grade into each other. However, Deprat was certain that both periods were represented because he found fossils from both. There are numerous specimens of *Ptychaspis walcotti*, a fossil trilobite from the Cambrian, and Deprat had found an example of *Trinucleus ornatus* known from Ordovician strata in Europe – one of the suspect trilobites. In his cross-section Deprat shows what he calls the base of the Ordovician near Lou-Tçai, including the bed containing the specimen of *Trinucleus ornatus*. His rationale for including the remaining beds on this section as Ordovician is the presence of a fossil called *Spirifer tonkinensis* which Henri Mansuy had estimated at the time to be also Ordovician (although Deprat records in 1915 that another palaeontologist, Frech, thinks it more recent).

Jacob returned to the same site in 1921, and included a similar section in his paper (Jacob, 1921). Jacob found specimens of the Cambrian fossil *Ptychaspis walcotti* where Deprat had indicated.

But, crucially, he also found some in another bed situated *above* Deprat's Ordovician series. This meant that the whole series up to the second *Ptychaspis* bed at least, must be Cambrian in age. So, not only was Deprat's fossil possibly of European provenance, it could not in any case have been found where he claimed to have found it, since these rocks are not Ordovician. Jacob writes:

> We found the same *Ptychaspis walcotti* in abundance in some new reddish schists, 1 kilometre in horizontal distance above the red bed . . . *It occurs, in all cases, in the middle of the suggested Long-Co series and above the beds which would have provided the* Trinucleus ornatus *since recognised as being of foreign origin* [original italics] . . . We consider the whole of the Chang Poung series to be Cambrian.

This was a compelling piece of independent evidence pointing to Deprat's guilt. However, in Durand-Delga's view, 'A precise analysis of the texts [of the two papers] shows that Jacob committed a serious error of interpretation.'

Jacob had, according to Durand-Delga, misunderstood Deprat's 1915 paper. This is not altogether surprising. The naming of the different series, and the numbering of the strata in the texts and on the figures, are extremely confusing. Jacob was guilty of misreading Deprat's section against the evidence in the field. The accusation that the suspect fossil came from a Cambrian formation was, it turned out, false (Jacob had gone to the wrong location) – though it stood almost unchallenged for seventy years. To quote Durand-Delga, 'However Jacob has an excuse for his error: Deprat's text and illustration are somewhat confusing.' Durand-Delga also reminds his readers that other trinucleus fossils have been found in north Tonkin since Jacob published his paper.

Having been accused of being planted in strata older than Ordovician, the *Trinucleus ornatus* from Dong Van has also been suspected of being from younger strata. This suggestion has come about because of the presence of fossil fish remains in adjoining beds. This may have been the discovery which changed Henri Mansuy's mind about the presence of Ordovician strata in north Tonkin, and thereby precipitated the whole affair (see page 88). In his 1915 paper 'Contribution à l'étude des faunes de l'Ordovicien et du Gothlandien du Tonkin', Henri Mansuy had discussed the fossils in the formation where *Trinucleus ornatus* had been found by Deprat:

> There are some argillaceous schists, containing fragments of ostracoderm fishes, which succeed the sandstone schists of *Trinucleus ornatus*. The ventral, median and lateral scales discovered in this horizon are very similar in their proportions and in the small star-shaped tubercules which cover the whole surface, to the corresponding parts of *Asterolepis* EICHWALD of the Old Red Sandstone [a famous Devonian formation]; other fragments, of less importance, show an alveolar structure, which by this peculiarity resemble species placed in the genus *Homosteus* ASMUSS. The stratigraphic level of the Ostracoderm schists, situated between the *T. ornatus* schists and the *Goniophora* sp.schist which themselves precede the *Spirifer tonkinensis* schists, the first of Ordovician age, and the second of Ordovician or lower Gothlandian, demonstrate that the ostracoderm fish preceded the lower Devonian period in the Palaeozoic of the Far East.
> (Mansuy, 1915b)

In other words, immediately above the bed containing the *Trinucleus ornatus* (an Ordovician fossil), were beds containing fish scales or bony plates which were very similar to those of Devonian armoured fishes (known as placoderms). Then above the fish beds were beds containing *Spirifer tonkinensis*, thought by Mansuy to be Ordovician as well. The explanation that Mansuy proposed, was that these ostracoderm fishes must therefore be Ordovician, since they were sandwiched between two 'known' Ordovician fossil beds.

The problem with this logical analysis by Mansuy is that, although some fishes were known from the late Silurian of Scotland, the earliest fossil placoderm fishes then known occurred in the lower Devonian period – i.e. later than both the Ordovician and the Gothlandian or Silurian periods. Mansuy acknowledged this difficulty in his last phrase, above, where he is suggesting that ostracoderm fishes (which are a sub-group of the placoderms) must have appeared earlier in the Far East than elsewhere. He cites support for this suggestion by referring, in a footnote, to a discovery by Charles Walcott: 'It is known that M. Walcott has come across the remains of ganoid fishes in the Ordovician of Colorado.' Walcott had published his account in 1892, but it is fair to say that this was looked on with scepticism by the geological world until discoveries in the 1930s showed that certain fishes did evolve as early as the Ordovician period.

Dr Philippe Janvier of the Muséum National d'Histoire Naturelle in Paris is an expert on Palaeozoic fishes, and has studied their occurrence in Vietnam for the past fifteen years. He has pointed out that, although some forms of fish are found in the Ordovician, those that Mansuy identified and figured are definitely Devonian species. Since these are directly above the bed where Deprat claimed to have found *Trinucleus ornatus*, that bed too is probably Devonian or at youngest Silurian in age. Even if we accept that the *Trinucleus ornatus* was apocryphal, this still leaves the problem of *Spirifer tonkinensis*, an apparently Ordovician fossil, occurring above the bed where the Devonian fish remains were found. We saw earlier that when Deprat wrote his paper in 1915, the age of this fossil was a matter of dispute between Mansuy and another palaeontologist. But in 1916 Mansuy had a radical and crucial change of mind about the age of many rock formations in northern Indo-China (see page 88). In view of its importance it is worth repeating the quote from Mansuy's paper:

> . . . most of the fauna in Tonkin considered up to now, on the basis of stratigraphic observations, as being of Gothlandian

> age, sometimes even Ordovician, undoubtedly combines all the traits, all the characteristics of Devonian fauna. All of these facts, all of these certainties are in complete contradiction to the observations made on the ground. Taking into account hesitations, incorrect interpretations, inevitable errors and relying on the most convincing palaeontological data, one is brought to the conclusion that a general revision of the principal stratigraphic data is needed, in particular that of the lower Palaeozoic of northern Indo-China. (Mansuy, 1916)

This change was based principally, though not exclusively, on Mansuy becoming convinced that *Spirifer tonkinensis*, which was found throughout the region, was a Devonian fossil. This key fossil is now classified as *Euryspirifer tonkinensis* and may in fact include several different brachiopod species. It is now thought to be restricted to the early Devonian of Tonkin, Yunnan and Szechuan.

So where does this reassessment leave Deprat's 'Ordovician' *Trinucleus ornatus*? Durand-Delga argues that we should view Mansuy's 1916 change of mind with great suspicion. Mansuy's reasoning is a little odd since he cites 'stratigraphic observations' as both pointing to Gothlandian and Ordovician attributions, and as indicating the need for a revision of these attributions. All the field observations were, in any case, made by Deprat, and Durand-Delga argues that this paper was Mansuy's way of clearing the ground to make the accusations of fraud against his colleague – and presumably to remove himself from any suspicion.

If, on the other hand, we believe that Deprat was guilty of fraud, then there is another difficulty. As Philippe Janvier has suggested, it would have been very odd of Deprat to 'plant' an Ordovician fossil in a bed when he knew there were fragments of fossil placoderm fish (which were generally known as being no older than Devonian) in the horizon immediately above. It may be that Deprat also knew of Walcott's 1892 paper, and took the presence of fish as early as the Ordovician period as a possibility; but we should not take it for granted that because

Mansuy knew of this paper then Deprat did too. Just as likely the presence of *Spirifer tonkinensis*, an apparently Ordovician fossil, in the bed above convinced Deprat wrongly that these were Ordovician strata.

It must be said that Professor Durand-Delga believes it possible that Deprat did recover an example of *Trinucleus ornatus* from this area. He cites Lantenois as stating in 1927 that there is no Ordovician in the region since the Devonian rests directly on the Cambrian (presumably following Mansuy's reassessment). In contrast, Durand-Delga points out that: 'Saurin (1956, p.60) reports that to the east of Chang-Poung, the "San-Kian-Tchai" series described by Deprat (1915) is authentically dated as lower Ordovician, which fact enables us "to maintain the validity [of the Lou-Tçai series] proposed by Deprat".' The discussion of this fossil is, eighty years after its appearance, far from over.

Durand-Delga's overall assessment of the fossil investigation at the time of the affair is that the Expert Committee of the Société Géologique de France did not do a good job. Apart from de Margerie, they did not relish the task and did not have the time to do it properly. Only Jules Bergeron had the expertise to investigate such a complicated affair. 'The arguments used to condemn Deprat were light and superficial, and only gained weight through the intervention *sans nuances* of the senior figures of French geology.'

This last point is supported in Durand-Delga's paper by the wealth of correspondence which he obtained and published for the first time. This shows the extent to which the geology 'establishment' rallied together to rid themselves of Deprat, even after the official charges against him had been dropped. Finally, Durand-Delga asked, what 'If Deprat were guilty'. First, why would he have done it and, second, how? After all the twists and turns we are back to the basic questions at the root of every crime movie – motive and opportunity. As far as motive is concerned, Durand-Delga points out:

Apart from Lantenois, who claimed that Deprat had made

sensational use of the fossils (this can hardly be supported, except for the two fossils from Nui Nga Ma) no one else has suggested the point of the proposed fraud. His reputation was already established from before 1913; in France the patrons of the science knew Deprat and appreciated his work; he had prizes from the Académie des Sciences and the Société de Géographie, and abroad he had been nominated as Vice-President of the Canada Congress in 1913. It is hard to believe he would jeopardise all this. Studying his life as a whole seems to exclude such a possibility.

And as for opportunity – the fossils themselves would have had to have been brought from Europe. So either Deprat took the fossils with him when he first went to Indo-China in 1909, or they were sent on to him later. If the former, then did Deprat know what types and ages of rocks he was likely to come across in Indo-China? His specialty was the relatively young rocks of the Mediterranean basin. Why would he have taken fossils from the lower Palaeozoic – particularly as Cambrian and Ordovician rocks were not definitively known in Indo-China before he discovered them? Also Deprat had never been to Bohemia or any of the other locations in Europe from where the fossils were alleged to have come. He would therefore have had to buy, or even steal the specimens in Europe, put them in his overloaded baggage, keep them hidden in Hanoi for several years (either at home, unless the family were all in on the fraud, or at the Service Géologique where others would have seen them); then take them with him on long expeditions into the field, before placing them among others he had collected. If, on the other hand, the fossils came later, then who would have sent them from Europe? Deprat would have needed an accomplice who had been sworn to secrecy throughout the affair. Even a dealer would surely have come forward when the affair erupted. And in any case a package of fossils arriving in a tight-knit place like Hanoi would have been noticed. After exhaustive and painstaking research, Professor Durand-Delga concludes that the case for fraud had not been made and that Deprat had been treated unjustly.

Some of the suspect fossils, found by Sigal in 1989 at the Collège de France, were passed to palaeontologist and trilobite expert Jean-Louis Henry of the University of Rennes. In 1994 he published the results of his own studies of three of what he called 'The Trilobites of the "affaire Deprat"'. Henry's paper is a critical response to Durand-Delga's, which Henry characterises as 'an attempt to rehabilitate his [Deprat's] reputation'. In Henry's opinion all three of the trilobites that he examined (the two from Nui Nga Ma and one from Yunnan) 'really come from Bohemia, where such forms are well known in the upper Ordovician'. Henry makes two points: first, that the determination of the species themselves is agreed by all, and is not in dispute; and second, that substitution by Mansuy can be ruled out at least in the case of the fossils from Nui Nga Ma. Henry concedes that 'it is nevertheless possible that some third party [i.e. someone other than Deprat or Mansuy] could have introduced spurious fossils into the collected material. At first sight, it would appear that such a hypothesis cannot be ruled out in the case of certain Cambrian or Silurian trilobites.'

On the specimens themselves, Henry writes that where Durand-Delga tried to argue that similar fossils had been found in Indo-China or Asia, he was mistaken. The old generic name of *Trinucleus* now covers about forty different genera, so old finds described as *Trinucleus* do not support Deprat's finds at Nui Nga Ma. In other words, trilobites which are identified as *Trinucleus* are not as closely related as was once thought. The finding of another trinucleus trilobite is therefore not an indication of the legitimacy of Deprat's finds. As for the *Dionide formosa* which Deprat said he found in eastern Yunnan, this species is from a particular period (the Caradoc and Ashgill stages) of the upper Ordovician, which is now known to be absent throughout that region.

Henry also notes that Cambrian trilobites had been found in

Yunnan and these finds were published in 1905 and 1907. Deprat therefore knew that there were Cambrian fossiliferous beds in Yunnan (though not Indo-China) before he left France. Most collections of trilobites in European museums and colleges have only European species – so if Deprat *had* wanted to take some specimens with him, these would have been the only ones available.

Henry states his belief that the motive for the frauds was to enable Deprat to propose precise and irrefutable dating of strata, where new species finds would have made this much more difficult. Once this had been done, then 'stratigraphic correlations and interesting palaeogeographic conclusions arose out of this fraud'. In other words, Deprat dated the rocks using European species and was then able to propose a marine link between Europe and south-east Asia in the lower Palaeozoic on the basis of these same fossils. Henry also had an interesting explanation for Mansuy's delay in making the accusations:

> In the early years of this century, numerous trilobites – regardless of their geographic location and geological sections from which they had been recovered – were ascribed to species that had been defined from deposits in Bohemia, Great Britain and North America. Plate tectonic interpretations were unknown at that time. Because of this, we should not be surprised that Mansuy's suspicions came rather late.

Palaeontologists initially matched their finds to species from Europe, using them as their benchmark. It was only when Deprat's finds were repeatedly in exact accordance with European species that Mansuy became suspicious.

Despite the fact that there are affinities between trilobites of the lower Palaeozoic era in the regions that were part of, or associated with, the great continental mass of Gondwanaland (including southern Europe and south-east Asia), Henry points out that these occur only at the generic, not the species level. Families of trilobites ranged across this ancient marine environment, but individual species remained local. In addition, all of the trilobites that Deprat reported from the Silurian and Ordovician of Indo-China and Yunnan were species known from Europe, while species of Ordovician trilobite that have since been found in Indo-China do not appear at all in Deprat's collections.

Henry's work is a timely reminder of a good principle of science – that 'similar' is a dangerous word. Primo Levi wrote in *The Periodic Table*:

> . . . one must distrust the almost-the-same, the practically identical, the approximate, the or-even, all surrogates and all patchwork. The differences can be small, but they lead to radically different consequences, like a rail-road's switch points; the chemist's trade consists in good part of being aware of these differences, knowing them up close, and foreseeing their effects.

As for chemistry, so for palaeontology. On the other hand, Henry was not able to overcome the central difficulty of scientific induction – just because no one has found these fossils, or rocks of this age, in a particular region does not mean that they never will.

Deprat's other work has once more come under examination in the past few years. In 1994 Maurice Lys of the University of Paris-Sud, who had written an addendum to Durand-Delga's 1990 paper in which he re-appraised Deprat's work on fusulinids, now published a full-length paper on the subject. The introduction was written by Michel Durand-Delga and by Jacques Sigal, who had found the trilobite fossils of the Deprat affair, as well as his fusulinid thin sections, at the Collège de France from Indo-China in 1989. The box of fusulinid slides had been sent back to France in 1933 for Jean Gubler to study at the Sorbonne, where they had remained until Jacob's retirement as Professor in 1948. They were then reunited with the other Deprat material at the Collège de France in Paris, and transferred to storage at Meudon in 1960. They had been assumed lost for fifty years, and came to light quite by chance.

Lys's conclusions overturned the earlier opinions of both Madeleine Colani and Gubler. Deprat's work on fusulinids was given formal approval once again:

> As for palaeobiogeography [the reconstruction of continental positions and movements using fossil data] I believe that Deprat was a pioneer in the ideas that are actually current in the subject at present; didn't he venture to 'claim' that the microfaunas found in Indo-China could be identical to those from Japan? There is abundant evidence to prove that, not only do they reach Japan, but that most of them reach the Palaeotethys in southern Tunisia!

Lys gave the following summary of Deprat's work on fusulinids and of his standing in this field:

> It is possible for me, after scientific analysis of Deprat's scientific work, to give an informed judgement on the scientific importance of J. Deprat, which I consider clearly proven; he has, among the world specialists – our Russian colleagues as well as those from Japan and China – an enviable reputation which certain critics have wished to diminish, if not destroy . . . It is my duty – and one close to my heart – to honour his memory among the community of geologists, in recognition of his scientific probity and the great service which he gave to us.

Interest in the Deprat affair continued in 1997. Dr Philippe Janvier, a palaeontologist with long experience of working in Indo-China, wrote an article in the journal *Nature* recalling the affair. The article was essentially an historical review of *Les Chiens aboient*, Deprat's own account of the affair. But it gave Janvier the opportunity to give a resumé of the affair itself. New information given by Janvier once again concerns the site at Nui Nga Ma (now known as Nui Nguu Ma). Although *Les Chiens aboient* appears to be an accurate account of the affair, Janvier writes: 'yet the story of his discovery of an additional Ordovician trilobite in Nui Nga Ma in March 1917 remains contentious: neither I nor any Vietnamese palaeontologist has ever found fossils on this hill'. Janvier's considered conclusion is that 'Whatever sympathy one may have for Deprat, one must assume that the specimens are indeed apocryphal unless proved otherwise by new field investigations.' He adds finally his perplexity at Deprat's motives: 'And why would he have ruined a promising career with such a useless deception? It seems entirely at odds with his personality and the integrity of his other work.'

The following year, 1998, Dr Robin Lacassin with other French and Vietnamese geologists investigated an important aspect of the geology of south-east Asia which Jacques Deprat had first put forward in 1914. In the region around the basin of the Rivière Noire, to the west and north-west of Hanoi, Deprat had come across a major unconformity which seemed to be widespread. An unconformity is an abrupt break in the continual layers of strata, which shows that there was some sort of break in the deposition of the material which formed those strata. In other words, something happened to interrupt the laying down of rock-forming material, which was then resumed at a later date. In this case, rocks of Palaeozoic and Triassic age had been laid down in a continuous sequence, and had then been disturbed – folded, faulted, tilted and chemically altered. On top of these strata a series of red beds was then unconformably deposited.These red beds came later and showed only mild disturbance compared to the beds underneath. Deprat had proposed, therefore, that there had been a major disturbance of the Earth's crust across the whole region of south-east Asia some time after the deposition of the lower beds, and before the formation of the red beds. Because he believed the red beds to have been late Triassic in age, and the youngest of the underlying beds to have been early Triassic, then this major disturbance must, according to Deprat, have occurred in the Triassic period. This disturbance became known as the Indosinian orogenesis, and the idea was developed by Fromaget in 1941 and Sengor and Hsu in 1984, though, as Lacassin says, 'This concept of large collisional deformations of Triassic age comes from the pioneering work of Deprat.'

Lacassin notes in his paper (Lacassin *et al.*, 1998), 'As no detailed field description of this hypothetical unconformity has been published since Deprat, we attempt here to reinvestigate the structure of some of these red bed basins.' Once they arrived in the field these geologists, working eighty-four years after Deprat, found that, far from being inaccurate, invented, confusing or even hastily compiled, his work was a sound guide to the geology of the region: 'In northern and central Vietnam, the clearest descriptions of tectonic structures are those of Deprat. His detailed and factual cross-sections proved to be highly reliable in the field.'

In general the Lacassin team supported the view that there was a 'compressional event' – i.e. some kind of disturbance caused by tectonic blocks moving together – which altered the older Triassic and Palaeozoic rocks, and brought about the unconformity that Deprat had recognised. They were uncertain how large-scale this event was, as it did not seem to have brought about the really major changes that would result from continental collision and mountain-building. They also mention that the overlying red beds are now thought to be at least as young as Cretaceous, so the event cannot be dated as precisely as Deprat had proposed. It might even have been late enough to have been part of the deformation caused by India's collision with Asia, which threw up the Himalayas.

The important point here is that, while Deprat's pioneering work on the tectonics of south-east Asia is being tested and subjected to revision, it is being recognised as the first real attempt to explain the tectonic history of the region, and as the reference point for all the work that has followed. Dr Lacassin has since expressed his opinion of Deprat's tectonic work: 'My own view is that he [Deprat] was a great naturalist who had an important respect for observations.'

There is one other aspect of the Deprat affair that does not fit easily into this chronology because it is rarely referred to in writing, though it is occasionally discussed by those with a keen interest in the affair. We have seen Deprat referring with disapproval to Lantenois being caught up in an *affaire Eulenbourg* – a homosexual relationship – with 'a coolie of the lowest rank'. We do not know whether Henri Mansuy was homosexual, but the suggestion, based on circumstantial evidence, opens up a conspiracy theory which needs discussion. The theory is that Deprat's outspoken disapproval of Lantenois's and Mansuy's sexual activities would have put them in danger of professional discipline or worse and therefore would have given them a motive for conspiring against him. The problem with this notion is that Deprat, apart from the letter quoted on page 142, never referred to this subject. In *Les Chiens aboient* he is scathing about every aspect of Lantenois's character, but the only distant allusion to his homosexuality in the book is that when he left Indo-China for France he took a young Indo-Chinese male servant with him. There is no reference at all to Mansuy's sexuality. The hoary old idea that homosexual men are likely to form some sort of conspiracy just because of their sexuality has, thankfully, been discarded. In this case there is no evidence that Mansuy and Lantenois together felt under threat from Deprat, and that this was therefore likely to be a motive for any such conspiracy.

It seems unlikely that this will be the last word on Jacques Deprat, his life, his work and the 'affair of the trilobites' – indeed the preparation of this book has stimulated further argument on the subject. Jean-Louis Henry has suggested that micro-palaeontological analysis of the suspect fossils should be carried out, and there is always the possibility of more discoveries in

Indo-China. But whatever new discoveries are made and whatever new evidence comes to light, at least we now have the perspective of eighty years, during which self-interest has given way first to collective guilt, and then to the passionate curiosity that this intriguing man deserves.

9 *Other Lives*

On 7 March 1935, at three o'clock in the morning, Herbert Wild and Henri Duboscq left Pau by car, in the direction of Lescun. They had planned to make a tour of the Ansabère Massif (Mt Ansabère, and the North and South Aiguilles d'Ansabère) and of the peak known as the 'Table of the Three Kings'.

After crossing the frontier at the Petragème Pass, also called the Anso Pass, they began a flanking walk on the Spanish slopes, to the west of Mt Ansabère. It was about noon. The snow was icy and hard like marble, after a warm southerly wind had been followed by a sudden drop in temperature. Both men pulled their skis behind them, by means of a rope. They were equipped with ice axes and crampons.

Finding themselves in a risky position above a rock escarpment, and the slope becoming steeper and steeper, they decided to drop down and descended diagonally, facing the slope, towards a gully which cut into the rock face.

At that moment, Wild, who was ahead, lost his balance and slid towards the nearby escarpment. His fall was extremely fast. Hampered, no doubt, by the string which held his skis, and which perhaps brought about his error, he was not able to use his ice axe with any effect, and disappeared over the vertical drop. (The crucial factor in the accident was, it appears, the slipperiness of his woollen gloves on the dry handle of the ice axe.) He fell about fifteen metres on to a rock ridge which broke his spine. He was still alive and completely conscious; he did not die for several hours.

Having got down to him, Duboscq made a sledge out of skis, and towed his friend until nightfall. Once he decided that his friend's body was not at risk of being buried by a snowstorm, he went on alone in the direction of Anso, the nearest Spanish village, about twenty kilometres away. In the course of the night, in the strange and complicated terrain, Duboscq ended up in the wrong valley, and arrived on the morning of the 8 March, not at Anso in Aragon, but at Isaba in Navarre.

The authorities in Isaba declared that the accident was outside their jurisdiction, and Duboscq was taken under escort to Anso, in whose commune the accident had taken place. (The Spanish authorities are very strict in such cases. The companions of the victim of an accident are, in general, imprisoned at least until the autopsy.) It was from there that he departed once again on the 9th, with a group of admirably dedicated local mountaineers, to bring back the body of his friend. On the 10th a storm erupted that lasted several days and buried the mountain beneath more than a metre of fresh snow.

Herbert Wild is buried in the small cemetery of Anso.

This article appeared in a mountaineering magazine, *La Montagne*, in early 1936. It was written by Robert Ollivier, who was one of the most prolific and important Pyrenean mountaineers of the twentieth century. Some years later Jean Ritter gave a fuller account of the aftermath of Wild's fall (Ritter, 1993). It seems that Wild did recover consciousness enough to apologise to his friend for causing him such inconvenience. Duboscq constructed a makeshift sledge out of skis and attempted to bring his companion down the side of the mountain. But then Duboscq, no doubt exhausted, lost his footing on a slope, and let the sledge fall. Wild, already close to death, was killed in this second fall. No longer able to use a sledge on the rough terrain, Duboscq then carried Wild's body on his back. He towed and carried his friend for a total of nine hours in bitter cold, eventually reaching a mountain cabin. He left Wild's body there, and walked for twelve hours to reach Isaba. Duboscq was taken to Anso and was, as Ollivier suggested he might be, held in detention by the Spanish authorities until the cause of his companion's death could be formally established. Duboscq had telegrammed Pau with a request for help. Three friends arrived, including a surgeon, Albert Tachot. Once Wild's body was brought down to the village, the authorities insisted that an autopsy be carried out by a local doctor, assisted by Tachot. Ritter then describes the scene that unfolded:

> Under the bell-tower of the church, the body was placed on a trestle. The carpenter brought a saw to open the top of the skull. The curious children were kept at a distance . . . Several men stood behind them, hoping to be of some use. Some women appeared and looked quickly without daring to linger . . . The two doctors then cut open the rib cage down the sides using shears, to uncover the scapular girdle. The cause of death being duly elucidated, Duboscq was set free.

The scene beneath the church bell-tower in the mountain village was, as Ritter says, worthy of Goya.

In his contemporary account of this tragic accident, Ollivier gives no hint of the peculiar past or the true identity of the man who had come to call himself 'Herbert Wild'. But he gave a much fuller account of the recent life of this remarkable *montagnard* in an appreciation published in another mountaineering magazine, the *Bulletin des Pyrenées*:

> Following the fatal accident that occurred last February [actually March] on the Ansabère Massif, numerous articles have revealed the life of Herbert Wild to the public . . . All these pieces have spoken of his passion for the mountains. But

> it is the duty of one of his '*camarades de cordée*', to describe here in more detail the passionate Pyreneist that he became during the last years of his life, after having pitched his tent and placed his shoes on most of the great mountain ranges of the earth. The infinite charm of the Pyrenees conquered him . . . and, having spent a little of that inexhaustible energy which so characterised him in only a few seasons with us, Herbert Wild left, in the memory of the mountaineers who had the chance to know and appreciate him, the fond memory of a powerful and original personality. (Ollivier, 1935)

On most of his expeditions Herbert Wild was accompanied by his friend Henri Duboscq. These two men in their fifties were among the veterans of the mountaineering fraternity – but they had an inexhaustible energy which put their younger colleagues to shame. Ollivier recounted one of their round trips:

> In July 1933, they left on foot from La Raillère (1,149m) at 16:30, reached the Wallon refuge and, towards midnight, passed by moonlight through the Port du Marcadeau. They descended into Spain. Dawn found them on the peak of Mt d'Algas (3,045m). From there they reached the summit of Mt Arualas (3,060m), then dropped, losing 700 metres of altitude, towards the Enfer lakes, climbing again to the Brèche Sarrette, from where they climbed Mt Enfer (3,081m). They descended again to La Raillère in the evening and finally travelled back to Pau by car: a walk of twenty-five hours, plus 3,300 metres of elevation. Not considering his journey sufficiently full, Wild immediately developed his photographs.

These two veterans became something of a legend among the *montagnards*, Duboscq generally restraining Wild from even more daring adventures. Tragically Henri Duboscq himself was killed just three months after Wild, on 7 June 1935, in an accident on Pic Long, also in the Pyrenees.

In his appreciation Ollivier wrote of Wild: 'Endowed with

great courage, and an extraordinary agility for his age, he was always the companion that any mountaineer dreams of having by his side . . . A tireless companion who did not know – or would not show – any physical or moral weakness, Wild was in a mountain refuge or in camp, the most charming of comrades.'

Ollivier pointed out that the Pyrenees were tough mountains, not simply for climbing, but because of the distances that had to be walked often with heavy packs, the danger of tornadoes and the difficulties of finding shelter.

> With Wild I never knew any sense of discouragement. The strength of the veteran sustained, by his example, the faith of the young mountaineer. And when bad weather forced us to stay in camp, or our trip finished a little early and we took a pleasant rest in the camp, he would tell, without ever boring us, of his distant travels in Indo-China. Sometimes as well, without the least pedantry, he would show us how to read, in the limestone of the rockfaces, in the structure of the crumbling ridges or peaks, the geological history of the Pyrenees. His poetic soul, imprinted with a sort of scientific mysticism, gave this history an epic scale. Moreover his enthusiasm for the sublime sights of the mountains was so contagious, that I never enjoyed the beauty of the Pyrenees so much as when I was with him.

Ollivier ends with this poetic elegy to a man whom he clearly found remarkable:

> The summer season is approaching. Once again, on the familiar paths the steel-tipped shoes will make their marks, the ice-axes will clatter against the rocks. We will find again the brilliant light of the high mountains, the wild rock-faces, the blue glaciers. But in our climbing parties one place will remain empty: that of a small, lively figure, with an energetic face and clear gaze, a gaze full of vision, in search of which he had walked over the most beautiful landscapes in

the world, and of which the last sight became the icy wastes of Ansabère.

Herbert Wild lives on though in the annals of Pyrenean mountaineering. As recently as 1982, his name was cited for his work opening up new routes: 'In 1912 Jean d'Ussel with Castagne and Haurillon as guides, made the first crossing of the Tempestades arête; ten years later Arlaut and Laffout claimed the Salenques arête, and in 1934, Ollivier and Wild linked the two to create a major traverse of about seven hours duration on delightful granite' (Reynolds, 1982).

At the beginning of his appreciation, Ollivier mentioned Herbert Wild's literary achievements. When he died Herbert Wild was a novelist and short-story writer with an established reputation in France. He had won acclaim and awards for a series of books about colonial life in Asia. His last book, *La Paroi de glace*, was the first of his novels set in the Pyrenees. And this ending is really only the beginning of the story of Herbert Wild – novelist, mountaineer and good companion. For Herbert Wild was also Jacques Deprat, precocious student, pioneering geologist, explorer, and – according to history – scientific fraud.

To connect the stories of Jacques Deprat and Herbert Wild we need to go back fifteen years to November 1920. The Deprat family was then living in the town of Nevers on the River Loire in western Burgundy. They were given cheap lodgings by Marguerite Deprat's relations and lived off their small savings. Jacques Deprat had been educated and trained as a geologist, but there was no chance of his getting any work in that sphere. It is not clear how many options were open to him, but whatever his choices, Deprat decided to try to make a living by writing fiction. His first attempt, *Le Conquérant*, was published in 1924 under the imprint of 'Les Chevaliers'. This was a form of self-publication which was financed by his friends the Liberts. The publication had exactly the right effect, as the book – a depiction of life among miners in Tonkin before 1910

– was picked up and republished by the prestigious Paris publishing house Albin-Michel. Jacques Deprat decided to adopt a pseudonym, and from now on all his novels and stories were to be published under the name Herbert Wild. In fact it seems that Herbert Wild became more than a *nom de plume*. It was effectively another identity for Deprat, and it was by that name that he became known in the literary and mountaineering worlds. It is not clear where the name came from. To the British reader it seems a quintessially English name of the pre-war period – straight out of the pages of P. G. Wodehouse or John Buchan. There is some suggestion that Deprat wanted to show a certain freedom and energy in his writing, which led him to the English or German name 'Wild'.

Encouraged by Albin-Michel, Herbert Wild embarked on the writing and publication of *Les Chiens aboient*. The title comes from what Wild describes as an oriental proverb: 'Les chiens aboient, la caravanne passe.' This suitably enigmatic phrase ends the book, and might be thought to encapsulate Deprat's philosophical attitude to the whole business – the disturbance was temporary and has passed, life goes on. The *roman-à-clef* was not a huge success – it sold around 2,500 copies – but it made an impact in Hanoi and among geologists in France. In fact Herbert Wild's novels did not sell in large numbers, but they were clearly well respected and he was able to make a living, supplementing his income by writing short stories for literary magazines. By the time *Les Chiens aboient* was published in 1926, Wild had already published five short stories in the magazines *Le Temps* and *Les Débats*, and a collection of stories entitled *Dans les replis du dragon*, as well as his debut novel *Le Conquérant*. In the next nine years he wrote a further ten novels and volumes of stories, two of which were published after his death. Most of his fiction was concerned with life in Asia, and the combination of European and Asiatic cultures clearly fascinated him. It was also clear that he felt intellectually and emotionally drawn to Asian life, and particularly to Japanese and Chinese culture, which he often compared favourably to European and American. Michel

Durand-Delga reports that he even began to dress a little like a Chinese sage, growing a thin wispy beard.

Between 1926 and 1930 the Deprat family moved from Nevers to Moulins and then to Yseures. Then in 1929 came another event that was to change Herbert Wild's life yet again. It seems that at this time he was just about managing to scrape a living from his writing. An old friend of his, M. Jourdan (who appears in *Les Chiens* as 'Lordan'), had just returned from Indo-China, where he made a lot of money out of the Hanoi to Yunnan railway. Jourdan heard about Wild's work and his precarious existence and offered him and his family an apartment on the avenue Alsace-Lorraine in the Pyrenean town of Pau, rent-free. They were to remain in Pau for the rest of Herbert Wild's life – a life that was increasingly divided between the mountains and his writing. In 1930 Wild's novel *L'Autre race* was cited for the Prix Goncourt. In March of the following year it won the Prix des Français d'Asie, worth 25,000 francs, beating, among others, André Malraux's *La Voie royale*. This enabled the family to move to their own house on the avenue Trespoey.

Herbert Wild had an up-and-down relationship with his publishers Albin-Michel. From time to time they sent back a manuscript for rewriting, or occasionally refused one altogether. They seemed to want him to write more commercial works. By 1932 *L'Autre race* had sold 3,700 copies, and another eight volumes had sold between 1,000 and 3,000 each. Wild was predictably annoyed by their attitude, but they usually managed to patch up their differences. In late 1934 he was revising the manuscript of a novel and a short story was being considered as the basis of a film screenplay. At the time of his death a new novella was about to be published in a literary magazine run by Albin-Michel, and two novels, *Monsieur Joseph* and *La Paroi de glace*, were published posthumously in 1936. The latter was issued by a new publisher, Editions de France, which may have been as a result of a rift with Albin-Michel just before Wild's death.

Wild had been encouraged in his writing by the well-known writer Claude Farrère, and Farrère continued to support him and to introduce him to a growing circle of literary acquaintances. Wild wrote essays as well as stories and novels, and gave lectures at literary conferences and gatherings. He was particularly in demand to give public lectures on China and Indo-China all around the south-west of France.

It is interesting to note that Wild/Deprat's literary friends were drawn from the 'nationalist' or right wing of French literary life. France in the 1920s and 1930s was a highly politicised and politically convoluted society. The success of the Russian Revolution and the later rise of fascism and of expansionist forces in Germany, France's traditional foe, set off a host of paradoxical responses in France. Socialists who had believed in the futility of war became convinced that German fascism must be fought tooth and nail, while French 'nationalists' saw Hitler as a bulwark against Communism, and a potential ally in suppressing the left in their own country, and so opposed war. This simplistic analysis is intended to show that political feelings were both complex and running high. Some of Deprat's literary friends later became collaborators with the occupying German army and one, Paul Chack, was executed for crimes against France. The one thing we might learn is that however much we study a person's life, habits, friends, beliefs, we still can never predict how they will behave in a totally new situation. We do not know what Herbert Wild's response to the German occupation would have been. He might have fought it with the courage he showed elsewhere, he might have welcomed it, or he might have gone on with his life in Pau and tried to ignore it. He died five years before anyone could find out.

Herbert Wild was not a perfect disguise for Jacques Deprat. He used this pseudonym on *Les Chiens aboient* and knew that the geological world would easily make the connection between his two identities. In fact some of his old colleagues had followed his career with interest. After reading about Wild's death in 1935, an engineer named Albert Bordeaux, who had known Charles Jacob in Indo-China, wrote to Jacob at the Sorbonne suggesting that a request should be made to an organisation called the Société des Amis des Sciences for a pension to be paid to Mme Deprat.

> You have heard no doubt of the accident which recently caused the death of Herbert Wild in the Pyrenees. I have previously spoken to you about him and I recall your impression that what had taken place in Indo-China had been somewhat exaggerated. As well as that, he was a man of high *valeur*, who was well thought of by M. Termier, and who showed a great fortitude in accepting his rather cruel fate, and in resolutely beginning a new career. He was on the road to greater and greater success. Prix des Français d'Asie, highly regarded by Governor Pasquier [now Governor-General of Indo-China] whose letters I know about, translated into many languages, and with an extraordinary and likeable conversation . . . Do you believe that we should ask for a pension for Mme Herbert Wild/Jacques Deprat? The request, presented by you, would I believe overcome any objections. And this would be a reparation of the great wrong, perhaps even injustice, which caused him to be sacked from his post in Indo-China.

Jacob evidently did not think this a good idea. We do not have his reply, but Durand-Delga quotes from Bordeaux's next letter:

> Allow me just some brief comments. I can well see a little of the reason for Wild's error. He wished to support with facts a hypothesis which was close to his heart, telling himself that the proof would come in time . . . Wasn't it said of Cuvier that he introduced several false bones into his reconstructions? But he was right in the end. And there will have been others. In the end the severity was great, a career ruined . . .

All in all, Herbert Wild had an interesting, fruitful and

productive literary career. He established himself as a member of France's literary scene and as an intelligent and perceptive writer of fiction and non-fiction. From a standing start at the age of forty he lived off his writings for the next fifteen years. In 1920, sacked in disgrace and left without work and without prospects, Jacques Deprat would surely have settled for that.

But now, just as we have circled back through the story of Herbert Wild and Jacques Deprat and arrived at the end of this eventful life, we find that this extraordinary man has one more surprise in store for us, for, in one of the fictional works published after his death, *Les Skis invisibles*, Herbert Wild committed the chilling act of describing the accident that was to kill him. Not only that, he seemed eager that the piece should appear as quickly as possible – i.e. before his death. This piece is taken from *La Revue hebdomadaire* of 16 March 1935:

> Hardly two weeks ago – on Wednesday, 27 February – I received a visit from the charming Herbert Wild, traveller, explorer, novelist, story-teller but above all perhaps, *mountaineer*, devoted to the unceasing exploration and to the celebration of the *Pyrenees* . . . Herbert Wild, who had travelled over much of the world, wanted no more than that; to be a lover and a poet of the mountains. He claimed that the Pyrenees were more mysterious, more forbidding, more difficult to master than the Alps, and that the true mountaineer must go there. Readers of *La Revue* will remember having read here last summer, delightful and colourful pages written by him, overflowing with his love of the Pyrenees. I had not seen him for several years: he hadn't aged at all, but rather had regained his youth. His lively and mischievous expression, which seemed to contain something of the brightness of the high mountains, reflected his ingenuous passion: 'Just think, in the last year I have done nearly eighty first ascents!' By this they mean in their jargon, I believe, climbs never before attempted . . .
>
> Blushing, not with the modesty of a man of letters who

fears a misunderstanding or a rejection, but with the modesty of a lover obliged to reveal one of his secrets, he offered me a manuscript: 'Would you like to publish this? . . . It is a short story, very nice, very *mysterious* . . . But you must publish it quickly.' Just to tease him a little, I objected that the skiing season was almost over, that it would be better pehaps to wait until next year. 'What do you mean, "over"?' he replied. 'The skiing season in the Pyrenees lasts until May! And anyway it is a wonderful subject. You must not let it go cold.'

I took my leave of the piercing gaze of Herbert Wild . . .

How could anyone resist this child of the mountains. I sent his story to the typesetters, intending to read the proofs myself . . . Indeed I have just read them . . . But with such a tightening of my heart, after having read in my morning paper: 'The writer Herbert Wild was the victim of an accident while attempting to climb the Pic des Trois Rois in the Massif d'Ansabère. *As a result of circumstances not yet explained*, the writer fell from a height and was killed . . .'

Did he know himself why there was so much haste to see this *mysterious* tale, wherein he describes his own death, appear in print? Did he know that, like his hero, he would pay for his love with his life?

François Le Grix, Directeur-Gérant

The story which followed this statement was published in two instalments. Entitled *Les Skis invisibles* it concerns two men who climb and ski in the Pyrenees together. The story is narrated by one of the men, who tells how the other is slowly driven mad by sightings of a set of ski tracks in the snow of the mountains. The tracks appear as if from nowhere – hence the title of the piece. The reader is never sure whether these tracks actually exist or not, and the story is a skilful evocation of the effect of the landscape, climate, air and isolation of the high mountains on rational perception. The narrator watches his friend Silhen follow these 'phantom' tracks into ever more dangerous places:

> When I arrived above the deep gorge that plunges towards the river, I could see at the bottom of the enormous slope a single minuscule point sliding like a drop of water down a pane of glass. And I recognised Silhen, launched on a wild descent. Almost immediately he disappeared into the wooded area that rises up high into the Combe Balour.

The possibility that Silhen will be killed in the pursuit of these tracks becomes, in the eyes of the narrator, inevitable. At the end of the story, he sees Silhen ski to the lip of a precipice and go over the edge:

> I removed my ski bindings, I retrieved my ice axe from my bag, and I descended cautiously, down the slope towards a rocky overhang which allowed me to see down to the bottom of the escarpment. There was a thirty metre drop on to the rocks below. And at the bottom of a glacier which was punctured everywhere by the rock, I saw a dark shape lying on a sheet of snow. It was what I had been expecting. I turned and called to the others, 'He is at the bottom, down there.'
>
> I climbed back up towards them. They were pale and more shocked than me – I was already prepared for this event. It took us at least a quarter of an hour to get to him. He still had his broken skis on his feet.
>
> The doctor examined him. 'He died in the fall,' he said. 'He did not suffer.'
>
> Pau, 11 October 1933

Not only, it seems, did Herbert Wild describe his own death with a considerable degree of accuracy, he also pressed Le Grix to publish the description as soon as possible – presumably so that he would still be alive when it appeared. It is all a little too thick with apparent intent to be totally coincidental, while being ambiguous enough to allow for almost any possibility. Even in his death Herbert Wild or Jacques Deprat retained his ability to disturb the world and to unsettle our notions of what we know about each other. Whether Herbert Wild intended to die in the manner of his fictional creation we will never know. But Le Grix was surely right to say that, in his art he was expressing something that he felt deeply in himself – that one day he would pay for his love of the mountains with his life.

The striking out of his old life had enabled Deprat to make a new one for himself. The end of Jacques Deprat, geologist, was a crisis in his life, but from it he managed to manufacture an opportunity. He was three-quarters broken by the shame of the world, so he finished the job himself and started afresh. It is hard to overestimate the degree of resilience this must have required. He chose, after all, not to shut himself away, but to embark on a working life in full public view. A writer's work is exposed to the opinions of others in ways that few other occupations are. To have been publicly disgraced once and then to enter the fray again must have been a difficult step to take. But perhaps Deprat was encouraged by the hand that fate had dealt him. He did not have much choice, he did not have much to lose. Our lives are shaped by incremental and accidental forces working a kind of drip effect to make us what we are, and to make us do the things that we do. During the course of the 'trilobite affair' Deprat had deluded himself into believing that he could control and shape events through his actions and the exercise of his own will. But his catastrophic defeat had paradoxically given him the chance to be in control of his own fate. At the age of forty he could, within limits, be exactly who he wanted to be. By erasing his past, the affair had prevented it from polluting his future. He could start with a clean slate on to which he could transcribe the story of a new life.

Perhaps it is best to see Herbert Wild in the place where he came to rest. After a life of troubles and wanderings, he had returned to a life in the mountains. The Pyrenees were like the Jura of his youth, and like the mountains of Yunnan and Haut-Tonkin before their memory became infected by the affairs of the world. But Wild did not look for a life of ease in the mountains. On the contrary he was endlessly, tirelessly energetic. Is it too simple to see this restless energy as an act of purgation, a cleaning out, a shedding, a leaving behind of the impurity of the past? Or was it that Deprat was finally truly happy in the Pyrenees – writing novels, tramping the mountain paths, pushing himself to the limit? It was in many ways an enviable life. Had he found his true place – was Herbert Wild, as well as being his invention, actually the real Jacques Deprat?

Herbert Wild was pulled for several hours across the Massif d'Ansabère in the early hours of 7 March 1935 by his friend Henri Duboscq. No doubt he knew he was dying and that his death would not be long in coming – this was not a time for self-delusion. He perhaps had the chance to consider all he had done and all he had been. In his early life Jacques Deprat had expressed the wish to be both a scientist and an artist, and said that these two things existed within him. In the end he did become both, but not at the same time, and not in circumstances he would have chosen. These things may not be exclusive, but they surely demand an overwhelming priority in a person's life and in the life of their mind. We might ask whether Deprat's artistic vision of the world was incompatible with, and even dangerous to, his scientific vision. In the early years after the affair Deprat wished to revenge himself on those who had done him wrong. The publication of *Les Chiens aboient* was an attempt to do that, but ten years on and his life as a writer became a kind of redemption. Whatever had gone before was best dealt with neither by confronting it nor ignoring it, but by making something potentially greater out of his life.

Epilogue

It was never intended that this book, or its author, should pass judgement on Jacques Deprat. If this 'investigation' of the Deprat affair was begun with the hope of finally discovering precisely what happened in Indo-China, the search for undeniable evidence of guilt or innocence soon became a prolonged attempt at understanding – and it has often been remarked how uneasily understanding and condemnation sit together. The unearthing of the background to the affair adds, as we have seen, moral complexity to an apparently simple case. The more we know of the affair, the more we increase our understanding, and the less importance we attach to the discovery of its central fact. The complexity of Jacques Deprat himself is more intriguing than the simple fact of his guilt or innocence. Even Deprat himself may have come to see this. After all, is it worse to suffer disgrace for an act which you did not commit or to live with the knowledge of your own guilt and utter foolishness?

And yet that central fact remains and the guilt or innocence of Jacques Deprat hovers over every aspect of the affair. Every argument that we can make about Deprat's or Lantenois's or Mansuy's actions, and every justification or consideration we can bring to the events of the affair, has an element to it that is just beyond our reach. We might predict that this unknowingness would cause us to feel frustration at not knowing the 'true story'. But in another sense it gives a deeper dimension to the affair and both forces and helps us to widen our understanding. It is too easy for us to relate histories in full knowledge of the 'facts', and to form our visualisations of the 'characters' of the people involved, by relating the events in which they participated and the acts which they perpetrated. Within the story of the Deprat affair, Jacques Deprat resists this naïve notion, and shows us the limitations of such a programmed approach to understanding the past. No matter how much we think we know about Jacques Deprat, this knowledge cannot grant us the privilege of assessing his guilt.

To judge Jacques Deprat would be to risk simplifying him – something that no one deserves, least of all a man who made such efforts to show that life could be taken in more than one way. Nevertheless, in this case, we have the problem of an unfinished story. If this is the story of Jacques Deprat, then it can satisfactorily end in March 1935 with the death of Herbert Wild on a mountainside in the Pyrenees. But if it is the story of the 'Deprat affair', then it needs something else – a resolution. Jacques Deprat never had his day in court, in front of an independent judge with a skilled advocate cross-examining Lantenois and Mansuy. If he had, he would have been able to severely embarrass his accusers. He would have shown how the secret sending of fossils from Indo-China broke Lantenois's promise and the most basic rules of evidence. And he could have shown up the inconsistency at the heart of Cayeux's expert testimony, and how his legal rights had been systematically denied. All this might not have mattered. He may have been found guilty 'beyond reasonable doubt'. But would the outcome of another Commission of Inquiry have brought us any nearer to the truth?

Deprat's defence had the incoherence of a guilty man's. The changes in his story and his wild accusations all gave, and still give, the impression of desperation. But we have already asked whether desperation is necessarily a sign of guilt. If we consider this for a moment we can see that an innocent man might have acted in the same way, when faced with a series of events for which he had no explanation.

It is worth remembering again, that even if Deprat had been found guilty by a legal tribunal, his first 'scientific' defence would still stand. Just because these fossils have not been found in Indo-China before does not mean that they never will be. On the strict logic of this argument we could never know *for certain* that Deprat was guilty. It is tempting to say that Jacques Deprat took the secret of the affair with him to the grave, but this would be unfair to him. He gave his own version of events at great length and vigorously protested his innocence. Deprat's position is a curious inversion of the scientific defence that he himself outlined. In his case, his only version of the story that would be believed by everyone would be a confession. Without this we remain open to argument.

The most plausible, or more accurately the least implausible, explanation of the events in Indo-China is that Jacques Deprat placed the fake fossils himself. But recent experience has taught us that plausibility is the starting point of almost every miscarriage of justice, and the desire for resolution its driving force. We have a need of stories, and stories have a need of meanings and of endings. We are vulnerable, are we not, to closure? Jacques Deprat's guilt would itself present a different set of implausibilities, as Michel Durand-Delga has so persuasively pointed out – such a high degree of advance planning, long-term deception and great risk of discovery, for so little reward. We are thereby faced with at least two possible versions of events, each of which is unlikely – but one of which undoubtedly happened. We are back to the point where facts are wanted to make the unlikely real, and back to that unfilled and endlessly fascinating absence at the centre of this story.

Acknowledgements

It is impossible to overstate the debt which this book and its author owe to two French geologists. Professor Michel Durand-Delga, formerly of the Universities of Paris and Toulouse, was, as is clear from the preceding pages, the pioneer in modern research into the Deprat affair. His energy and expertise in tracking down unpublished documents and in scouring the scientific and personal records of all those involved has been remarkable. Dr Philippe Janvier of the Muséum National d'Histoire Naturelle in Paris has worked in Vietnam over the past fifteen years, is a passionate and well-informed student of the history of geology, and has a long-term interest in the life and work of Jacques Deprat. Both Professor Durand-Delga and Dr Janvier have been extremely generous and patient in providing me with documents, maps and photographs, as well as answering numerous questions by letter and in person, and in pointing me towards other sources where necessary. Our long meetings in Paris were both an enormous pleasure for me personally, and an invaluable help in my researches. They also each took the trouble to read the manuscript and correct certain factual errors. This book would simply not have been possible without the enthusiastic co-operation of these two distinguished scientists.

In addition I would like to thank the following correspondents who have willingly given help and information: Alan Cameron, Professor John Flower of the University of

Kent, Kev Reynolds, Sam Collett, Jean Ritter and Jean and Pierre Ravier. Mrs Margaret Ecclestone of the Alpine Club Library in London was particularly generous with her time and was of great help to me, as was Mme Ozanne, librarian of the Société Géologique de France in Paris. The staff of the Geological Society library, and of the Royal Society library in London, were, as usual, extremely efficient and helpful.

The comments on the French education system in Chapter 1 draw heavily on the work of Theodore Zeldin (see References, page 239). The story of the Deprat affair is drawn from published and unpublished sources and from Deprat's own account in *Les Chiens aboient*. Inevitably it goes over much of the same ground as Michel Durand-Delga's 1990 paper on the subject. I have tried to tell the story from a broader perspective and, while I have leaned on Professor Durand-Delga's researches where necessary, I have not always drawn the same conclusions. I have described the detailed arguments over the two most important fossil sites. For the others, I have used extended figure captions on pages 146 to 149 as a guide for those who wish to delve deeper in to the primary literature on each specimen. While once again thanking all of the above for their generous help and co-operation, I should emphasise that any errors in this book are, of course, my own.

Roger Osborne
Scarborough, 1999

References and Sources

Name and date references are given in the text where necessary. Where it is obvious which publication is being referred to (as in Chapters 7 and 8) then a formal name, date reference is not always given, in order to avoid repetition. References to personal correspondence and those official unpublished documents not listed here can be found in the *Références* section of Durand-Delga (1990). Readers might find it easier to access Durand-Delga's 1995 paper, which is really a summary of his earlier paper, though with an addendum comprising a response to Henry's 1994 paper.

Adams, Frank Dawson (1938), *The Birth and Development of the Geological Sciences*, Williams & Wilkins, New York. Re-issued (1954) by Dover, New York.

Birembaut, A. (1963), 'La Géologie', in *Histoire de la Science*, M. Dumas (ed.), Encyclopédie la Pléiade, Paris.

Broad, William, and Wade, Nicholas (1982), *Betrayers of the Truth*, Simon & Schuster, New York.

Cayeux, L. (1919, unpublished), 'Rapport sur l'étude comparée du quartzite à Dalmanites, rapporté par M. Deprat du Nui-Nga-Ma, en 1917, et des quartzites siluriens du Mt. Drabow (Bohême)', archives of the Académie des Sciences, Paris.

Colani, M. (1924), 'Nouvelle contribution à l'étude des fusulinidés de l'Extrême Orient', *Mémoires du Service Géologique de l'Indochine*, vol. 11, fasc. 1.

Congrès Géologique International (1914), *Compte-Rendu de la XIIe session, Canada 1913*, Imprimerie du Gouvernement, Ottowa.

Conrad, Joseph (1895), *Almayer's Folly*, Unwin, London.

Davies, H. R. (1909), *Yun-nan, the Link Between India and the Yangtse*, Cambridge University Press, Cambridge.

Deprat, J. (1899), 'Etudes micrographiques sur le Jura septentrional', *Mémoires de la Société d'Histoire Naturelle de Doubs*, vol. 1.

Deprat, J. (1905), 'Les dépôts Eocènes Néo-Calédoniens', *Bulletins de la Société Géologique de France*, series 4, vol. 5.

Deprat, J. (1912a), 'Etude géologique du Yun-nan oriental: géologie générale', *Mémoires du Service Géologique de l'Indochine*, vol. 1, fasc. 1, 1.

Deprat, J. (1912b), 'Sur la découverte de l'Ordovicien à *Trinucleus* et du Dinantien dans le Nord-Annam et sur la géologie générale de cette région', *Comptes-Rendus de l'Académie des Sciences,* t. 154, pp. 1452–4.

Deprat, J. (1912c), 'Etudes des fusulinidés de Chine et d'Indochine et classification des calcaires à fusulines', *Mémoires du Service Géologique de l'Indochine*, vol. 1, fasc. 3, 3.

Deprat, J. (1913a), 'Sur les terrains paléozoiques de la Rivière Noire', *Comptes-Rendus de l'Académie des Sciences,* t. 156, pp. 579–81.

Deprat, J. (1913b), 'Les fusulinidés des calcaires Carbonifériens et Permiens du Tonkin, du Laos et du Nord-Annam', *Mémoires du Service Géologique de l'Indochine*, vol. 2, fasc. 1, 2.

Deprat, J. (1913c), 'Note sur les terrains primaires dans le Nord-Annam et dans le Bassin de la Rivière Noire (Tonkin) et sur la classification des terrains primaires en Indochine', *Mémoires du Service Géologique de l'Indochine*, vol. 2, fasc. 2, 1.

Deprat, J. (1913d), 'Etude préliminaire des terrains triasiques du Tonkin et du Nord-Annam', *Mémoires du Service Géologique de l'Indochine*, vol. 2, fasc. 2, 2.

Deprat, J. (1913e), 'Les charriages de la région de la Rivière Noire sur les feuilles de Thanh-ba et de Van-yên', *Mémoires du Service Géologique de l'Indochine*, vol. 2, fasc. 2, 3.

Deprat, J. (1913f), 'Les séries stratigraphiques en Indochine et au Yunnan', *Mémoires du Service Géologique de l'Indochine*, vol. 2, fasc. 2, 4.

Deprat, J. (1914a), 'Etude comparative des fusulinidés d'Akasaka (Japon) et des fusulinidés de Chine et d'Indochine', *Mémoires du Service Géologique de l'Indochine*, vol. 3, fasc. 1, 3.

Deprat, J. (1914b), 'Etude des plissements et des zones d'écrasement de la moyenne et de la basse Rivière Noire', *Mémoires du Service Géologique de l'Indochine*, vol. 3, fasc. 4.

Deprat, J. (1915a), 'Mode de formation de deux centres volcaniques japonais, l'Aso-San et l'Asama-Yama, comparés à des centres volcaniques d'âges géologiques anciens', *Comptes-Rendus de l'Académie des Sciences*, t. 161, pp. 30–2.

Deprat, J. (1915b), 'Sur la découverte du Cambrien moyen et supérieur au Tonkin, au Kwang-Si et dans le Yun-nan méridional', *Comptes-Rendus de l'Académie des Sciences*, t. 161, pp. 794–6.

Deprat, J. (1915c), 'Les fusulinidés des calcaires Carbonifériens et Permiens, du Laos et du Nord-Annam', *Mémoires du Service Géologique de l'Indochine*, vol. 4, fasc. 1.

Deprat, J. (1915d), 'Etudes géologiques sur la région septentrionale du Haut-Tonkin', *Mémoires du Service Géologique de l'Indochine*, vol. 4, fasc. 4.

Deprat, J. (1916), 'Sur la découverte d'horizons fossilifères nombreux et sur la succession des faunes dans le Cambrien moyen et le Cambrien supérieur du Yunnan méridional', *Comptes-Rendus de l'Académie des Sciences*, t. 163, pp. 761–3.

Deprat, J. (1917a), 'Exploration géologique de la partie du Yun-nan comprise entre la frontière tonkinoise, le Kwang-si et le Kwei-tcheou', *Comptes-Rendus de l'Académie des Sciences*, t. 164, pp. 107–9.

Deprat, J. (1917b), 'L'Ordovicien et le Gothlandien dans le nord du Tonkin et le bassin du Haut Iou-Kiang (Chine méridionale)', *Comptes-Rendus de l'Académie des Sciences*, t. 164, pp. 147–9.

Deprat, J. (1917c), 'La zone frontale des nappes preyunnanaises dans les régions de Bao-lac et de Cao-bang', *Comptes-Rendus de l'Académie des Sciences*, t. 165, pp. 243–6.

Deprat, J. (1917d), 'Sur la présence du Cambrian inférieur à l'ouest de Yunnan-fou', *Comptes-Rendus de l'Académie des Sciences*, t. 165, p. 564.

Deprat, J. (1917e), 'Sur la présence du Permien à Hongay et la structure de la bordure de la région rhétienne du littoral tonkinois dans les baies d'Along et du Fai-tsi-long', *Comptes-Rendus de l'Académie des Sciences*, t. 165, pp. 638–40.

Deprat, J. (1918), 'Les lignes directrices de l'Asie sud-orientale, dans leurs rapports avec les éléments anciens et les géosynclinaux', *Bulletins de la Société Géologique de France*, series 4, vol. 17, pp. 284–300.

Deprat, J., and Mansuy, H. (1910), 'Résultats stratigraphiques généraux de la mission géologique du Yun-nan', *Comptes-Rendus de l'Académie des Sciences*, t. 151, pp. 572–4.

Durand-Delga, Michel (1990), 'L'Affaire Deprat', *Travaux du comité Français d'histoire de la géologie*, series 3, vol. 4, 10, pp. 117–215.

Durand-Delga, Michel (1995), 'L'affaire Deprat, plaidoyer pour la réhabilitation d'un géologue proscrit', *Mémoires de la Société Géologique de France*, new series, vol. 168, pp. 87–95.

Duras, Marguerite (1984), *'L'Amant'*, Les Editions de Minuit, Paris; English translation by Barbara Bray (1985), Collins, London.

Duverne, Gustave (1932), *Sur les routes du monde: Paris–Hanoi–Saigon*, Fournié, Paris.

Feist, Raimund, and Courtessole, Robert (1984), 'Discovery of Upper Cambrian Series Containing East Asian-type Trilobites in the Montaigne Noir (Southern France)', *Comptes-Rendus de l'Académie des Sciences*, t. 298, series 2, 5.

Fromaget, J. (1927), 'Etudes géologiques sur le nord de l'Indochine centrale', *Bulletins du Service Geologique de l'Indochine*, vol. 16, fasc. 2.

Fromaget, J. (1941), 'L'Indochine Française, sa structure géologique, ses roches, ses mines, et leurs relations possibles avec la tectonique', *Bulletins du Service Geologique de l'Indochine*, vol. 26, fasc. 2.

Furon, R. (1955), 'Histoire de la Géologie de la France d'Outre-Mer', *Mémoires du Muséum de l'Histoire Naturelle (Paris)*, t. 5, pp. 171–5.

Gillispie, C. C. (ed.) (1970), *Dictionary of Scientific Biography*, Scribner, New York.

Greene, Mott T. (1982), *Geology in the Nineteenth Century*, Cornell University Press, Ithaca and London.

Gubler, J. (1935), 'Les Fusulinidés du Permien de l'Indochine', *Mémoires de la Société Géologique de France*, new series, no. 26.

Guides Modrolle (1912), *Hanoi et ses environs*, Hachette, Paris.

Habert, A. (1918, unpublished), 'Enquête préliminaire, affaire Deprat: Résumé et conclusions', archives of the Académie des Sciences, Paris.

Hall, D. G. E. (1981), *A History of South-East Asia*, 4th edn, Macmillan, Basingstoke.

Henry, J.-L. (1994), 'The Trilobites of the "Affaire Deprat" ', *Alcheringa*, vol. 18, pp. 359-62.

Hinsley, F. H. (1962), *The New Cambridge Modern History; vol. XI 1870–1898*, Cambridge University Press, Cambridge.

Hutton, P. H. (ed.) (1986), *Historical Dictionary of the Third French Republic, 1870–1940*, 2 vols, Aldwych Press, London.

Huxley, T. H., ed. Huxley, L. (1900), *Life and Letters of Thomas Henry Huxley*, Macmillan, London.

Jacob, Charles (1921), 'Etudes géologiques dans le Nord-Annam et le Tonkin', *Bulletins du Service Geologique de l'Indochine*, vol. 10, fasc. 1.

Jacob, Charles, and Bourret, René (1920), 'Itinéraire géologique dans le nord du Tonkin', *Bulletins du Service Géologique de l'Indochine*, vol. 9, fasc. 1.

Janvier, P. (1997), 'In retrospect: *Les Chiens aboient*', *Nature*, vol. 389, 16 October, p. 688.

Karnow, Stanley (1991), *Vietnam: A History*, revised edn, Pimlico, London.

Lacassin, R. *et al.* (1998), 'Unconformity of Red Sandstones in North Vietnam: Field Evidence for Indosinian Orogeny in Northern Indo-China?' *Terra Nova*, vol. 10, pp. 106–11.

Lantenois H. (1907), 'Note sur la géologie de l'Indochine', *Mémoires de la Société Géologique de France*, series 4, vol. 1, fasc. 4.

Lantenois, H. (1917), 'Ecrasements et charriages dans la région de Chapa, près Laokay (Tonkin)', *Comptes-Rendus somm. de la Société Géologique de France*, pp. 190–1.

Lantenois, H. (1927, unpublished), 'Remarques sur les travaux du Service Géologique de l'Indochine', archives of the Académie des Sciences, Paris.

Le Grix, François (1935), *La Revue Hebdomadaire*, 16 March, pp. 288–9.

Little, Archibald (1910), *Across Yunnan: A Journey of Surprises*, Sampson Marston Low, London.

Lys, Maurice (1994), 'Les Fusulinida d'Asie orientale décrits par J. Deprat: révision et mise en valeur de la collection-type', *Cahiers de micropaléontologie*, new series, vol. 9, no. 1.

Mansuy, H. (1912), 'Etude géologique du Yun-nan oriental: paléontologie', *Mémoires du Service Géologique de l'Indochine*, vol. 1, fasc. 1, 2.

Mansuy, H. (1913a), 'Paléontologie de l'Annam et du Tonkin', *Mémoires du Service Géologique de l'Indochine*, vol. 2, fasc. 3.

Mansuy, H. (1913b), 'Nouvelle contribution à la paléontologie de l'Indochine', *Mémoires du Service Géologique de l'Indochine*, vol. 2, fasc. 5.

Mansuy, H. (1915a), 'Faunes Cambriennes du Haut-Tonkin', *Mémoires du Service Géologique de l'Indochine*, vol. 4, fasc. 2.

Mansuy, H. (1915b), 'Contribution a l'étude des faunes de l'Ordovicien et du Gothlandien du Tonkin', *Mémoires du Service Géologique de l'Indochine*, vol. 4, fasc. 3.

Mansuy, H. (1916a), 'Faunes Cambriennes de l'Extrême Orient méridional', *Mémoires du Service Géologique de l'Indochine*, vol. 5, fasc. 1.

Mansuy, H. (1916b), 'Faunes Paléozoiques du Tonkin Septentrional', *Mémoires du Service Géologique de l'Indochine*, vol. 5, fasc. 4.

Mansuy, H. (1919), 'Catalogue général par terrains et par localités, des fossiles recueillis en Indochine et au Yunnan', *Bulletins du Service Géologique de l'Indochine*, vol. 6, fasc. 6.

Mayeur, J. M., Rébérioux, M., and Foster, J. R. (1988), *Cambridge History of Modern France,* vol. 4, *The Third Republic from its Origins to the Great War 1871–1914*, Cambridge University Press, Cambridge.

Ngo Vinh Long (1973), *Before the Revolution: The Vietnamese Peasants Under the French*, MIT Press, Cambridge, Mass.

Ollivier, Robert (1935), 'Herbert Wild aux Pyrénées', *Bulletin Pyrénéen*, vol. 216, avril–mai–juin, pp. 63–5.

Ollivier, Robert (1936), 'Accidents de Montagne en 1935: Herbert Wild, Massif d'Ansabère, 7 mars, 1935', *La Montagne*, series 4, vol. 4.

Pillola, Gian Luigi (1990), 'Lithologie et trilobites du Cambrien inférieur du SW de la Sardaigne (Italie): implications paléobiographiques', *Comptes-Rendus de l'Académie des Sciences*, t. 310, pp. 321–8.

Press, Frank, and Siever, Raymond (1986), *Earth*, 4th edn, W. H. Freeman,

New York.
Price, Roger (1987), *A Social History of Nineteenth-Century France*, Hutchinson, London.
Reynolds, Kev (1982), *Mountains of the Pyrenees*, Cicerone, Milnthorpe.
Ritter, Jean (1993), 'Le drame d'Ansabère', *Revue Pyrénées*, no. 174, pp. 183–203, no. 175, pp. 331–48.
Saurin, E. (1956), *Lexique Stratigraphie International*, vol. 3 'Asie', fasc. 6a, 'Indochine', p. 80.
Sochurek, Howard (1989), interviewed by Harry Maurer in *Strange Ground: Americans in Vietnam, 1945–1975*, Henry Holt, New York.
Société Géologique de France, *Comptes-Rendus du Conseil*, 9 Dec. 1918; 13 Jan. 1919; 24 Feb. 1919; 8 April 1919; 4 Nov. 1919.
Société Géologique de France, *Comptes-Rendus de la Commission du Bulletin*, 5 Jan. 1918; 4 Nov. 1918; 18 Nov. 1918.
Société Géologique de France (1919, unpublished), 'Affaire dite des trilobites: Rapport de la commission speciale', archives of the Académie des Sciences, Paris.
Termier, P. (1917) [Presenting Deprat (1915d) to the Société Géologique, includes remarks by Douvillé, de Margerie and Jourdy], *Compte-Rendu sommaire des séances de la Société Géologique de France*, 1917 vol., pp. 21–4.
Termier, P. (1929), *La vocation de savant*, Paris.
Termier, P. and Deprat, J. (1908), 'Le granite alcalin des nappes de la Corse orientale', *Comptes-Rendus de l'Académie des Sciences*, t. 147, pp. 206–8.
Vassall, Gabrielle (1922), *In and around Yunnan-fou*, Heinemann, London.
Wild, Herbert (1926), *Les Chiens aboient*, Albin-Michel, Paris.
Wild, Herbert (1927), *Le Colosse endormi*, Albin-Michel, Paris.
Wild, Herbert (1930), *L'Autre race*, Albin-Michel, Paris.
Wild, Herbert (1935), 'Les Skis invisibles', *La Revue hebdomadaire*, 16 March, pp. 289–307, 23 March, pp. 418–42.
Wild, Herbert (1936), *La Paroi de glace*, Editions de France, Paris.
Zeldin, Theodore (1973–7), *France 1845–1940*, vol. 2, Oxford University Press, Oxford.

The author and publishers would like to thank the following for permission to reproduce photographs: the Deprat family for pictures of Jacques Deprat; Popperfoto for pictures of Hanoi and Yunnan-fou; Société Géologique de France for photographs of Henri Mansuy, Honoré Lantenois, Pierre Termier, Alfred Lacroix, Henri Douvillé and Emmanuel de Margerie; Kev Reynolds for pictures of the high Pyrenees at Vignemale and Lescun.

Index

Index

Index

Index